I0684282

HOMECOMING

BOOK 3

THE SECRETS OF CLAYTON COUNTY

DON WOOLDRIDGE

DPW PUBLISHING
PHOENIX, ARIZONA

| COPYRIGHT

Copyright ©2013 by Donald Wooldridge. All Rights Reserved.

Published by D&PW Publishing, Phoenix, Arizona

PRINT: ISBN-13: 978-0615957760 (Custom Universal)
ISBN-10: 0615957765

All rights reserved. No part of this book may be used or reproduced by any means, graphic, electronic, or mechanical, including photocopying, recording, taping or by any information storage retrieval system without the written permission of the author.

Requests to the Publisher for permission should be addressed to 215 N Power Rd, # 428 Mesa, AZ 85205-8455.

Limit of Liability Disclaimer of Warranty. While the Publisher and author have used their best efforts in preparing this book, they make no representations or warranties with respect to the accuracy or completeness of this book and specifically disclaim any implied warranties of merchantability or fitness for a particular purpose. No warranty may be created or extended by sales representatives or written sales materials. The publisher and author are not engaged in rendering professional services, and you should consult with a professional where appropriate. Neither publisher nor author shall be liable for any loss or profit or other commercial damages, including but not limited to special, incidental, consequential or other damages.,

For general information on other books written by this author contact: Donald Wooldridge at 215 N Power Rd, # 428 Mesa, AZ 85205-8455.

Printed in the United States of America
10 9 8 7 6 5 4 3 2 1

Cover design by Wheatmark Press

| ADVANCE PRAISE

I finished reading The Homecoming about a week ago and am still thinking about it. It was that good. The struggles each character experiences – individually and collectively – brought me closer to them. For me to "feel" that connection with the characters in a book determines whether or not the read is a good one! Wooldridge has done a fine job of bringing the characters to life – not only by the challenges we all sometimes experience at some level or another - but he has loaded the pages with a few twists and turns that plucked me right out of my rather stationary life into a world of emotional involvement and interpersonal relationships that mimic life in a most believable manner. Another great job by Wooldridge. Having read the first two books of the trilogy, I hate to see this family saga end; the story begun by Sarah with her first venture to Clayton County, was a joy to read as Wooldridge drew it to a close. Following her life as a wife and mother has not been a chick flick – it has been warm, poignant, funny and real! Highly recommended.

~ T. R. Stearns, EdS

One has an advantage, I suppose, in reading the final book in an author's trilogy. The first test in reading any story in a series is whether the author has written the story so that it stands on it's own... should I not have had the privilege of reading the preceding books. Although I knew of the progression of this family's life... Wooldridge thoroughly supported the story as a stand-alone – intertwining a sufficient amount of the back story to not leave me wondering, "What the hey?" What did occur, however, was alert me to the fact that if I were, indeed, a first time reader of Wooldridge's Trilogy, his writing was rich enough I was titillated... wanting more of that back story. I would want to read the first two books and then wrap up with a re-read of Homecoming to see if I enjoyed it as much the second time around... noting I infrequently read a book more than once.

Homecoming is the continuing saga of Kent and Sarah Crodin... keeping their love and relationship alive in the midst of their diametrically different children finding their own pathways in life. Needless to say, just as Kent and Sarah often journeyed the less traveled roads of life... so do Wendy and Teddy. Will the wild child Wendy ever conform to her mother's wishes for being anything more than a Daddy's girl; will Teddy ever move beyond feeling awkward and inadequate and compelled to take risks with the one person intended to remain his best-friend and life partner? We see Zoey grow into her beauty and develop a core strength to live her life outside Clayton county; we see her return to claim what is necessary to fulfill her.

As far as a steamy romance story goes – this was not the objective of the writer; in reality, relationships are the ever-evolving integration of personalities, and Wooldridge achieved just that as Kent and Sarah maintained a life-long commitment to each other, while watching their offspring begin their own journey in life and love.

~ A Weber | Literary Strategist

| DEDICATION

This story is dedicated to Adel Parker of Guttenberg, Iowa.

| ACKNOWLEDGMENTS

This novel would not have been possible without the interest and assistance of family and friends. A special thank you to the following people, who contributed their time and expertise in the development of this novel.

Marty Mitchell
Pat Shetler
Barbara Sjekora
Barbara Smerud
Anna Weber
Patricia Wooldridge

| PROLOGUE

Sarah Hunter was a big city I.R.S. agent assigned to the small community of Clayton, Iowa. Her job was to investigate five residents whose IRS returns seemed to be defying the 1982 IRS Bartering law requiring a barter to be reported as income. She quickly discovered that life in Clayton was not as black and white as IRS regulations.

Despising the country, Sarah escaped her father's dairy farm to go to the big city of Chicago, as soon as she could. Earning degrees in accounting, Sarah fulfilled her dream to be a city girl. Accustomed to the finer things in life, she lived in partnership with her affluent boyfriend, Andy Counts, and helped him entertain clients for his prestigious accounting firm.

Unhappy with her assignment, Sarah hoped to sneak in and out of the sleepy town without fanfare. It didn't happen. On her first day, she found herself in a most unlikely place — a tavern — being introduced to a gathering of local citizens. Sarah learned that the residents were more than neighbors to each other; she realized they were loving friends who took care of each other in ways that couldn't be measured by IRS rules.

However, Sarah was forced to meet potential tax resisters on their own turf. She hunted mushrooms in high heels with Peter Wulfric, was caught in the rain checking catfish traps with Norm Fisher, and had to literally jump into the local dentist's fishing boat so he couldn't avoid her interrogation.

Each day Sarah was drawn closer to the lives of the local people. They included realtor Vickie Banks, restaurant owner Wilma Frisbie, and her most unlikely confidant "Weird" Warren Nickel. Then there was Kent Crodin, a tall, handsome man Sarah found attractive. On her first day in town, she vowed to avoid him… and any possible romantic trouble with her boyfriend.

Clayton's troubles and natural disasters became Sarah's as well; the longer she stayed, the more she was entwined. Each tragic event pushed Sarah closer to the townsfolk and Kent, who saved her life during a tornado. On Sarah's last night, before returning to Chicago, a man in the shadows gave her a precious gift, meant for another woman, together with a prophesy she was leaving her heart in Clayton.

The next day Kent proposed marriage. Shocked and confused, Sarah ran away, lamenting the fact that she'd just met the right man, in the wrong place.

Finally, with her rose-colored glasses gone, Sarah saw her cheating boyfriend, vindictive boss, and the city of Chicago, as they truly were— manipulative and deceptive. Sarah felt cold, after having been warm with Kent. She felt distant, when she had been welcomed in Clayton. Sarah was crushed, realizing she had made a terrible mistake.

Giving up everything to follow her heart, Sarah returned to the most unlikely of places, Clayton, Iowa. While her marriage to Kent Crodin was strong, their dreams were shattered as life tested them. The FBI arrested her and sent her off to jail. Lightning destroyed his business. Her first baby became the most challenging daughter any mother could imagine.

A pretty blonde, Wendy was the most stubborn, independent and mischievous tomboy there could be. While Sarah endured the embarrassment Wendy caused her, the townsfolk laughed at her antics. Who wouldn't?

When Kent delivered a foal, he bartered his veterinary services for a barrel racing quarter horse named Ginger. When he gave Ginger to Wendy, she began to develop a sense of responsibility. Then, at age thirteen, Wendy spent a week with her Aunt Rita, shopping and visiting salons and spas… being transformed into a beautiful young woman that shocked her parents.

Sarah patted Rita on the shoulder. "Well Rita, you did it. I cannot tell you how long I've tried to get Wendy to start acting like a young woman. You're a miracle worker. I'm so grateful."

Rita looked up at her from her wheelchair. "Don't be too grateful. More problems are on the horizon . . . boys. "

"Boys," she repeated. "I thought this was the hard part?"

"I'm afraid not, dear. It's just beginning."

CHAPTER 1

Spring 2001

The rumbling sound of Tommy's truck split the silence of the night. When lights swept across the window, Sarah got up to turn the yard light on. She saw sixteen-year-old Wendy watch Tommy leave, then turn toward the house, give her a little wave, and walk toward the barn.

"Kent."

"Uh-Huh."

"I'm going to the barn to help Wendy."

He looked up over the top of his book. "You think that's wise?"

Sarah walked out the door. Wendy was leaving her horse's stall carrying a bucket when she entered.

"What's up, Mom?"

"Oh, I just thought I'd give you a hand with Ginger."

"Don't need help. Just checking her water before bed." Wendy turned away and, hung the bucket on the waterspout.

Sarah was not going to be ignored. "Wendy, where have you been? You were supposed to be home an hour ago."

"Just talking, Mom."

"What would you two have to talk about this late?"

Wendy turned her back again, rolled her eyes and sighed. She was used to this when her mom was unsettled. Nervous, over-controlling. Ugh! She wished she'd just stop it.

Turning to face her mother Wendy told her, "You know Mom, we talked about marriage, having babies, where we'd live and work. Stuff like that."

Nonplused by Wendy's comment, Sarah watched her take the water bucket into the stall and waited until she reappeared. "You know, your childish absurdities don't work anymore young lady. I'm talking woman to woman here."

Leaning on the lower half of the stall door, Wendy looked at her mother. "Ok, woman to woman? Then, let me tell you something. I will never have sex with any boy in this town. I'm not taking a chance of having his baby, then living in a trailer and raising kids while he tries to make a living at the lumber mill, fishing, or any other meaningless job." Wendy walked around the door, locked it and turned toward her mother. "I'm leaving this town first chance I get, Mom, so get used to it."

The look in Sarah's eyes could have bored a hole through Wendy. "We'll see about that, young lady. Now, get to bed."

ଓଞ

The aroma of manure blended with the odor of horses, cows, and sheep, creating an atmosphere only a member of Future Farmers of America, or their parents, could appreciate. When Teddy saw the time on his dad's watch showed eleven-thirty, he tugged his dad's hand, "Can I go to the midway, Dad?"

Kent squeezed his hand firmly to prevent his escape. "No son, this is Wendy's day. She has two events and you're going to see them with us."

Sarah interrupted them. "Kent, come quickly, I found some good seats."

He and Teddy followed her to the folding chairs near the front of the stage for the beauty pageant. People flowed in from all sides of the tent to fill the remaining seats.

Teddy wiggled and squirmed in his chair trying to see between people's heads and shoulders. The lights came on, getting everyone's attention. The master of ceremonies walked to the podium. It was none other than Doc Bendenhoff, the town dentist. Short and stocky, Doc entertained everyone in town with his fits of foolishness. Who could forget the time he tried to make turtle soup and the turtle bit his finger, forcing him to close his office until it healed.

"Ladies and Gentlemen, it's my pleasure to welcome you to the annual Clayton County Fair and the crowning of the 2001 Poultry Queen. At this time, I'd like to get these lovely semi-finalists out on stage. Let me introduce you to our first semi-finalist, Miss Samantha Blake."

As Samantha walked on to center stage Sarah reached for Kent's hand and held on tight, causing him to look over at her.

"Are you all right?"

"Just saying a prayer, that's all."

"You can't be serious?"

When Samantha had taken her place, the master of ceremonies announced, "And now, introducing our second semi-finalist, Miss Cindy Calhoun. Come on out, Cindy."

"Kent, I just don't want to see Wendy's stubborn independent streak under the lights in front of all these people."

He kissed her hand and returned it to his lap. "Honey, she'll do fine. You've got to relax."

Then, Doc Bendenhoff could be heard again, "And our third semi-finalist, Miss Wendy Jo Crodin.

"It must be a mother thing. She's just so unpredictable."

"Shhh." He said pointing to the stage. "Here she comes."

There was the tall, sixteen-year-old Wendy, striding confidently to center stage. She was stunning. Wendy had grown her blonde hair long so she could wear it in a rolling wave over her shoulders and onto her spaghetti strapped blueberry dress. The thigh length skirt made her beautiful tanned legs looked even longer as she walked confidently in high heels.

What a chore it was to get that girl to take off her boots and practice wearing heels around the house. Thank God, she did.

"Ladies, you all look very beautiful. I'm sorry only one of you can win. Today, in the last event to determine our winner, we'll be asking each of you to answer a question. It will be up to our judges to evaluate the quality of your answer, and tally their scores from today with those of the previous two days of competition. Of course, the highest score will determine which of you will be crowned our new 2001 Clayton County Poultry Queen. Ok, let's get started."

The three nervous girls looked at each other and whispered, "Good Luck."

"Samantha Blake, will you please step up to the microphone."

Wendy and Sam were not close friends, but Sam was well liked and known for being smart. She was the one to beat.

"Samantha, here's your question: "How would you define trust?"

Samantha looked at her hands for a moment, smiled at the crowd of folks leaning forward in their seats expectantly. Then she spoke, "I think trust is reflected in the way someone behaves toward you when your back is turned. It's like when you're away from home. You always know you can trust your parents to care for you and come to your aid if you need help. That's what trust means to me. Thank You."

Loud applause followed as she stepped back to join the other two girls. Doc turned and smiled at the remaining two contestants.

Wendy was impressed with Sam's answer. She didn't want to be next. She preferred to hear Cindy's answer.

"Cindy Calhoun, it's your turn. Please step up to the microphone. Here's your question: How would you define love?"

Wendy was startled.

Oh, my God. She's laid every boy in town. This ought-a be good.

Cindy wasn't shy, and took right off describing her definition of love. "Love is a feeling that comes from the heart. It's warm and thrilling and simply wonderful. I feel love from my parents. I feel love from my grandparents. And someday, I hope to meet a man that makes my heart feel the same way about him. Oh, not now, of course. It's way too soon, I haven't even finished high school. But, you know, later. Like when I'm more grown up. Then I'll be ready for love."

The audience appreciated her effort, but the applause sounded more polite than enthusiastic as Cindy stepped back to join the other girls.

Doc smiled as he turned to look at Wendy. "Wendy Crodin, will you please step up to the microphone? Here's your question: How would you define maturity?"

Sarah squeezed Kent's hand and bowed her head. "Of all questions for her to answer."

"Shhh."

After a few seconds of thought, Wendy answered the question. "It's been my experience that when I come to a crossroad in my life, I've had to decide whether to hold dearly to the past or meet the challenges of the future. Maturity for me was letting my childhood stay in the past." She took a deep breath, and continued. "Most of you have learned that too, haven't you?" The audience laughed in agreement. "And," she added warmly, "I embrace each and every day of my future knowing that if I falter, my parents are always behind me for support." Applause and approval from the audience washed over her along the way back to join the other girls.

Kent pulled Sarah's hand to his lap and patted it saying, "Now, what'd you think of that?"

She looked up at him, "Oh, it was beautiful. I never thought I'd hear words like that come out of her mouth."

"I'm not surprised. You probably put them there and didn't know it."

Doc Bendenhoff spoke again. "Thank you, Wendy. Now, the judges will tally their scores, while the band plays for us."

They never heard the name of the song, but the tune was pleasant enough. Everyone was riveted on the judges.

"Mom," Teddy asked, "Why does this take so long. Wendy's the prettiest. Just give her the trophy and let's go to the midway. "

"Listen, you're gonna be here 'til it's over, so sit still and be quiet."

Teddy knew Zoey had been waiting for him, that is if her parents let her get away. Who knew Wendy's queen-for-a-day thing was going to ruin his plans.

CHAPTER 2

The judging seemed to drag on much longer than necessary. Sarah leaned her head on Kent's shoulder for comfort, and said, "Even if she doesn't win, we can tell her the answer to her question was superb and very mature."

Before he could respond, Doc spoke to the audience. "Ladies and Gentlemen, the judges have completed our contestant's scores and we have a winner. First, let me say that all of these young women are winners, and worthy of representing Clayton County. But now, it's on with the show."

"Let me introduce our third place finalist, Miss Cindy Calhoun."

When the applause died down, he said, "And now, one of these two remaining ladies will be crowned the 2001 Clayton County Poultry Queen. The runner-up will receive an award of $250, while our winner receives an award of $500. So, without further ado, it's my honor to introduce you to our new 2001 Clayton County Poultry Queen..."

"Here goes," she said, squeezing the blood out of Kent's hand.

"... Miss Wendy Jo Crodin. "

Sarah raised their hands and screamed, "She won! She won! "

Wendy shook with excitement as tears welled up in her eyes.

"Ladies and gentlemen, I present this Golden Chicken to our new Poultry Queen, Wendy Crodin. Congratulations Wendy."

The crowd cheered, and her mother jumped up and down hugging everyone around her, while Kent made sure Teddy didn't slither off into the crowd. "That's a trophy, Dad? Wendy dressed up for that stupid chicken?"

They worked their way through the crowd toward the stage to meet Wendy.

Sarah was the first to hug Wendy. "Oh, Honey, I'm so happy for you."

"Daddy!" Wendy said, spreading her arms for a hug.

"You are beautiful, sweetie."

"Hey sis, who took first place, you or that stupid chicken?"

"Shut up jerk." Wendy fired back.

He just grinned, and walked away flapping his arms like a bird, singing, "My sister's the chicken queen, cluck, cluck, cluck."

Wendy was glad he left, but still had to take a shot at him, so she hollered, "Teddy, if you wanna' be a turd, why don't you go lay in the grass?"

Kent tapped Wendy's shoulder. "That's enough. You only have half-an-hour before you show Ginger in the riding competition. You should get going. Hand me that trophy, I'll take it to the truck."

"Holy cow! Mom, where are my boots and jeans?"

"Right here in the bag, Dear. I'm sure there's a ladies room nearby where you can change. I'll go with you and take your dressy things with me. Let's hurry. "

αβ

The crowd in the arena looked anxiously at the gate where contestants entered the ring. Seated in bleachers surrounding the half acre dirt floor, the only protection from the elements was the overhead canopy. Sometimes used for auctions, the latent animal odors were shooed away by a light breeze through the open sides. Everyone had heard how beautiful Wendy looked when she was crowned Poultry Queen. Now they were waiting to see that tough little girl they had watched grow up. Billy Geitz was also in the crowd, rooting for Wendy to win too. She had no idea he was watching her. However, he'd had a crush on her since elementary school, and only meant to tease her when he flipped her new braids to get her attention. Then, all the other boys in the hallway joined in and wouldn't stop. That's when Wendy knocked three boys down and started punching him. Billy's pride was hurt worse than his face. Unfortunately, Wendy never gave him the time-of-day.

Mounting Ginger, Wendy checked her stirrups, then tapped the horse's flanks, crossed the start line and they were in the arena. First Wendy had to walk Ginger at a slow steady gait around the ring. Next, they had to trot around the ring while the judges evaluated both horse and rider. There were other reining maneuvers that were easy for Ginger. The tough part was the row of cones, where Wendy had to ride Ginger without reins.

They rode to the head of the line of cones. Wendy dropped the reins onto Ginger's neck and placed both hands onto the saddle horn, just like the rules said. Without a sound, Wendy squeezed Gingers flanks with both heels, and they slowly started to move ahead.

At the first cone, Wendy pressed her left knee into Ginger, and they moved right between the cones. Pressing her right knee against Ginger she moved left between the next set of cones. It went perfectly. Ginger was doing great. To win, they had to finish cleanly.

But it wasn't to be. As Ginger turned away from the last cone, her hind foot knocked it over. No winner today. They got second place, which seemed to please Wendy. She'd had a great day.

CZ &O

As they approached Ginger's stall in the livestock barn, there was a crowd of boys vying for Wendy's attention.

She nonchalantly groomed Ginger, as though she needed it, encouraging the attention but brushing it off as easily as the boys offered it.

Sarah smiled, remembering her teen-age years. *Good for her. She deserves some attention.*

When her parents approached, Wendy told the boys, "Gotta go guys. See you later."

The boys dispersed and Wendy turned to her parents. "Where have you been? I thought you'd never get here."

"Looked to me like you were having fun," her mother replied.

"But Mom, I gotta go. I've got a date."

"Who asked you for a date?"

"Randy."

Concerned at the thought of her young daughter going on a date with a boy she didn't know, Sarah asked, "Do I know him?"

"Yeah, Randy Wagner. His mom works at Mueller Ford."

"Oh, yes. I do know them. Sure, it's fine to go with him. But we're not going to rerun last night. If you're not home by eleven, Randy will be your last date. Understand? Come to think if it, isn't he eighteen?"

Wendy knew where this was going. "Yes, Mom, he's eighteen. He's got a car. You know, like that's how we're getting to the movie."

"Explain to me why Randy would want to be with a younger girl like you?"

Wendy twirled around in front of them; arms outspread as she said, "Because he said I was the hottest cowgirl at the county fair."

Sarah put her hands on her hips. "Oh, he thinks so, does he? Well, I've got a piece of advice for the hottest cowgirl at the county fair."

"Yeah, what's that?"

"Make sure to keep your boots on, Missy"

Wendy stomped her foot, looking at her mom fiercely. "Mom, how could you say that? Don't you ever listen?" She turned and went down the aisle of the livestock barn in a huff.

"What's so hot about her?" Teddy asked. "She smells like a barn."

| CHAPTER 3

Sarah was sleeping on the couch by the stairway when Kent entered the living room. "Wake up. "

She lifted her heavy eyelids just slightly. "What time is it?"

"It's after midnight and they're over an hour late. A bad rainstorm started a while ago and I'm worried about them."

Sitting straight up, she blinked. "Wendy's not home yet? I warned her not to be late, again."

"I think they're in trouble."

Her eyes were open wide. "What kind of trouble?"

"I don't know, but I'm calling the sheriff."

As he turned to go to the CB radio Sarah bounced off the couch and followed. She listened in as Kent and J.R. talked about accident reports that didn't include Wendy or Randy. J.R. promised to notify the Highway Patrol, so more eyes would be watching out for them. Then he asked, "Are you sure those two aren't snuggled up somewhere trying to stay warm in this rainstorm?" J.R. chuckled, "Know what I mean?"

"Give me that." Sarah grabbed the mike out of Kent's hand, "Now, J.R. you listen to me. If that's the way you deal with teenagers lost in the night, then you've got no business being a Deputy Sheriff. "

"Oh, Geez. Sorry, Sarah, didn't know you were listening in. Didn't mean it that way."

"I'll bet you're sorry. Just keep your opinions to yourself, and go find my daughter."

Shaking his head and grinning at her, Kent hung up the mike. Walking to the closet by the back door, he pulled out his Carhartt overalls and knee boots.

Watching him curiously, she asked, "Just what are you doing?"

"Well, Hon, those kids couldn't have been in an accident or J.R. would have known about it. So, I'm going out to search for them."

"Not alone you're not. I'm going with you."

"Sarah, you can't. You have to stay here and let me know if they come home. I'll be alright. I think they either broke down or slid off the road somewhere. I'll take the boom truck in case I have to pull'em out."

CR EO

The first place Kent searched was Lookout Point, a teenage make-out spot overlooking the Mississippi River. It was a half-moon parking lot high on a bluff overlooking the Mississippi river. Kent and his friends always joked that they were going there to watch the submarine races. But they never attended without a girl in their arms.

The rain was coming down heavily, so most of the tire tracks were washed away. Still, he observed slight depressions between a set of tracks. They seemed out of place. Standing in the rain shining his flashlight on them Kent pondered what could have made the marks. Were they footprints? He couldn't be sure, so those were the tracks he followed.

CR EO

"Are you ok, Wendy?" Randy asked.

"No. I'm wet, cold, and scared to death. My parents are gonna kill me."

"I know. I hope you don't think I planned this."

Wendy grunted and pushed the truck. "Why would I think that? Or, do you always take your first dates out in a rainstorm and make them push your truck home?"

Laughing helped them ease the tension a little. "Wendy, this just sucks. I wanted you to have a good time."

Wendy turned her head to listen down the road. "Hey, do you hear something?"

ೞ೦

The kids appeared in his headlights as he drove up behind them. As he got closer, Kent could see them standing behind Randy's truck, wet and muddy. Immediately radioing the sheriff to let him know he'd found them, he heard, "Thank God, are they alright?" from Sarah, listening in on their base radio. "Yes, they're alright." Kent replied before he got out of the truck.

"Daddy." Wendy yelled, as Randy hung his head, and wished he were invisible.

Kent sloshed across the road towards them. "What seems to be the problem?"

Though Randy was afraid of what Wendy's dad would do, all six-foot-six of him, he didn't shrink in the face of her father. "Well sir," he said, "we were at Lookout Point, I'm sorry we did that sir. When we wanted to leave, my truck wouldn't start. Honest."

Kent was watching Wendy's reactions as Randy talked. He saw no drama, or nervousness to indicate otherwise. "Well, no sense standing out here getting soaked. Let's get in my truck."

Settled in his tow truck, out of the rain, he glanced over at the two cold, wet teenagers.

I don't think Sarah needs to worry about these two having much of a romantic evening. They're scared to death.

Reaching out his hand, he asked, "Wanna give me your keys son and I'll try to start your truck?"

As he got into the pickup and turned the key, he heard absolutely nothing. No starter. No solenoid. No sound at all. He returned to the kids in the cab of his own truck. "Dead battery, Randy. Why'd you decide to push it in this weather, anyway?"

Wanting to take Wendy on a date again, Randy was straight with her dad. "Well sir, to tell the truth, we didn't want anyone to know we'd been to Lookout Point."

Kent chuckled. "Son, I'd be surprised if you didn't go to Lookout Point. Everyone has."

Feeling a jab in his ribs, he looked down at Wendy. She was glaring up at him, whispering strongly. "Daddy, I can't believe you said that."

He just grinned at her.

"Well, guess I'd better get your pickup on the hook and take you home. "AAA trucker to base. You copy?"

Sarah jumped up from her chair. "Yes, what in the world is going on?"

"All's well. The kids had mechanical troubles. I'm going to drop Randy and his truck home. Then we'll head for the house."

"Please don't be too long. It's late and dangerous out there," Sarah said, as she remained standing by the CB radio.

"I know. Why don't you call Randy's folks and let them know what's going on. I'll hook him up now. Over."

"10-4." Sarah left the mike and went to the phone to call the Wagner's.

CR&

After Wendy's dad left to hook up the truck, Randy whispered to Wendy. "I'm so nervous, Wendy. What's your dad going to do to me?

Watching her dad through the rain-blurred window Wendy replied, "I don't know Randy, but he doesn't seem that mad to me."

"Maybe he's just waiting until we're all in here together?"

"Maybe. Just keep quiet and let me do the talking if we have to, ok?"

"Ok."

ଊ ଈ

Kent got directions from Randy to his house. After unhooking the truck, he asked Randy if he'd like him to stop by the next day to replace his battery. Afraid to spend any time alone with Wendy's dad, Randy said, "No, thank you. My dad will help me."

Kent and Wendy left and headed for home. Wendy jabbered continually about how it was just an accident. They hadn't spent that much time at Lookout Point. She and Randy hadn't done anything bad.

Kent interrupted her. "Settle down, Honey. It was just an unfortunate incident. But I do have a suggestion."

Wendy looked him curiously. "What's that Daddy?"

"Finish buttoning your blouse before we get home."

Wendy was shocked. Looking down at herself, she felt the heat from her face blushing, and buttoned the three top buttons of her blouse.

She continued to hang her head, ashamed and embarrassed. Wendy peeked at her Dad out of the corner of her eye, waiting for the other shoe to drop. It didn't.

Sarah seemed distraught when Wendy and Kent arrived. "Wendy Jo, didn't I tell you to be home by eleven? "You should know better than to let a boy take advantage of you like this."

Instantly Wendy was ready for combat. "Hey, that's not fair. I told you I don't do that stuff. Why is it so hard for you to believe me?"

Kent tried to intervene. "Now, now, you two settle down and listen to me. Honey, the boy's battery died. They were scared to death we'd think the worst, so they tried to push his truck to a safe place." He chuckled. "I think our Randy Wagner thought I was going to kill him or something."

Wendy looked up at him. "He did, Dad. He was really scared"

Sarah spoke to Wendy with an edge in her voice, "Well, can you imagine what went through my mind while you were missing?"

Kent raised his hands and walked between Wendy and her mother. "Ladies, ladies, ladies. It's late. He turned to Wendy, "You're cold, wet and muddy. Get upstairs, take a hot shower and go to bed."

Sarah wasn't letting her drag mud through her house. As Wendy went into the kitchen, she called out to her, "Throw those clothes in the washroom first. I don't want mud all over the house."

Once Wendy was gone, Kent looked at Sarah. "And how about you, do you need to cool off?"

Not appreciating the remark, she turned away to leave the porch, "I'm just fine, thank you."

Kent followed her into the house.

As Wendy ran up the stairs, she stopped and looked back at her father. She didn't know why he had done it, but she was grateful he warned her about her blouse, and kept her out of a jam with Mom. He was her hero.

CHAPTER 4

Teddy had stayed too long fishing and was afraid he'd be late for work at Wilma's Café, again, so he pedaled his bike as fast as he could. He cut into a driveway and across the corner of the yard trying to save time. When he shot into the street again, a horn and screeching tires startled him, but he continued to race down the street.

When a car pulled alongside he just pedaled harder trying to beat it to the next intersection.

Whrrrrrr. The siren's blast almost burst his eardrums. Sheriff J.R. Norvus angled his patrol car to the curb, cutting him off and forcing him to stop.

"What are you doing, J.R.?"

" I'm going to be late for work."

"Trying to control a menace. Do you know I can give bicycle riders a ticket?"

"What for? I can't speed on a bike."

"Reckless driving, son. Cutting through yards, running a stop sign, and cutting off that driver."

"You're not giving me a ticket for that are you?"

"No, but I could. Consider this a warning. Your sister made a fool of me more than once with her mischief, and I'm not letting another Crodin kid do it to me."

Teddy was furious. "J.R., you can't take it out on me just because Wendy caused trouble. That's not fair. "

"Fair or not, I've got you in my sights, and I ain't letting you get away with anything. Now, get going, and obey the law or you'll have two tickets."

⋘⋙

Wilma had bussed tables and was putting dirty dishes into the sink when Teddy entered through the back door. She turned toward him with a scowl on her face.

"Well, nice of you to show up for work, Teddy. What is this, maybe the third day you're late in two weeks? A lot of kids would like your job, you know, if you find it so hard to show up on time."

"Wilma, I'm so sorry. J.R. stopped me because he didn't like the way I was riding my bike. I told him I had to get to work, but I had to listen to his lecture first."

Wilma shook her head. "So now the sheriff made you late. That's one helluva excuse. Once more, son. If you're late one more time, you're out of a job.

Teddy put on his apron and started bussing tables, scared of Wilma and angry at J.R. But mostly, angry at his sister, Wendy.

⋘⋙

When Teddy got home after work, he went straight to Wendy's bedroom, which was painted a saddle brown to match her burnt pine bed frame. The walls were covered with pictures of rodeo cowboys and horses. Her cowboy boots were tossed on the floor. The only semblance of order was her straw cowboy hat resting on a bed post.

She looked up as he opened her door. "Get lost, Brat. I'm sick."

Teddy entered her bedroom and closed the door. "Good. Gives you time to think about this. I'm going to be your worst nightmare, Sis."

"You already are," she said between coughs.

"What did you do to piss of J. R. so bad that he's threatening me?"

"Poor baby. The sheriff doesn't like you?"

"Yeah, all because of you and the trouble you caused. He just threatened to give me a ticket for the way I rode my bicycle."

Wendy rolled onto her back and covered her chest with a pillow. "So now he knows you're crazy, too. Big deal."

"What did you do, Wendy, that's got the sheriff so pissed off?"

She blew her nose, hoping to gross him out. "None of your business."

"I can find out, you know."

"Then go do it, dweeb. Now, get outta my room. I told you I'm sick."

"Watch your back, Wendy. You haven't heard the end of this."

ᏣᏍᎲ

Zoey walked down the path to the fishing hole noticing the big grey clouds moving fast across the sky. She didn't feel a wind yet, but knew she would soon. She guessed it would rain overnight. Reaching the end of the path, she walked through the opening to the fishing hole. Teddy already had his hook in the water when he heard Zoey and looked her way

"Where have you been?" He asked.

"Oh, Mom made me do some chores before I could leave. I think she knew where I was going, and tried to mess with me."

"Well, you're here now. Better hurry, fish are bite'n."

As she prepared her fishing pole, Teddy noticed the size of her fishhook. "Better put on a smaller hook. That's too big for the fish I'm catching.

"Ok. Thanks." She took out her pliers and cut the bigger hook off the line.

With the smaller hook in her hand, Zoey tried to thread the line through the eyelet. It wasn't working with her hands trembling like they were.

"Hey. What's wrong with you? You never have trouble threading a hook."

Keeping her head down, she didn't want to look at him. "Just nervous I guess."

"About what?"

"Oh, stuff."

Shaking his head, he asked, "Is this girl stuff again?"

Zoey nodded, "Yeah."

"What is it this time?"

Glancing at Teddy, she said, "It's hard to tell you."

Like a great orator, Teddy threw his head back and declared, "Really? Let's see. You told me about the first time you pooped in a potty; you told me when you saw your mom and dad naked; you told me when Buster barfed on your mom's new couch and you cleaned it before she ever saw it. So, what could make you so nervous now?"

"I want to kiss."

Teddy was stunned. "What?"

She still didn't look at Teddy. "Yeah, I want to."

Fixing his gaze out over the creek, he asked, "Why are you telling me?"

Zoey threw her line in the water and turned to Teddy with a smile, "Because I want you to kiss me."

He turned away to focus on his bobber.

Folding her legs under her, Zoey looked out over the creek as she talked. "Well Teddy, all the girls in school are talking about the boys they've kissed. And, I'm the only one who hasn't kissed a boy. I feel stupid and left out. I just want to do it so I know what they're talking about. Will you kiss me, Teddy?"

"Holy cow." Teddy said as looked at her. "I've never kissed a girl. Are you sure you've got the right guy?"

"Yes. If I'm going to kiss boys, I want you to be the first."

He stiffened. "You're not going to give up until we do it, are you?"

She smiled at him. "No, I want to do it."

"Well, Mom always told me if I have to do something I don't like, it's better to just get it over with. So, I'll kiss you if it'll make you happy."

Zoey was excited to be kissed, and watched Teddy set down his fishing pole, lean toward her, and place his hand on her thigh. She pursed her lips like she'd seen in the movies and waited with anticipation. Teddy kissed her on the check.

She was upset and slugged his shoulder. Already off balance, Teddy fell back.

"That's not a kiss," she said.

"Is too."

"Is not. That's how my Dad kisses Mom when he leaves for work. It's not a real kiss."

Teddy shrugged his shoulders. "So now what?"

Putting her finger to her lips, she told him, "On the lips, silly. That's a kiss."

"Oh, Geez."

So they sat with their hips together and arms around each other. Their lips touched lightly, but Zoey pulled him closer so she could feel the warmth. After a few seconds, Teddy pulled away.

"Whew. That ought to do."

It sure did. She felt warm all over. It was exciting. Her pulse pounded in her chest. Her lips tingled.

Teddy interrupted her blissful feelings. "So, now that you've been kissed, you gonna fish or what?"

Zoey felt warm and excited about her first kiss, but knew she'd pushed Teddy far enough for one day.

"Yeah, let's fish."

CHAPTER 5

Since they'd both been sick with bad colds and chills, it was Wednesday before Wendy saw Randy again, It was when he boldly drove into their farmyard after school and walked right up to the door. Wendy held her breath and watched her mom closely.

Sarah looked out the screen door. "Well, what do we have here?"

Wendy replied nervously, "It's Randy, Mom."

"I see." She got up and opened the screen door before Randy could knock, opening it wide so he had to backtrack. She stood facing him with one hand on the door and the other on her hip. "Well, well. Who are you, young man?"

Thumbs in his pockets and looking her in the eye he answered. "Randy Wagner, Mrs. Crodin."

Without a smile, she asked. "And, what is your business?"

Wendy lowered her head in her hands to hide her face. Her mother was treating Randy like a burglar.

Randy didn't flinch. "Well, ma'am, I've come to apologize for the trouble I put you and your family through during the storm."

Now, Sarah acted surprised, "Apologize?"

Randy stood his ground.

Wendy peeked between her fingers. Good job, Randy. Hang in there.

"Yes ma'am. I have too much respect for Wendy to strand her out in a storm like we did. And I'm sure it worried you. Please forgive me. I would like to take Wendy on another date, you see."

Letting loose of the door, it slammed shut. Now both hands were on her hips. "Do you think you could do that, young man, without disrupting our whole family?"

Randy turned hoping to see Wendy through the screen door. He couldn't. He looked back to her Mom. "I'm sure I can, ma'am."

"Anything else to say for yourself, Mr. Wagner?"

"No, ma'am. I'll be off now. Thank you for hearing me out."

Randy turned and was down the porch steps, into his truck and out the lane.

When Sarah entered the kitchen, Wendy shook her head. "Geez, Mom, could you be any bitchier? He didn't deserve that."

"I guess I could have, but I learned what I wanted."

"Which is?"

Sarah sat across from her. "I've learned you have good taste in men."

Wendy looked up from the table at her Mom. "You're impossible. You just made Randy feel like crap, so you can say I have good taste in men?"

"Yes, Honey. Plus, I can tell he's responsible or he wouldn't have come here at all. He's honest. He didn't try to BS me. He's got backbone. And, he has respect for you. That boy comes from good parents."

Wendy was shaking her head as she listened. "Are you going to do this to every boy I date?"

"Not at all. But this one must really be attracted to you."

CB&CO

Kent put his hands between his head and the pillow. "From what I hear you were pretty hard on young Mr. Wagner today."

"Maybe. But you know Wendy's version is going to be twice as intense as reality."

He rolled toward her. "I feel sorry for the boy. He had a rough night with his date and her dad. Then he has to face the snarling mother. Woulda scared the hell outta me when I was his age."

Sarah pushed away from him. "Who said I was snarling?" Then she laughed as she curled up to sleep.

಄

Spring was wetter than usual, and everybody was sick and tired of the rain. Heavy thunderstorms would roll in, dumping three to five inches of rain before they left. Adding the snowmelt turned fields into ponds, highway ditches like canals, and the streets of Clayton as deep as children's wading pools.

Sarah's family wore their rubber knee boots everywhere they went. She demanded they leave them on the porch to keep the mud out of the house. It reminded her of the time Wilma made her take her snow boots off at the door of her café. She had resisted then, but now understood Wilma's logic.

At supper all they talked about was the rain, and the Mississippi River rising.

Kent got up to refresh his drink. "You know, if this rain doesn't stop we're going to be in big trouble."

"Does it make that much difference?" Sarah asked.

He turned to answer her. "You bet it does. You've seen it crest over the flood wall before. And that was in normal years. You add this rain to the snow melt and the river is going to rise like you've never seen before."

"What do the guys say at the barbershop, Dad?" Teddy asked.

Returning to his seat at the table he said, "Same thing. Roy's preparing for it already."

"Guess I'd better talk to Wilma about it, too, huh?"

"Son, I'm sure she has a plan just like Roy. Nothin' new to them."

CЗ ഇ

"Wheeee-oooooo, weeee-errrrrrrr-weeeeee-errrrrrrr."

Startled, Sarah sat up in bed. "Kent! What is that?"

Kent wiped the sleep out of his eyes, leaned up on his elbow and said, "The lock and dam's new siren. The river's at flood stage."

With her hand over her racing heart Sarah asked, "Do they have to do that in the middle of the night?"

"The river doesn't wait for anybody. Get the kids up, we've gotta go."

As they got out of bed, she still didn't comprehend. "Where are we going?"

"Sarah, we've got to go help sand bag. We can't stop the flood, but maybe we can protect buildings and businesses. Come on, we're wasting time.

When Kent had the kids in the kitchen, he started giving orders. "Everybody get your rain suits, rain hats and boots. Meet me at my truck. I'll get the shovels."

Sleepily Sarah and the kids complied. Wendy and Teddy got in the back seat, leaning against the windows trying to go back to sleep. Sarah was in the front seat when Kent tossed four shovels in the bed of his truck. Then they headed for town.

When they reached town Sarah thought the scene was bazaar. In the shadows of the night, she saw men unhooking a conveyer belt and pushing it down the middle of the street. Dump trucks were leaving piles of sand in the street, instantly soaking up four inches of water. Pickup after pickup was filled with pallets of white bags, their strings waving in the air.

"Kent, what do we do?" Sarah asked.

"Well, Wendy can shovel sand onto the conveyor. You and I can help fill bags and Teddy, you can carry and stack them."

As they got out of the truck, the kids followed reluctantly. They did what they were told; until Teddy saw the lights come on at Wilma's… he left his job and went straight to the café.

Poking his head in the back door Teddy asked, "Wilma, do you need help?"

Surprised to see Teddy, she smiled and said, "Well, yes I do. Someone has to feed all these volunteers. Get in here and help me."

CB&O

Wendy found herself at the conveyor with Billy Geitz and Randy Wagner, in the middle of the street, standing in three inches of water. A dump truck bed was raised, leaving a second load of sand beside them, so they backed away until it was empty. She looked at the boys and asked, "What are we supposed to do?"

"Shovel sand onto the conveyor so they can fill the bags when it rolls off the other end," Billy told her. "Two scoops then wait for about a foot or two before adding two more scoops. Otherwise, they don't have time to prep the next bag. Got it?"

Wendy nodded. "Yeah, I get it."

As the three of them loaded scoops of sand onto the conveyor, Wendy took interest in how the boys worked. Randy was like a rabbit, shoveling fast for fifteen minutes then taking a break. On the other hand, Billie was like the tortoise, working steadily with Randy and right on through Randy's break.

In his enthusiasm, Randy started adding a third shovel full of sand to each pile on the conveyor. It wasn't long before they heard complaints from the baggers. "Hey, stop that. There's too much sand and we're wasting it."

"Randy," Wendy said. "You know that's too much sand, quit it."

Randy sneered at her. "Oh, to hell with it. I'm goin' to find an easier job." He threw down his shovel and walked away.

Billy watched him go and shook his head. "Never was much of a worker anyway. No loss."

ⳤⲃⲟ

Wilma was standing next to Teddy. "You watch these muffins baking while I go look for a cart of some sort. We'll take them out to the volunteers when they're cool."

The sun had come up so Teddy could see all the people working… filling and stacking sand bags. He saw all his classmates helping alongside their parents.

Man, there's goin' to be a lot of people to feed.

When Wilma returned, he asked her, "Wilma, is the café going to survive this?"

"Don't know, Son, but you and I are going to work until we have to shut her down and run."

Zoey burst through the back door. "Hey, can I help?"

Wilma looked at her and smiled. "Well, lookie here. A little angel of mercy. Yes, you can help. Tell you what, I found two carts, so each one of you can fill them with muffins and deliver them to the volunteers."

"Cool," Zoey said with excitement. "Come on. You go north and I'll go south."

As Zoey passed Roy's barbershop, she saw a man carrying a five-gallon water jug over his shoulder and a sleeve of cups. There were other men in Roy's so she figured they were doing the same thing.

| CHAPTER 6

"Wilma. You won't believe what I heard." Teddy said as he rushed into the café with his cart.

"I can't imagine. What did you hear?"

"Norm had a heart attack. The ambulance is there now loading him up."

Wilma stopped what she was doing. "Good Lord, he really did?"

"Yeah. They're locking the place up."

Wilma went back to work. "Well, given the circumstances, probably wouldn't hurt any."

He couldn't believe Wilma didn't get it. "But, Wilma, they can't close his business now. We need boats. It's goin' to be the only way to get around."

Wilma shook her head. "Now, settle down. Someone will figure it out."

"But, I already did. I'm going to run it while he's gone. I can't stay here; I've got to help Norm."

Wilma was not happy about that idea. "What? You can't leave me now. In case you forgot, you work for me, not Norm. Now, you get over here and help me. Someone else can help Norm."

"I can't Wilma. I know his place too well. Nobody knows it like I do. I have to help him."

Zoey pushed her cart through the back door and saw Teddy and Wilma shouting at each other.

"Hey, what's going on?" Zoey asked.

Wilma was still angry when she spoke to her. "He thinks he needs to abandon us to go help Norm."

She didn't understand. "Why, Teddy?"

"Norm just had a heart attack. There are boats to rent and his place to take care of. I've got to go help him."

Turning to Wilma Zoey said to her, "Don't worry about him. I'll stay here. I won't leave ya'."

Wilma turned her back on him. "Harrumph."

Teddy left the café and headed down the street to Norm's Bait and Tackle Shop.

It was a dreary walk through the water under heavy dark clouds and a wind off the river. The only one in town who knew where Norm hid his key, Teddy pulled the plant out of a terracotta pot by its stem. Retrieving Norm's hidden key in the bottom he opened the shop. Everything was the same as he remembered. The flood was straining the floating docks to their limits. Teddy was most concerned about the boats. Only five minutes after he'd opened people were asking to rent boats. Not knowing what Norm charged, Teddy decided on fifty dollars a day. The sheriff wanted two more boats. The Volunteer Fire Department wanted four boats. Locals rented the others, leaving Teddy standing on the dock with only personal boats bouncing in the waves and bumping the dock.

CB&CO

Zoey's shoes were soaked as she waded through ankle deep water pushing her cart full of hot dogs for the volunteers. She was tired, but not as tired as the people she saw filling sandbags. Teddy's mom noticed her and hollered out, "Zoey, over here."

Zoey grabbed a couple hot dogs for Teddy's mom and dad and waded their way.

"Where's Teddy? Sarah asked. "We haven't seen him for hours."

Pointing toward the boat dock she said, "When we heard about Norm's heart attack he went to run his business. He's there now if you want him."

"Is he ok?"

"Sure he is. Teddy can take care of himself," Zoey said proudly.

CR&

Teddy wasn't sure what to do. The dock wasn't going to stay tethered as the river rose, and the boats were going to get damaged or rip off and float down river. He had to do something, so he went to Norm's office and started calling all the slip renters he could find.

"Yeah, I know Norm's in the hospital, but that's not what I'm calling about," he'd say. "Your boat's taking a beating here, and people still want to rent boats. If you'll let me rent yours for fifty dollars a day I'll split it with you. You'll make a little money and your boat will be safe. What do 'ya say, 'go,' or 'no go'?"

Well, it was 'go' for all the owners and Teddy had no trouble renting their boats. That solved the first problem. Now for the second one.

The floodwater kept raising the dock higher and higher, straining the one-inch ropes. Teddy figured that if he cut the ropes tethering the docks in just the right way, he could swing the dock around so the river would push it into shore. Which was first and in what order would make all the difference. Teddy loosened all the ropes toward the shore so the dock would have room to swing. Starting the chain saw, he cut the first rope at the end of the dock. Then he cut one on the opposite side. Back and forth, he worked his way from the channel side of the river toward shore. His heart was pounding and his nerves were on edge. Teddy knew one mistake and this whole thing would be down river and crushed in the locks, him included.

When the dock started to turn, Teddy found the tautest rope and cut it. Then the next and the next. Bouncing on the heavy waves he rode the dock like a rodeo cowboy until it was finally shoved into the shore. Teddy had done it! Norm's dock was saved, if it would only stay there. Standing on the dock with chain saw in hand, Teddy let the reality of what had just happened sink in. He was proud, but exhausted. Realizing there was nothing more for him to do, he jumped onto the shore and walked to Norm's shop to stow the chain saw and lock up. Then Teddy headed for Wilma's.

⊗⊗

While Zoey was a very good helper, Wilma missed Teddy. He had the energy for this job that she didn't anymore. She'd put a lot of time and effort into bringing him up in the business, and he'd done well. Excellent cook, he was. Wilma was flat tired and close to the end of her rope when Teddy rushed through the back door.

"Hey, I'm back."

"And I suppose you want me to welcome a traitor with open arms? Leaving me high and dry? Do I need to have a heart attack too, before you'll help me?"

"Oh geez, Wilma, don't be so dramatic. First you gotta' have a heart."

Wilma rushed up to Teddy and threw her arms around him. "Why you little whipper-snapper, I oughta ring your neck. But I'm tired, so I'm going to sit down. Get to work."

"Yes, ma'am. Don't mind if I do."

⊗⊗

The town folks did all they could, but the flood was the worst in a hundred years. After thirty-two straight hours the river rose high enough to stop the sandbagging operation. Pumps were now in use to relieve the stress on the community.

The Crodin family dragged their tired and dirty bodies into Kent's truck. Sarah sank in her seat and leaned her head back to rest. "You know," she said to anybody listening, "this mess is going to last for weeks."

"Yeah, I know," Kent replied.

"Businesses will be closed, and we'll have to go out-of-town to shop. And I'll bet the cleanup will be as bad as the sand bagging."

"Yeah, Mom," Teddy remarked. "But at least Norm survived his heart attack. He should be home next week."

"Lot of good that's going to do him," she said. "Where's he gonna live? Wilma has moved to her sisters until the café can be opened again."

Kent looked back at Teddy. "And, Roy went to his brothers."

"Just think," Sarah added, "All the kids in town will get cabin fever having to stay home with their mothers until the schools could open again."

On that note, Wendy and Teddy spoke in unison, "Not going to happen, Mom."

CHAPTER 7

Sunday, two months later

"I told you it was a dumb idea. You almost died."

Looking through the slits of his swollen eyelids Teddy could barely see Zoey. She sat in a chair next to his hospital bed with her legs folded under her and her arms crossed tightly across her chest. He could see her scowling face looking at him.

He tried to hold his head up to see her. "It wasn't dumb. We saw everything we wanted to and never were caught. It was Kenny that ran into the beehive and knocked off the lid."

Rolling her eyes and shaking her head in disbelief, Zoey replied, "Yeah, as if you didn't know there are a million honey bees on old man Shone's farm."

"I knew that. We were careful. And I would have gotten away if I hadn't tripped on a rock."

"Look what it gotcha'. You've got a ga-zillion bee stings and a broken arm. Was it worth it to snoop around his place? Huh? Oh, and guess what? Old man Shones' was home after all. He's the one that saved ya' and carried you back to his house to get the bees off ya'."

"He was? He was supposed to be gone. No one had seen him for weeks."

Dr. Carr entered the room with Teddy's dad, the local veterinarian, and of all people, Willard Shones, owner of the farm the kids had snuck onto this morning after church.

"Will you excuse us, Zoey? I need to treat our patient here."

She got off her chair and started to leave the room as Dr. Carr pulled the curtain around Teddy's bed. The doctor's chatter was loud enough that no one noticed Zoey didn't actually leave the room. Quietly walking around the curtain, she looked between the wall and the curtain's edge. She had to, of course, because Willard Shones hardly ever came to town and this had to be a special occasion for him to visit the hospital. Zoey just had to know what he was doing.

Teddy's dad was the first to speak. "Well, Doc, Willard here is sure this ointment will cure the itching and swelling so we brought some to try."

Dr. Carr looked at Willard. "Have you ever used this ointment before?"

"Yup. Used her plenty of times on myself, don't ya know. I get bit from time to time by them bees."

"Ok, then," Dr. Carr remarked. "Why don't you go ahead and treat his bee stings, and we'll watch. Ok?"

"Just fine with me, Doc," Willard answered.

Zoey saw Willard open a baby food jar. The stuff in it looked sorta gray and green. It was a color Zoey had never seen.

"Now, see here," Willard, said as he applied the ointment on each of Teddy's bee sting welts, "It's not necessary to cover the whole welt, just the stinger part. This here ointment works its way into the wound and heals it."

Kent watched with interest. "I like that, Willard. Makes the ointment go a long way, doesn't it?"

Willard smiled with pride, "Yep, just a little dab'll do ya'"

Dr. Carr then asked Willard, "I've seen a little of how you use this. Would you mind if I try? I have four more boys with bee stings and I'm sure you won't want to treat all of them. Let's see if I've got the hang of it. Ok?"

"Sure, Doc," Willard said as he handed over the bottle of ointment.

Zoey stood quietly watching Teddy's face for signs of pain. That gooey stuff must not hurt 'cause he didn't flinch. When the three men turned to leave his bedside, she slid toward his bed, stopping in her tracks when she heard a new voice in the room.

"J.R.," Teddy's dad said. "What brings you here?"

"Just doing my job, Kent. Issuing trespassing citations for these boys."

There was a pause that made her nervous, so Zoey squatted down and hid at the side of the bed.

Teddy's dad broke the silence. "Now, J.R., do you think that's necessary when all these kids were doing was satisfying their curiosity? It would be mean spirited to fine them."

"No sir. I'm sorry, Kent, but your daughter made a fool of me and with this election coming up, I'm not letting anybody do that to me again."

Dr. Carr entered the conversation, saying, "Sounds a little vindictive to me, J.R."

"Call it what you want, I'm just enforcing the laws on the books. Now, here's his citation, Kent. I trust you'll see to it that Teddy gets it."

When Zoey was sure they were out of the room she stood up to look at the gunk they'd put on Teddy's bee stings.

Feeling her presence, Teddy moved his hand to the edge of the bed. "Is that you, Zoe?"

"Yeah."

"I thought you'd left," he mumbled.

She didn't touch his gooey hand. "No, I want to see this stuff on your bee stings. Does it hurt?"

"Naw, can't feel a thing."

"You'd better hope it works."

"They said it will."

"Yeah, but adults say anything just to make kids feel better. Well, I gotta go home for supper."

"You gonna come tomorrow?"

"Only if I run out of intelligent people on the planet to talk to."

"Hey, that's not fair."

Zoey walked past the curtain to leave. "Oops, hello, Mrs. Crodin!"

"Hello Zoey. How's our patient coming along?"

"Just as dumb as ever," she replied.

Thinking Zoey had said 'numb', Sarah asked,

"His head or his body dear?"

Mrs. Crodin's mistake tickled her. "Both if you ask me. Sorry, but I've gotta go. Nice to see you ma'am."

"And you, Zoey."

As their cute neighbor left the room, Sarah stepped around the curtain to see Teddy.

CRSO

After telling Dr. Carr goodbye, Kent turned to Willard, "so what in the world is this stuff?"

Willard grinned. "This ain't nothing new Doc. I've been making it for years fer bee stings, skin rashes and such. Pretty damn good stuff, if I say so myself."

Kent looked at the jar of ointment. "I don't doubt that, Willard, but the scientist in me needs to know the ingredients. What do you use to make it?"

Opening the door at the hospital exit Willard said, "Plantain mostly. Easy to find in these parts. If you put a leaf in your mouth and chew it so there's some spit on it, you just rub a bee sting and it won't hurt anymore."

"Willard, if all you have to do is chew plantain, why do you make an ointment?"

"Well," he said looking at the jar of ointment in his hand, "the plantain only takes care of the stingin' part. I use four other plants for the healin' part."

"Come on, Willard. There's five plants in this? You're starting to sound like an Indian medicine man."

"It's true." Willard started to count them out on his fingers. "You got yer echinacea for disinfecting; witch hazel for the itching and inflammation; then there's camfrey's protective coating fer skin healin'.

"So, what's the fifth one?"

"Aloe Vera. It hydrates the skin, but when I put all this in a blender, it's the thing that makes the pasty part.

Kent was becoming more curious by the minute. "I really want to see how you make this ointment, Willard. Could we do that someday?"

"Sure, son, just name the day."

They turned into Willard's farmyard. Before Willard got out, Kent said, "Well sir, we'll see if your concoction does any good for those kids. In spite of what you've said, I'm still curious about what chemicals are in that jar. Can I take it to my lab and investigate some?"

Willard handed him the jar of ointment. "Here 'ya go. Let me know whatcha find."

"I will. See you later, Willard."

Willard stepped out of the truck and closed the door. "Thanks for the ride."

CR BO

Leaning against the bathroom doorframe, Sarah waited for Kent to finish brushing his teeth.

"What's up?" he asked her reflection in the mirror.

"I just have a question. When you were a kid, were you as adventurous and mischievous as Teddy and his friends seem to be?"

He turned to face her. "Yes, as I recall, I was. Never had anything happen like this bee incident, but we had our narrow escapes."

Sarah shook her head and declared, "Young boys must be bored out of their minds to do such stupid stuff. I don't get it."

He put his finger under her chin and raised her head. "Honey, it's all very simple. Young boys are just establishing their boundaries. They go until they fail, then draw a line they never cross again.

"Kent Crodin, if that's the logic behind it all, it's absurd." Leaving the bathroom, she got into bed. "Anyway, how was your day?"

He slid into bed. "Mine? I spent the day with a medicine man"

Sarah rolled across the bed and put her chin on his shoulder. "So, doctor, did you think your education was over?"

"Of course not. I just didn't imagine I'd be involved in herbal medicine.

"It certainly can't hurt. Good Night."

CR&O

It had been three days since Sarah had engaged in a meaningful conversation with Kent. He needed a break. She walked from the house through the veterinary clinic and opened the door to his lab.

"Hey, Doc. Are you ever going to come up for air?"

Startled from his deep thoughts, Kent smiled at her. "Yes, I suppose I should."

"Well, I've got a cold beer out on the porch waiting for you." With a wink and a flirty little hip movement, she said 'Suit yourself,' as she closed the door.

Soon after she settled into the porch swing with a glass of wine, Kent showed up.

"And the mad scientist comes out of his cave, blinded by the light of day and fearful of earthly beings."

He took a slug of the beer she had promised. "Oh come on, I wasn't working that long was I?"

Sarah leaned forward to look at him. "You've been obsessed with that ointment of Willard's. Just what are you doing?"

He shook his head. "I've been trying to overcome a roadblock. I can separate the elements in his ointment, but I can't analyze them. I've tried all I know, with no results."

"You're trying too hard."

Kent turned to her. "Trying too hard? How do you mean that?"

Putting a hand on his thigh, she said softly. "Honey, you don't have to do this all by yourself. There are labs and specialists at Iowa State that can help you. Why haven't you asked for their help?"

Sitting up with renewed energy Kent said, "You're right. Why didn't I think of the university lab? I'm going to call tomorrow and make arrangements to take this ointment to their lab. It's much more sophisticated than mine." Leaning over and kissed her on the cheek. "Thanks, Honey."

Sarah raised her eyebrows as she looked at him. "Are you going to take Willard with you?"

"Willard?"

She patted his hand. "Yes. It's his concoction, he'd love a road trip, and I'm sure he's never seen a laboratory.

CHAPTER 8

The weather cleared two days later, providing a beautiful day for a road trip. Kent opened the door of his pickup, stretched his left leg full length and rested it on the hinge between the body and the door. Fifteen minutes ago, Willard had waved from the porch saying he'd be just a minute. He hadn't seen him since.

When he did show up, Willard had a basket full of weeds with him, and put them on the seat between them.

"This here's them weeds you asked me to pick. Got three of each, just like you said."

"Very good, Willard. The scientists will want to separate the compounds of the actual plant material you have there, as well as separating the elements of your ointment in a centrifuge. I suppose it'll help them match up the test results and identify the chemical elements."

"Whoa, now. Are we gonna talk this way the whole day? Cause I didn't understand half of what you just said."

"No Willard, we won't. You let me handle the technical talk, and I'll let you handle the questions about your weeds, ok?"

"Yep. I wanna enjoy this adventure, not be confused all day. Coulda stayed home and done that."

CB ∞

The large buildings on the campus of Iowa State University mesmerized Willard.

Kent smiled as he watched Willard acting like a little boy. "Well, Willard, welcome to Iowa State University."

Willard looked at buildings as far as he could see. "How the hell do you find anything here? This place is huge."

"I suppose it gets easier the more time you're here. Don't worry, I know where we're going."

They drove through campus so Willard could see the sites. Then Kent turned south towards the veterinary medicine facilities. Willard was trying to see everything at once, but he stopped to gaze at the central campus landscape.

"Holy smokes. That there is pretty!"

"It is, Willard. Actually it was picked as one of the twenty-five most beautiful campuses in the country, back in '91."

"Sure can see why. That was worth the trip, son."

Kent drove another five minutes before he pulled up and parked at the Veterinary Medicine Complex.

Willard looked up at the four-story building and asked, "This building is taller than the trees. How high up do we have to go to see these people?

"Fourth floor, Willard."

Willard looked at him with a questioning look. "Well, how do we get there?"

Kent smiled and put his arm over Willard's shoulder. "The elevator. I'll show you. Ever been in one?"

Willard was hesitant. "Nope."

They walked into the building to an area where people were standing.

Something went 'ding' and Willard watched people rush into a box. The door shut and they were all gone.

When the next bell rang, the doors opened again. Kent patted Willard on the shoulder. "Come on, Willard, here's our elevator."

Willard backed up a step, shook his head and said "No. I ain't gettin' in that box."

Kent was caught off guard. "Why not, Willard?"

"Dang it." Willard pointed to the elevator. "That thing doesn't have windows. I ain't getting in there."

"Are you claustrophobic, Willard?"

Willard looked surprised. "No, I'm Presbyterian."

Kent gave in as he laughed. He could see it was no use discussing elevators with Willard, and they were wasting time. "Ok then, we can walk up. Do you want to do that?"

"Sure."

Dr. Steinhouse greeted Kent and Willard and walked them to the lab where the tests on Willard's ointment and plants would be made. Willard was overwhelmed with the sanitation required in the lab; it'd never do on his farm. He was also fascinated with the walls made of glass.

"Won't you please make yourselves comfortable here?" Dr. Steinhouse asked, showing them into a faculty lounge. "We'll test the ointment first. The plants, I'm afraid, will take longer. You may not want to wait for that, Kent."

Understanding the time involved, Kent said, "We do have to be home this evening. Let's see what happens, ok?"

"Sure." Dr. Steinhouse answered as he stepped out of the lounge.

They were comfortable enough, but the wait was boring. So they took a walk on campus. Willard had questions, and Kent did his best to answer them. It was a kind of game. It wasn't too strenuous on Willard, but Kent sure had to work at digging up answers for some of the simplest questions.

The two had just returned to the fourth floor faculty lounge when Dr. Steinhouse came into the room.

"Gentlemen, I have some good news, and then something I don't think you want to hear."

Kent smiled and stood to greet the doctor. "So, what have you found?"

"We've separated the ointment and identified the chemical compositions. Here's a list of what we've identified. We found glycosides, allantoin, and acids, namely amino, cichoric, caftaric, and Gallic. It'll all make some sense when we're done with the plants."

"How's that coming, Doc?"

"Slow at best. Not only are we trying to identify their chemical makeups, but the concentration in each plant will be important too. I'm afraid we're looking at two or three more days to accomplish that."

Kent turned to Willard. "Well, Willard, we're done here. Let's head for home."

Dr. Steinhouse held up his hand to stop him. "Listen, before you leave, can you and I talk?"

Kent was surprised. "Sure, what's up?"

He looked toward Willard and replied, "Alone, if you don't mind."

"Well, ok." Motioning toward the door, Kent asked Willard, "Would you mind waiting outside for a few minutes? We won't be long."

Willard obliged and left the room.

"Please sit down."

Seated again, Kent asked, "What's on your mind, Doc?"

Dr. Steinhouse sat up straight, placed his hands on his knees and said, "I want to offer you a job."

"What?" He said as he leaned toward Dr. Steinhouse. "Doc, I've got my own clinic to run. I don't want to move. Why are you asking such a thing?"

"Calm down. I know all that. I have a visiting professor position open, and I'd like you to take it."

Slumping back into his chair Kent asked, "Just what does a visiting professor do? And how often do they visit?"

Dr. Steinhouse had relaxed, now leaning on his knees looking at Kent. "I want you to teach research techniques. You're the best person at it I know. All I want is for you to teach a class every week or two during the semester. I need your help. Will you do it for me?"

Crossing his leg over his other knee, Kent leaned back and said, "I can't, Doc. I'd have to shut down my clinic each day. I assume visiting professors get paid, right?"

"Yes, of course." Dr. Steinhouse responded. "And I don't want it to ruin your business. I'm hoping it will supplement your income and help you develop a retirement career."

"A retirement career? Man, I haven't even thought of retirement yet."

"I know, but you've got to start sometime. Professorship takes time, Kent."

"Not now," Kent said. "Maybe later." He got up. "Doc, Willard's been waiting a while. I've gotta' go. Someday I may take you up on your offer, and thanks for your help in the lab. We appreciate it.

Dr. Steinhouse shook his hand. "Why don't I fax you the final results when we're done. There's no need to drive all this way again."

"Good idea, I appreciate it."

"Consider it done, then. Have a safe trip."

◌ ❦ ◌

The sunny day coaxed Willard into a nap giving Kent a quiet drive home. When they arrived in Clayton he dropped Willard off and drove home.

"How was your trip?" Sarah asked.

"Excellent. Got good information, and more will come in a few days. Thanks for the idea." He hugged and kissed her.

Sarah pointed to the phone, "I almost forgot. You have a message from Oly."

"What did he want?"

She was at the refrigerator, getting things out for supper, and said over her shoulder, "He wants you to join him for a beer."

Putting his hands on Sarah's waist, Ken leaned on her shoulder and asked, "How long do I have before supper?"

"An hour would be fine."

Kent chose to across the field to Oly's place instead of driving, and met him on his back patio.

"Hello, Doc," Oly said, greeting him.

"Hi, Oly. Good timing you know. I need a beer.

"Figured you would."

Taking the beer Oly offered, Kent sat in one of the Adirondack chairs and asked, "How are your sales coming along?"

"They were really good until we started experiencing this weird rash on sow's teats."

"A rash, huh? Where'd that come from?"

Oly sipped his beer, and then looked out over the landscape. "Have no idea, Kent. Just started this season when the piglets were born. Damned sows won't nurse."

Deep in thought for a moment, Kent said, "I've never heard of such a thing."

"Is there anything you can do to help?" Oly asked.

"I don't know, Oly."

The conversation turned to Kent's work at the clinic, their children, and of course Teddy's episode with bee stings and a broken arm. That's what sparked an idea.

"Say, Oly. I just might have something to help you. When Teddy was in the hospital Willard brought in an ointment that dried up the welts and burning in the bee stings."

Oly nodded, "Yeah, I remember hearing about that."

"Well, I was at Iowa State today getting some lab work done to analyze his ointment. Scientifically speaking, I don't know what it is, but I wonder if it would have any effect on these sows?"

Oly sat up, excitedly. "Man, I'll try anything. We've got nothing now."

"Well, on your way to work tomorrow, stop by the clinic and I'll give you a sample to try. It only took a day to work on the bee stings, but I don't know what it'll do in your case."

Oly was pleased that he had something to offer his customers. He handed Kent another beer and the conversation was much more informal until suppertime.

Kent patted Oly on the shoulder as he left. "Thanks for the beer, Oly. I've got to get home for supper."

CHAPTER 9

Rushing into the house, Wendy went to the living room and announced, "Daddy, she's ready."

Kent looked at Wendy with a matter-of-fact expression. "What's she doing, Honey?"

"She's restless and squatting and just nervous as a cat."

"You should be able to handle it. It's not your first time you know."

"Yeah, but Daddy, I want you to help."

"I will. Let me know when she starts to deliver, ok?"

Wendy's shoulders sagged as she left for the barn.

Having observed the conversation, Sarah felt it was time to share her point of view. "Are you proud of yourself, Doc?"

He was surprised. "What?"

"That was you daughter asking for your help, you know."

"Honey, I've delivered hundreds of foals. It's no big deal."

"That may be a doctor's point of view, but as a father you just blew it."

"Oh, come on."

"Kent, this is Wendy's horse. It's her first time delivering a foal. She doesn't need a doctor, she needs her father."

Frowning as he laid his book on the end table, Kent stood and looked at her. "You're right. That was the doctor speaking. This may take a while, so don't wait up for us."

He left the house to join Wendy in the barn.

CR ಬಿ

Wendy jumped off the hay bale she was sitting on and threw her arms around him. "Oh, Daddy, thanks for coming. I am so lonely and scared out here. I don't want anything to go wrong with Ginger"

Kent held her close, feeling her nervousness. "I'm here to help, Honey. We'll make sure that nothing happens to her. When was the last time you checked her?"

"Just before I came to the house."

"Ok, why don't you sit down and relax. I'll look in on her."

Cautiously, Kent looked around the door of the stall. Ginger was circling her stall, and breathing heavily. It looked to him like she was close to lying down and starting delivery. Looking back at Wendy, it appeared she needed more attention than Ginger. He returned, sat on the hay bale with her, and held her hand.

"She should begin delivery soon. I don't think we'll have to wait long."

Wendy squeezed his hand. "I'm so glad you're here, Daddy."

"You've been through this before. Don't get nervous about it. Just do what you know how to do, and I'll be right beside you to help."

"I'm not so sure I can."

"Well, I am. You'll do fine."

They waited in silence, hearing only their own quiet breathing and intermittent snorts from Ginger.

This is a lousy time to ask, but I'm never alone with Daddy much.

"Daddy, can I have a car?"

Kent was surprised. "Do we have to talk about this now?"

"Well, what other time are we alone?"

"Good point."

Wendy turned a little to face her dad. "I've wanted one for a while now. I need a car for school, rodeo events and stuff."

"Honey, I think I've already done that. My truck is available if you need to drive during the day, and mom doesn't use her truck much in the evening. That should be enough, don't you think?"

Wendy sighed. "But Daddy, I want my own. Won't you buy one for me, too?"

Throwing his arm around Wendy and hugging her, Kent said, "I understand that you want one of your own, but you'll have to do it on your own."

"But Daddy, I don't have any money like Teddy does."

He rose to check on Ginger and saw she had laid down to start delivery.

"Wendy, people that don't have money often barter for what they want. You could too, you know."

"I don't have anything to barter."

"You will in about an hour."

"What? You want me to barter Ginger's foal?"

Sitting next to Wendy again, Kent explained. "Before the days over you're going to have two horses to feed and care for. Are you prepared to spend the time and money to do that?"

"I didn't think of that."

"I'm not surprised. However, if you scouted around a little bit you might find someone who wants a horse more than a car or truck. Then, when Ginger's foal is weaned, you could close the deal."

"Is that what you do, Daddy?"

"Many times, Honey. You should know that. That's how we got Ginger, remember?"

"Was that bartering?"

"Yep."

Ginger whinnied. Kent leapt off the hay bale with Wendy following. The foal's nose was barely visible. Ginger was delivering.

Wendy opened her dad's medical bag and removed two pairs of long latex gloves and a roll of adhesive tape. She put her's on and held them on her arm while her dad taped them. Then she did the same for him.

"Now's the hard part, huh, Dad?"

"Yes, and patience isn't something you have a lot of."

Wendy pretended to pout. "Hey, I'm getting a lot better at it."

She went quietly to Ginger's stall and looked around the gate post. "Daddy, the foal's almost out. We still have to wait for the afterbirth, right?"

"Yes. We'll make sure Ginger and her foal are healthy just as soon as they've bonded.

೮೫౸

Wendy wanted a car badly enough to spend a weekend making posters with a picture of her new foal. She loaded them into her mom's truck and headed for town.

"Hi, Wendy," Roy Cutler said, greeting her to his barber shop. "You here for another haircut?"

Remembering the last haircutting fiasco at Roy's shop, Wendy wrinkled her forehead as she looked at him and replied, "Never."

"So what brings you here?" he asked.

"Will you let me put up my poster, Roy? I'm trying to barter my little foal for a car or truck."

"Ah-ha. Good idea. Go ahead. Lots of guys will see it in here."

"Thanks, Roy."

Wendy hung her poster picturing Ginger's new foal, and headed off to Dave's Tavern to do the same. Then the hardware store, beauty salons, restaurants, even Wilma's Café. Wilma was reluctant, because she didn't allow advertising in her café, but she let Wendy put her poster outside on the window by the door.

School was another place where Wendy talked it up, wanting everyone to know she had a foal to offer for a car.

And that was it. She didn't know what else to do but wait. And wait she did. Three weeks passed without an inquiry.

Cง৪১

Sarah was the first person to be contacted. While Wendy was in school, a stranger pulled into the farmyard in a two-toned maroon and white Ford pickup. She watched a thin man in his thirty's step out of the truck wearing a cowboy hat and riding boots. She went outside to meet him.

"Hello, can I help you?"

The man shook her hand. "I'm Tommy Ryan, ma'am. I don't know if this is the right place or not. I'm wanting to see about a new foal Wendy Crodin is interested in bartering for a car."

"Oh, yes. You've got the right place, but I'm afraid she's not here; she's in school."

"I see. Any chance I can see the foal?"

Pointing toward the barn, she said, "Sure, follow me."

They walked to the barn and Ginger's stall so Mr. Ryan could see the foal. Tommy took a few minutes watching the foal, and then turned to her. "Does she have a name yet?"

Sarah laughed. "Oh, no. Wendy won't name her on purpose thinking that if she did she could never give her away."

Mr. Ryan looked back into the stall. "Well, she's beautiful."

"May I ask, Mr. Ryan, why you're interested in this foal?"

"Yes, I'm sorry I didn't say earlier. My daughter loves riding. The only horses she can ride are on a neighboring farm. Wants her own, you know."

"I see. And, why are you looking at a foal instead of a riding horse?"

Mr. Ryan smiled at her. "Actually, ma'am, I have the idea that her interest will either wane or get stronger if she has to invest her own time and energy into what she wants. If it all works out, they will have grown up together."

She smiled. "You know Mr. Ryan, that's sort of what we're doing with Wendy."

They left the barn and walked to Mr. Ryan's truck. "When does your daughter get home from school?" he asked.

Frowning, she replied, "I'm sorry, but it'll be a couple more hours."

Mr. Ryan got into his truck, and looked out, "Sorry, I can't wait."

Writing on a scrap piece of paper he handed it to her when he was finished.

"Here's my name and number, ma'am. Maybe she could call and set a time for us to meet. Do you mind?"

Sarah took his note. "Not at all. She'll be pleased that you came by."

Starting his truck and putting it in gear, he said, "Ok, then. See you later."

Sarah waved. "Goodbye, Mr. Ryan."

Cଃଞ

Wendy walked from the school bus looking glum. She was discouraged.

I thought by now lots of people would want to barter for my horse. Everybody wants to barter with Dad.

When she came into the house Sarah told her, "There's a note on the table for you."

Wendy dropped her backpack on the floor and picked up the yellow scrap of paper with the name Tommie Ryan, and his phone number.

"What's this about, Mom?"

"I thought you'd guess. The man's interested in your foal."

"He was here, " Wendy asked excitedly?

"Yes. Stopped by two or three hours ago. He saw the foal and wants you to call him."

"Does he want to barter, Mom?"

"I think so. He wants to come back. He wants the foal for his daughter."

"How cool. Can I call him now?"

"Whenever you're ready, Honey."

Cଃଞ

"105,000 miles? Wendy asked. "Isn't that a lot?"

Mr. Ryan just smiled. "Wendy, if it was any less you'd have to give me two horses for it."

63

"It seems old, and I don't have a job, Mr. Ryan. So, I don't have money to fix it all the time."

He handed her the keys. "She's solid as a rock. Go ahead. Take it for a drive."

Wendy and her mom went off in the truck for a test drive. Neither was an expert, but it seemed nice enough. When they returned, Sarah got out of the truck saying, "Well, Wendy. It's up to you."

"Everything looks really nice, Mom, except all those miles, but I don't think I can do better." She walked up to Mr. Ryan with the keys. "You've got a deal, Mr. Ryan. When do you want to pick up Ginger's foal?"

"How about Saturday? You won't have school, and I can find a helper. Take the truck home with you, now. I'll see you Saturday morning."

Wendy was so excited driving home. She bounced in the seat cheering, "I did it. I did it! Isn't this cool, Mom? My first barter and I got a truck. Wait 'til Dad hears about this."

Sarah had to smile watching Wendy act so excited. "I think he just did."

| CHAPTER 10

On Saturday morning the sun was coming up through the haze hanging in the sky when Teddy rode his bicycle to Zoey's house where she was waiting for him. Laying their fishing poles across the handlebars, the two thirteen-year-old kids peddled down the road side-by-side.

Focusing on riding the gravel road, Zoey asked, "So, why do you want to fish at the river all of a sudden?"

Teddy glanced at her. "Because that's where the big fish are biting. Everybody is catching fish there."

"Don't we catch fish at our secret spot?"

"Yeah, but only little ones. Do you know what it's like to catch a big walleye? Man, I wanna know."

She shrugged. "I suppose."

The three-mile ride took them to Scout Park, located at the Mississippi River's edge. Leaning their bikes against a picnic table, Teddy and Zoey jumped down from a rock wall onto the soppy, squishy riverbank. They had only one tackle box, the one Teddy had borrowed from his dad and tied to his bicycle seat. It had the big fish stuff.

After an hour, Zoey leaned her fishing pole against the rock wall and found a piece of stone big enough to sit on.

"What's wrong with you?"

"I'm tired of this." Pointing to the river she said, "All those guys out there are pulling fish into their boat and we haven't had a bite. This is stupid."

Teddy couldn't disagree. He looked out over the river and saw boats by the dam pulling in fish every now and then. "Maybe we could get out there, too."

"Sure. So where's the boat?"

A light went off in Teddy's head like the one Ford uses for a 'better idea'. "Grab your pole and come with me."

"Why?"

"Just come."

In only a few minutes of walking the riverbank, they came upon a fishing boat moored at a dock. "Put our stuff in here and I'll untie it."

"Teddy. This is Doc Bendenhoff's boat. We can't steal it."

"Come on, we ain't stealing. We're borrowing. Can't you see, he's not using it?"

"Oh, I don't know if we should."

"You wanna catch a big fish or not?"

"Yeah, I do."

He motioned for Zoey to get in. "Then, let's go."

When they rode up to the dam in their boat and anchored, the head shaking and chuckling among the other fishermen floated across the river in waves. Everyone knew whose boat they were using. Unconcerned, the kids rigged up their poles and started fishing for walleyes. About a half-hour later, Teddy felt the boat lurch. "Teddy. Teddy, Zoey yelled. "I got one!" Although he wanted the first fish, Teddy didn't have the heart to say so. He just watched her bring a beautiful walleye up to the boat so he could net it.

"Wow, nice catch."

"Thanks. Man that was fun. You were right. We can catch big fish here."

"Hey. Where the hell's my boat? Damn it. Who cut my boat loose?"

Zoey dropped her fish in the bottom of the boat as she jerked around to see Doc Bendenhoff screaming from his boat dock.

"Thought you said he wouldn't miss his boat," Zoey quipped.

"Guess I was wrong."

"Hey. Hey! What the hell are you kids doing with my boat out there?"

The laughter and chatter among the fishermen surrounding them didn't help Doc's mood.

Spotted by Doc, Teddy knew he had to answer him. "Hi, Doc. Just borrowed your boat to come out for a Walleye or two. We'll bring'er back soon."

"The Hell ya' say. So, what am I supposed to use?"

Zoey whispered to Teddy. "Why don't we go in and get him? Three can fish in this boat."

Teddy shook the idea off and yelled back at Doc, "Soon as I catch a walleye we'll bring your boat in."

Now the men in their fishing boats were belly laughing. No one could remember a time when Doc wasn't fishing with them, and now two kids had beached him. All he could do was stand on shore and holler like a stuck pig.

"What? You're going to pay for this Teddy Crodin! "

 C3 80

Doc walked off in a huff. Teddy finally caught a walleye, and the kids returned the boat to the dock. All seemed quiet as they walked across the park to their bicycles. Using the string in the tackle box, Teddy and Zoey were working out how to tie their fish to the handlebars when they heard a roar. It was Doc Bendenhoff, pounding across the park from his office. If it was a cooler day, they might have seen his head steaming and smoke coming out his nostrils. But it was hot and sunny, so the best Doc could do was look like a crazed buffalo.

"Stand right there you two." he said. "Don't you dare move."

Trying to ease Doc's anger, Teddy said to him. "Sorry about taking your boat, Doc. We just wanted to catch a big fish. And, you know, you weren't using it."

"Teddy Crodin, damn it! It doesn't matter if I'm using it or not. It's mine. Now, because of you every damn kid in town is going to think they can borrow my boat if I'm not in it."

"We're sorry, Doc," Zoey interjected. "We didn't mean to do that."

"Sorry isn't going to fix the problem. But I know what is. Here's the deal, I can report my boat stolen." Pointing towards the dam, Doc continued. "I can have every damn fisherman out there be witnesses that you're the thieves, and let the judge take care of ya'."

They looked at each other in panic, and Zoey said, "Man, borrowing a boat is getting pretty scary."

Doc let his threat sink in for a moment before he continued. "Or, I say or… you two rascals can come back here Saturday and paint my boat. Right here by the park where your friends and everyone in town can see what the cost is to borrow my boat. Now, which is it? I'm a busy man, and ain't got all day."

Both kids let out a sigh of relief in unison. "We'll paint your boat, Doc. Won't we, Zoe?"

"Yes, sir. Saturday we'll paint your boat. And, thanks for not telling the sheriff."

"It's gettin' hot these days. We'll start at 7 AM Saturday. Shaking his finger at them, Doc turned to leave saying, "Don't be late."

Plopping down on the seat of the picnic table, exhausted from the tension, they watched Doc amble back across the park.

"Pretty expensive fish, Teddy."

"Yeah, I know. But, you gotta admit, it was fun."

CB EO

If there were secrets in Clayton County, Teddy and Zoey's escapade wasn't one of them. Not only did their parents know, but almost the whole town knew. And, many of them made sure they were near Scout Park on Saturday to watch the painters. Why, the town hadn't seen such a crowd since the Fourth of July!

Doc hadn't mentioned they had to clean the boat first, but they did what they were told. They might do dumb stuff, but they weren't stupid. If that's what Doc wanted, that's what Doc was going to get. After all, he still worked on their teeth with his drills and stuff.

Sheriff Norvus appeared, of course, leaving the lights flashing on his car to draw attention as he walked across the park to Doc's side. "How much do you reckon your boat's worth, Doc?"

Doc was not pleased to have J.R. showboating at his party. "Why do you want to know that J.R.?"

"Well, it makes a difference whether I arrest Teddy for theft or grand theft?"

Doc was appalled. "What? J.R. you're not arresting anybody. You're just trying to get publicity for your re-election, and I'll not be a part of it."

"Now, what would make you say such a thing as that, Doc?"

Doc took J.R.'s arm and began to lead him back to his car. "Look, you've got my vote. And, I'll probably make a donation to your campaign. But I will not press charges against these kids. Go do something constructive. I've got this situation right where I want it."

CR&O

At 4 p.m., with Doc's approval, they were finished. Teddy and Zoey were so tired they could barely walk their bikes out of the park. They were resting on the steps of the barbershop when Roy Cutler closed up and locked the door.

Roy smiled. Two of the brightest kids in town looked like wet dishrags. "You kids worn out?"

Teddy looked over at him. "Yeah. It's going to be a long ride home."

Roy pointed to his truck. "Wanna' put your bikes in my truck? I'll give you a lift home."

Zoey jumped up with renewed energy. "Would you? Oh man, you're a lifesaver, Roy."

So, with a little help from a friend, they didn't have to ride the three miles home. Roy turned onto the highway. "Listen, Teddy, it seems you need to be busier than most kids, and I have an idea."

Leaning on the door, Teddy sat up when he heard the word 'idea'. "What's that?"

"Do you know anything about go-karts?"

He nodded. "Yeah, but I've never ridden one."

"Well," Roy continued, "I have a friend who has a two seat go-kart chassis for sale. I bet you'd love it."

That excited Zoey. "I know I'd love it, 'cause he could give me rides in it."

Teddy's eyes brightened and his eyebrows rose. "Roy, how much money does he want?"

"$300 dollars."

Looking toward Roy he asked, "Is that a good price?"

"Actually, it's cheap."

"Really? And all it needs is a motor?"

"Yep. You know, if you got a couple chain saw motors, a few pulleys and drive chains, you'd be good to go."

"Would you take me to this guy's place, Roy?"

"Yeah, we could do it tomorrow if you have the money."

Teddy shook his head. "Nah, don't have money." Then he looked up. "But I'll ask dad for a loan when we get home. I'll call you after supper."

Roy pulled into the Bondi's driveway. "Is Zoey's place close enough for you two?"

Teddy hopped out of the truck ahead of her. "This is fine Roy. I can walk across the field. Sure appreciate the ride."

"Yeah, thanks for the ride, Roy," Zoey said. "You're a lifesaver."

"Alright then. Get your bikes. Talk with you later, Teddy."

ରୁ ଅଧ

Teddy leaned his bike against the porch and stalked up to the door quietly to see if anyone was in the house.

"Are you having trouble opening the door, Teddy?" Sarah asked him as she continued to prepare supper.

He sighed and entered the kitchen. "No, Mom."

"Tired?" She asked.

"Yeah. I'm bushed," and he turned a chair around backwards crossing his arms on top and rested his chin.

She stopped to look at him. "So, did you learn your lesson?"

Teddy really didn't want to talk about it, much less answer his mom's question. It was good that Dad wasn't here, or he'd get both barrels.

"I guess so. We were just borrowing it. Doc wasn't using it. He just got all-possessive and stuff. You know, mad 'cause he couldn't go fishing."

She listened with her back turned as she worked. "Well, what did you expect?"

Kent walked into the kitchen ending the conversation. Which was great for Teddy. He jumped off his chair. "Hey, Dad, guess what I heard?"

He looked at his son thoughtfully. "I'd hate to guess. What did you hear?"

"Roy's friend has a go-kart chassis for sale. He said for $300 it's a great deal. Can I buy it, Dad?"

Kent glanced at Sarah to see what she knew, but only got a shrug of her shoulders. "What would you do with it?"

Getting more excited by the minute Teddy said, "Dad, can't you see it. Two chain saw motors, some drive chains, it would be cool. I can build it if you will just loan me the money. I'll pay you back, promise. "

When anyone in the family talked money, Sarah the accountant got involved, so she had to ask, "How are you going to do that, Teddy?"

"With my pay from the Café as a server. I'll even get tips, too." Teddy looked at his Mom, then his Dad. "Please."

"Nice try, son," he replied. "But, as I recall you're not ready for the server job. Has she started paying you for it yet?"

Teddy's enthusiasm was thwarted. "No." After a pause, Teddy looked up with bright eyes and renewed enthusiasm. "But she will."

"Tell you what, then. When you show me your first check as a server, I'll loan you the money."

CHAPTER 11

When Kent finished his work neutering a cat, he checked in with his receptionist. He was pleased to find that he had a fax from Dr. Steinhouse at I.S.U. It came a day earlier than he'd expected and Kent anxiously read the results:

Glycosides from plantain: 38% - reduces stinging and itching

Caffeic acid from Echinacea: 4% - acts as disinfectant

Gallic acid from witch hazel: 42% - Anti-inflammatory

Allantoin acid from camfrey: 9% - protective skin coating

Saponins from aloe vera: 7% - Hydration

Rushing to the house Kent burst in, "I've got it. I've got it! "

Startled by his outburst, Sarah asked him, "What is wrong with you?"

He paced the kitchen floor, looking at the paper in his hand. "I got the results from I.S.U. I know what's in Willard's ointment. "

"Oh, please sit down. You're acting like a child."

He stopped long enough to look at her and make a point. "But, now I know how to make it. Do you know what that means?"

She shook her head. "Yeah, it means I've got three children to raise. For Pete's sake, Kent, sit down. "

But he didn't. Pacing again, Kent rattled off his plans. "All I have to do is order these chemicals, mix a batch using these percentages, and it's ready for sale."

"Are you going to put it in something?"

"Oh, yeah. We'll package it too."

"I think it's wonderful you're so excited, but I'm smart enough to know you're doing nothing until you patent this potion of yours."

That stopped him. He plopped into a chair, looked at her and said, "Really? How much time does that take?"

Sitting across from him, Sarah could see Kent's disappointment. "It takes a while, but I don't know exactly. What I do know is if this stuff works, and you don't have a patent, someone can steal it overnight."

Sighing deeply, he asked, "So, how do we do this?"

Sarah put her hand on his and smiled. "Let's ask Warren. If he doesn't know everything, he knows everybody that's important. He's helped us before. Maybe he can help again."

When Sarah called, Warren was pleased to hear from her, and agreed to meet them after supper.

CB EO

"First, Kent," Warren Nickel said, "You've got your core patent. That would be your combination of chemicals, the blending, manufacturing and packaging processes. More difficult is what is called the vectors of claims and potential options."

Sitting on a hassock with his elbows on his knees, Kent tried to absorb all that Warren had been telling them. "Warren, vectors of claims is foreign to me. What is it and why is it important?"

"Well, vectors of claims are what protects your core patent from invasion. Each vector is a different form of your core patent. Like soldiers, these vectors are just slightly different from the one next to it."

Sarah was catching on, but not completely. "What would be the difference between one vector and another, Warren?"

"Not much. Just a slight change in the percentage of a given chemical would create a different vector. It takes a lot of time to do this, but it's critical to preserving your patent. The more little soldiers your competition has to wade through, the less apt they are to find your true formula."

Sitting back in the rocking chair, she asked, "Warren, you know we have no idea how to do this. Who can you recommend to help us?"

"I hate to say this, because you've had so much trouble in Chicago, but that's where the best one is. If you like, I can call and ask them to get in touch with you, so you can get started."

She looked at Kent, and he looked back. It was as if neither one wanted to be the one to make the commitment.

Sarah finally said, "This is your baby. What do you want to do? Go ahead, or drop the whole idea."

Kent certainly didn't like the sound of dropping the whole idea. Coughing to clear his throat he finally said, "Go ahead, Warren. Get in touch with him. I want to put this product on the market."

"Said and done," replied Warren. "Just one little thing to remember, Kent. This attorney is a her, not a him."

They thanked Warren and left for home. On the way, Kent was anxious for Sarah's support.

"You know, it's not that I mind working with a woman, but I can't do this and run a business. Will you manage this patent process for me?"

"Honey, I don't know any more about it than you."

"Yeah, but you're smart, you're an accountant, and you deal with details a lot better than I do."

She smiled. "So you think flattery is going to do the trick, huh?"

Taking her hand in his, he asked again, "Please? I want this to work, but I'm not prepared for it like you are."

Squeezing Kent's hand, Sarah replied, "Ok, I'll try. But no guarantees. We'll just see how it goes."

"Thanks, that takes a load off my mind."

CHAPTER 12

Teddy had learned to bus tables without disrupting the customers, and was pretty efficient. He'd even do the setups, trying to help Wilma all he could. Still, Teddy would end up with time on his hands watching her work both the kitchen and waiting on customers. He wanted to help, so one day he approached her.

"Wilma, can I take those plates out for you?"

"I guess so. Yes, that would be nice. It's for table four, soup and sandwich on the right, and the other on the left. Thanks."

He took out the meals, the customers thanked him, and he returned to the kitchen. "Is there more for me to take out, Wilma?"

"Say, what's this all about?" Wilma asked.

Teddy put his hands in his pockets and looked at the floor. "Well, to tell the truth, I'm bored. I don't bus tables all the time you know."

"Yeah, I know."

"Well, I see you're so busy," he finally looked at Wilma, "I wondered if I could learn to be a server."

She returned her attention to the grill. "That's not an easy job, you know. You'd have to learn a lot."

"That's ok, I really want to. I like working here, and I need the money. Will you teach me?"

Wilma looked at the young teenager with a glint in her eye, "Money, huh? What are you up to now?"

Weeell, I'm building a go-kart," Teddy said, looking at the floor again.

While flipping a couple burgers, Wilma asked, "I take it the sheriff doesn't know you'll be driving a go-kart around town?"

Teddy looked up quick. "You won't tell him, will ya'? I'd like to drive it here to work."

"No, son, I've got this hearing problem, you know." Wilma smiled and glanced at him. "I seem to be missing out on a lot of conversations lately."

Laughing at her mock hearing problem, he was grateful that she always covered his back. "Thanks Wilma. Thanks a lot. You know, I'll be a good server. Won't you give me a chance?"

Wilma placed french fries on plates. "I've got to think about it. Taking plates out to customers is a start. And, since these dishes aren't quite ready yet, why don't you take out the coffee pots and see if folks need a refill?"

Teddy was all smiles. At least Wilma was going to let him try! With a carafe of coffee in each hand, he was out on the floor, enthusiastic, talking to customers and refilling their cups.

CRSO

Niki Bondi quietly opened the door to her daughter's bedroom. She was lying on the bed with headphones on.

"Zoey."

There was no response, so she touched her shoulder.

Zoey looked up, saw her mom and removed the headphones. "Did you say something, Mom?"

Niki sat on the edge of her bed. "You've been sulking for days now. What is the matter with you?"

Zoey rolled on her side, put her hand under her chin and made a sour face. "I'm just bored, I guess."

"Well then, why don't you go over and see what Teddy's doing. You like hanging out with him."

"Can't, Mom. He's working at Wilma's."

"At this time of day?" she asked.

"Yeah, he's learning to be a server now. When we don't have school he works the whole day, breakfast to dinner. He won't be home until at least eight."

"Why don't you go see your girlfriends, Honey? You cannot spend all your time with him, you know."

Zoey planted her elbows on the bed and plopped her chin on her hands. "Why not?"

"Because, he isn't going to be around forever, dear. He'll grow up and move away like all the other boys."

Glancing at her mother she replied, "No, he won't."

Niki rubbed her back gently. "How can you be so sure?"

"Cause he's just like his dad. He'll be here forever."

Her mom tried again. "Honey, I still think you should go see your girlfriends for a while."

"Don't want to. They just laugh and make fun of me."

Niki shook her head. "Oh, now, now. I find that hard to believe."

Zoey got up off her bed and walked to the mirror. "They do. When we put on make-up, I look like a geek with glasses and lipstick on my braces."

Her mother stood and hugged her. "Oh, Honey, I'm so sorry. Your braces won't last forever."

"They already have, Mom."

"Well, ok then. Ride your bike to Wilma's and see how Teddy's doing?"

Her eyes brightened at the thought. "Good idea, Mom."

Niki was relieved to get her out of the house.

Cʒ✥♡

Zoey walked into Wilma's café and took a small two chair table. Teddy noticed her. "Hey. What are you doing here?"

"Checking out Wilma's new server. He's supposed to be cute and smart. Seen him around?"

He just smiled at her. "Nope. Must not have shown up. But, I'm here, so what can I get you?"

Throwing a smile his way she ordered a Coke. She didn't hang out at Wilma's Café much, and it was pretty cool. Zoey knew almost everybody in the café, and the old cooking stuff on the wall was neat to look at. Plus, she got to watch Teddy work. She noticed he had trouble keeping his pleated paper hat on. She had the urge to get up and push it back down on his head.

Zoey continued watching Teddy as he shoved the hat down over his curly hair. It looked good. Eventually, when it scooted up to the top of his curly hair, she thought it looked like a cruise ship beached on a rocky island.

When Teddy noticed it again, he'd shove the paper hat back down, and the whole beached ship thing would happen again.

Zoey wanted him to come by her table again. But she didn't know how to get his attention… some people would call out his name, and others would just raise their hand. Raising her hand made more sense, so she put her hand in the air. Teddy ignored her, but stopped at the tables of the coffee people.

She didn't like being ignored, so she got up and walked to the kitchen.

Wilma glanced at her when she entered. "Hey, Zoey, what can I do for you?"

Getting close to Wilma, she whispered. "You can tell me what coffee tastes like."

Wilma stepped back to get a good look at her.

"Why do you want to know that, child?"

"Well, if I order coffee then he has to come and refill my cup like the others, right?"

Wilma smiled, "What's happening now?"

"Nothing." Zoey put her hands on her hips and scowled. "He ignores me."

"My, oh my, we gotta' fix that now, don't we? Let's see, how does coffee taste. Well, it's a little bitter. I suggest a couple glugs of milk and a spoon full of sugar to make it taste better."

"That's what I should do?"

"Yep. Now why don't you go sit down and I'll get you some." Leaning out into the dining room Wilma called out to Teddy.

"Coffee at table eight, and don't forget the cream."

She was anxious to try her coffee and took a little sip. It had a strange taste that wrinkled her nose. But, she could bear it if it brought Teddy over to her table.

Her cup was about a quarter empty when he came by with the coffee pot, glanced at her cup, and walked past.

Zoey frowned.

Well, you don't even speak or anything. It's not like you don't know me.

She sipped and sipped more coffee. The next time he came by her cup was half-empty and Teddy finally stopped, gave her a smile, and asked, "Zoe, want a warmer-upper?"

She smiled sweetly "Yes, please."

He returned her smile. "You're welcome," then moved on to the next customer.

Zoey admired her handsome friend as he walked away. Then she took bigger sips of coffee.

CR&

Kent finished work, closed the clinic and went into the house. As he passed by Sarah to get a beer, he noticed her studying a piece of paper. "What's that you're studying?"

"Oh, just something you don't want to know about."

He sat at the table and studied her. "Why wouldn't I?"

Looking up at her, he noticed her sad eyes. "What?"

"Kent, Honey, I know how disappointing this is for you. The attorneys are saying you can't get a patent on Willard's ointment."

He flew out of his chair onto his feet. "What? Why can't we?"

"Somebody else makes it. It's been on the market for a few years. There's no way you can make the ointment without infringing on their patent."

He had already started pacing, trying to think. He stopped to look at her. "Well, do they say who it is?"

"Yes."

Kent was hurt, disappointed, and furious. "Tell me. Who is it?"

"It's a product called "Bee Balm.""

He spit out "Damn," as he turned and left the house, walking off the porch, through the farmyard, and into the soybean field.

Sarah gently laid the letter down, folded her arms on the table where she rested her head and cried.

| CHAPTER 13

The High School was abuzz with preparations for the Junior-Senior Prom. Boys were nervous, girls were anxious, and teachers couldn't keep anybody's attention in class. On Saturday morning Wendy ran down the stairs screaming. "Mom, that brat ruined my phone. "

Sarah looked up when she entered the kitchen, held up her hand and tried to continue her conversation on the phone.

Wendy bent as if she was in pain. "Mom, do something."

"Something's going on here, Roxanne," she said, "I have to go. We'll talk later." After hanging up the phone, Sarah turned to Wendy, "Wendy Jo, you are so rude."

"But, Mom, Teddy ruined my phone."

"Honey, how could somebody ruin a cell phone? It looks ok to me."

Wendy showed her mom the contact list on her phone. "Look. He changed the names. Now I don't know who's calling."

"Oh, it can't be that bad dear."

"Ok, would you know who's calling if their name was Camaro?"

"Camaro?" she asked.

Wendy was in a panic. "Yes, and there's Mustang, Firebird, Barracuda, Charger, and Cobra. He's changed all my friend's names to the name of a car. I'll kill him. "

"I'm so sorry, Honey, but I'm sure you'll figure it out."

"Mom. There's no time. The prom's three weeks from now and I don't have a date yet. How am I gonna' know if a boy calls me?"

CR&RO

Teddy just loved it that his sister was in a panic. Every time she got a text or phone message, she'd study it trying to learn who it was. When boys texted asking her to the prom, she wasn't sure who was asking. The strangest one was a poem.

Roses are Red
Violets are Blue
The sun rises and sets with you
My inspiration from you comes
So please, go with me to the Prom

"Mom, you won't believe this. Look."

Sarah sat on the couch next to Wendy and looked at her phone. "That's pretty creative, don't you think?"

Wendy gave her a pained look, "I'd never go out with a sappy guy like that."

Sarah patted her knee, "Don't be so harsh. You can tell he's an admirer, intelligent, and romantic. That's not sappy to me."

Looking back at the message, Wendy said, "Well, I don't even know who it is."

Sarah got up off the couch, "Come on Wendy. Get creative. He did, didn't he?"

So Wendy sent a text back, "How can I take your poetry seriously if you don't even sign it?"

Bing. Her phone signaled a message. "Chaucer"

Wendy's texted again, "Get real. I'd never dance with a boy named Chaucer. Show your face. Top of Billy Goat Hill, 7 AM Saturday."

Bing, she received his text. "C U There."

Wendy went into the kitchen to see her mother. Sitting at the table, she said, "Ok, I did it your way,"

Sarah stopped what she was doing and sat across from Wendy. "So, what did you do?"

"I figured if he was man enough he could meet me on Billy Goat Hill at 7 AM Saturday."

"Why there, Honey?"

"Because he'll have to hike up, drive a Jeep or ride a horse. Wimps can't make it up there, Mom."

"Aren't you being a little hard on the guy?"

Wendy jumped out of her chair. "I can't be seen at the Prom with Casper Milk Toast. My God, how embarrassing."

Sarah went back to what she was doing, "I guess sensitive guys aren't your cup of tea, huh?"

"A poet, Mom? Get real. "

C3 80

Wendy was lost in her thoughts while saddling Ginger for her ride to Billy Goat Hill.

If he's a manly type he'll drive a Jeep up the hill. If he's athletic he'll hike up the hill. If he's a wimp, he won't show. At least Ginger and I get a nice ride out of the deal.

It was a beautiful spring morning. The sky had cleared after last night's rain and everything smelled so fresh. She got a wicked smile on her face.

It'll be just that much harder for the guy to get up there now that it's muddy. Hope he doesn't show so I can back out easily.

Wendy followed the horse trail across the bluff to the top of Billy Goat Hill. As they got closer, Wendy was confused by what she saw. It looked like a horse and rider ahead. Her mouth dropped when she recognized the rider.

"Billy, what are you doing here?"

Billy Goetz rested his hands on the saddle horn. "Waiting for you, Wendy. Is it 7 AM yet?"

Wendy looked shocked. "You? You sent me that poem?"

Nodding, Billy answered, "Sure did. Will you go to the Prom with me now?"

Billy Goetz? I've never given Billy the time of day.

"Ah, I don't know what to say?"

Billy turned his horse away from the hill. "Tell you what, let's go for a ride and you can think about it. Maybe there's another hurdle or two you'd like me to jump over before you say yes."

Wendy was flabbergasted. Billy was into horses just as she was. She's known him all her life, even though they fought once. Who would ever know Billy wasn't a wimp.

Mom thought his poem was kinda nice.

They rode together and chatted about school; the upcoming prom; and what Teddy had done to her phone. Billy almost fell off his horse laughing at that. It was nice to have a riding companion, and somewhere along their ride Wendy made up her mind.

"Billy, let's take this trail. It leads to my house where we can water the horses before you go home."

"Fine with me."

When they reached her farm, Wendy and Billy led their horses to the corral for water. Then, Wendy took him up to the house.

Sarah saw them coming and was filled with curiosity. When they entered the house she asked, "Well, who do we have here?"

"Mom, let me introduce my date for the prom. This is Billy Goetz."

Billy was shocked that he got her answer in front of her mother.

"So nice to meet you Billy. You name sure sounds familiar."

Wendy grew self-conscience immediately. After all, her fight with Billie in sixth grade got her suspended. "We don't talk about that anymore. Mom. Just forget it."

She gave Wendy a curious look, and then returned her attention to Billy. "Did I just see you riding a horse, Billy?"

"Yes, ma'am. We have two of 'em actually, but Socks is the one I ride.

"Well, well. I guess you two have something in common. How nice."

"Yeah, it was pretty cool riding together," Wendy said, bubbling with enthusiasm.

Sarah gave Billy a warm smile. "Well, Billy, you're welcome here anytime." She turned to Wendy and said, "Now, why don't you two run along and care for your horses."

Wendy held Billy's hand as they left. She looked back at her mom with a proud smile and winked.

CB &

Their classmates were stunned when Billy and Wendy walked into the dance together. No one had ever imagined them being together. And she seemed so happy on the dance floor with Billy. Of course, all the boys that wanted her to be their date cut in on Billy. But it was no big deal to him, since he got to dance with their dates, cheerleaders, and candidates for Prom Queen.

One dance each and Wendy put an end to it. Grabbing Billy away, she made sure he was by her side the rest of the evening.

"Wendy, instead of staying until they turn the lights out, how about a walk along the river?"

"Oh, I'd like that. Let's get out of here."

There was enough moonlight reflecting off the river to make it a romantic scene. Holding hands and chatting, they looked comfortable together. When they did go home, Billy opened the door for her, let her out, and then blocked her exit, looking a bit unsure of himself.

"Is something wrong, Billy," she asked.

Quickly Billy planted his lips on Wendy's. When he stepped away he said anxiously, "I'm sorry, I didn't know if you wanted to or not."

Wendy kissed him again, and said, "Don't be. It was sweet. Goodnight, Billy."

| CHAPTER 14

It took all winter for Teddy to earn the money and buy the parts he needed to finish his go-kart. As soon as the snow melted, he test-drove it a few times, up and down the lane, with Zoey riding along. Her mother was worried about her daughter riding too fast, and Kent warned Teddy not to drive it on the rough gravel roads. Having a fast kart and no place to drive it frustrated him. They talked about it as they turned around at the end of the lane.

"This is boring, Zoe. I can't even open it up. I gotta find a place to drive wide open."

She pulled the top of her coat together to block the wind. "The airstrip on Abel Island would be perfect."

"Dad won't let me drive on gravel roads, and we'd have to do that to get there."

"I know Let's go up the lane again."

૬૩ ૪૦

At the supper table Teddy listened to his mom and dad plan to visit Aunt Rita Friday evening at her home in Bluffton. He saw his chance. They planned to leave at 4 p.m. and be home by 10 p.m. plenty of time for what he had in mind. All he had to do was tell Zoey.

After their parents had waved good-bye, Wendy went to her room and Teddy went to the shed. He pulled out the tilt-bed tow truck, and lowered it to load his go-kart. Then he went in the house and bugged Wendy until she screamed at him, "Teddy, leave me alone and never come back." Grinning, he didn't expect that she'd even miss him.

All that remained was to wait until it was dark.

Teddy flashed the yellow running lights twice so Zoey knew it was time to go. When she climbed into the truck, he had it started and the diesel engine was warming up.

Buckling her seat belt, she asked him, "Are you sure you know how to drive your dad's truck?"

"Sure? I've seen it done a hundred times."

Watching Teddy steer the truck and shift the gears, she said, "Just what I thought, you know how but you've never done it, right?"

"Right." He glanced at her, "Does that scare you?"

"I'm here aren't I? I think we should drive past town and come in on the North side so the sheriff doesn't see us."

"Good idea. If he sees this truck he'll think it's my dad making a service call, and follow us."

The island was isolated in spring, and Teddy didn't anticipate anyone noticing them on the airstrip. Abel Island was a busy place in the summer. The airstrip for private planes brought in visitors to the cabins lining the edge of the island. Visitors enjoyed the privacy as well as the small town atmosphere. Winter was the other busy time, when ice fishermen drove their cars and snow machines onto the bay between the mainland and the island.

The kids aimed the tow truck down the airstrip and turned on the headlights, spotlights, and all the overhead running lights. They'd never seen all the lights on, and it looked really cool. Teddy gave Zoey the new black helmet he'd bought her that matched his, and they climbed into the go-kart. At first, they drove slowly down the airstrip to ensure there was nothing unexpected they could hit. At the end, they turned around, and raced wide open to his Dad's truck.

"Woo-hoo!" yelled Teddy.

"That was great." Zoey shouted. "Let's do it again!"

They spent almost two hours racing up and down the airstrip, around and around in circles and figure 8's.

Teddy was having a great time, but wisely knew he'd better get home early so he wouldn't get caught.

They had to start the truck to operate the bed and load his go-kart. Nothing happened when he turned the key. Nothing. The lights had drained the battery.

Teddy was under the hood when Sheriff J.R. Norvus drove up.

"Hey, are we glad to see you, J.R. This battery's dead. Will you give us a jump so we can get my dad's truck home?"

The sheriff stood between the door and his car, resting his right arm on the roof. Well, the way I see it, you won't have to do that Teddy. You see, with all the violations I see here, you'll be spending the night in jail."

"What violations J.R.? We just need help."

J.R. walked slowly toward the kids, counting the violations on his gloved fingers. "Let's see here, one, we've got a stolen truck; two, an underage driver without a license; three, a go-kart that isn't street legal; and four, doesn't have a license; and five, trespassing on government property. That's just the violations I can come up with off the top of my head. Need I go on?"

"J.R., we weren't hurting anybody. Give us a break."

"The only break I can give you is this. I'll write these citations, you go to jail tonight, the judge hears your case and you pay the fines. Or, we can haul all this crap back home and talk to your dad about it."

Teddy kicked the dirt. "That's not a choice, J.R."

"Best I can do."

He stepped closer to J. R. and said quietly, "J.R., There's gotta be a way we can make a deal."

J.R. held out a stiff arm, "Hold on, Son. Are you trying to bribe me?"

Zoey saw things getting worse, and stepped between them. "No, no, J.R. you're not understanding him. Let me explain. First of all, we know nothing about this go-kart. It was here when we came, and it'll be here when we leave. We've got no idea whose it is."

"Is that so? I thought I heard he was building something like this."

Turning to Teddy she asked, "Is this your go-kart?"

Teddy knew she was smart, and he knew what she was doing, but it hurt to go along with her. "Ah, no, it's not mine." "See, J. R.," she said, her confidence building with every passing minute. "You wouldn't want to embarrass yourself by fining him, and hauling him off to jail for something he doesn't even own, would you?"

J. R. looked awkward and shook his head. "No, that wouldn't be good."

Pressing on she said, "So you see, J.R., all we need is a jump to start this tow truck, and you can forget about a whole night of paperwork. Please, will you help us start the truck?"

J.R. stiffened. He wasn't about to have a young girl tell him what to do. "I've got a problem with that."

"What's the problem?" she asked.

"You kids aren't old enough to drive. I've got to write you up for that. Underage driver violation." J. R. got out his pad.

Zoey waved her hands as if she was stopping something. "Ok, ok. Write the ticket. But when you're done with that, you'll have to write one for your son, Jerry."

J.R. was shocked. "The hell you say. I'm not doing that."

She spoke softly to J.R. as she stepped up beside him. "Oh, you don't know that your wife had him drive to the store and back for her last Wednesday after school? He's in our class, so he must be underage, too. Right?"

Getting more frustrated, J.R. stiffened and tried to act like he was in charge. "Listen here, are you trying to blackmail me?"

Turning her back, Zoey threw up her arms in exasperation, "J.R. if the truth's blackmail, then I guess so."

"Zoey Bondi, you're just talking in circles trying to confuse me. I haven't got time for this. Let's get your truck started so we all can get outta here."

CB ❧

As they drove off the island Teddy said, "You know, I really appreciate your help back there. But did you have to give away my go-kart?"

"Just think, will you? Those fines were going to cost you a lot more than that go-kart's worth. Plus a night in jail? And who knows what your parents would do."

The loss really hurt, but he knew she was right. Plus, he would have been in trouble if she hadn't stepped in to help. "Zoe, you're a pretty special friend. Thanks for keeping me out of trouble."

"It's ok," she responded. "That's what friends are for."

CB ❧

Thank God, his mom and dad weren't home when they drove in. Wheeling the truck around, Teddy backed into the machine shed just as headlights turned into the lane, lighting up the truck and shining in their eyes.

"Duck." Both kids slid off the seats onto the floor of the truck.

"Do you think they saw us?" Zoey asked.

"I don't know. I hope not."

They listened intently for his dad's truck to shut off, and then heard the closing of two doors. They were breathing heavily and their hearts were pounding. They were trapped until the screen door closed and they could escape.

They didn't hear it, and were afraid to peek over the dash to look.

She whispered, "What's happening?"

Before he could answer, they heard his dad holler out, "Teddy, don't forget to lock the truck when you get out."

They looked at each other with fear in their eyes.

"How did he know?" Zoey asked.

"I don't know. What am I going to tell him?"

"Just make up something. I've gotta get home before they see me."

"Go out the driver's door, so they only hear the door close once. Ok?"

She awkwardly crawled over the seat and past Teddy, opened the door and left quickly.

As nervous as he'd ever been, he slid out of the truck, locked the door and walked slowly to the house.

His mom and dad were in the kitchen when he entered. He could see his mom, but only his dad's back. Teddy tried to act normal, but he was shaking inside.

"Did you lock the truck, Son?" his dad asked.

"Yeah, it's locked."

"Thanks, good night."

Teddy breathed a sigh of relief and kept on walking, right out of the kitchen and up the stairs to the bathroom where he fell to his knees and puked.

Sarah smiled at Kent. "That was mean, you know."

"Yeah, I know, but it was fun."

"You're terrible. That boy's a nervous wreck."

"He should be. He'll get over it."

"Why would you do such a thing?"

"Honey, all fathers were boys once, and boys push the envelope. No one knows what they'll do. So the best we can do is let them know that we know, so they don't do the same stupid thing again."

Sarah shook her head. "Your male logic sounds like boy's dumb and dad's dumber. And men have the gall to complain about understanding women!"

| CHAPTER 15

Teddy was happy about the confidence Wilma had in him. It was his second week as a breakfast cook, and he loved it. Oh, there were times when he'd get things out of order, but he was getting a feel for putting meals together.

The part that pleased him the most was the fact that Wilma could work the floor and be with all her friends. That left the kitchen to himself, which suited Teddy. It was a great job, and nobody cared that he was only fourteen.

After work, Teddy headed home to catch up with Zoey. He knocked on her door and Niki, her mother, answered.

Looking through the screen, Teddy said, "Hi, Mrs. Bondi. Thought I'd go fishing, can Zoey come along?"

Niki shook her head. "She's not here, Teddy. Said she was going for a walk."

Teddy's shoulders sank. "Oh, ok. Thanks." He turned and scuffed his feet across the field, dejected.

Then he thought of a possibility. Their "secret spot."

CB ჴ

As Teddy neared the end of the path, he could hear sobbing. He slowed and entered the clearing cautiously.

Zoey was sitting with her arms folded around her legs. Her head rested on her knees as she sobbed. Teddy didn't know what to do. Should he hug her? Maybe she didn't want to be touched. Confused, he sat down next to her and stayed quiet.

Zoey eventually looked at Teddy. "Hi."

Teddy felt helpless, but didn't want to cause trouble, so he asked. "What can I do to help, Zoe?"

"Nothing."

Teddy wanted to put his hand on her back and rub it, but didn't dare. "What's eatin' you?"

Zoey turned her head to see Teddy, "My boobs."

Shrugging, Teddy asked, "What about'em?"

She sobbed again, "I didn't get the ones I wanted."

"Really. I didn't know you could choose."

Sitting up, she looked at Teddy. "You can't. You just get what you get."

Teddy shrugged. "And that doesn't make you happy?"

"All the other girls look like ladies, sexy and all."

Gazing out on the creek, Teddy suggested, "Maybe you grow slower than they did."

Zoey rolled her eyes. "No Teddy, you don't understand. You either do or you don't"

"You do or don't what?"

"Look sexy."

"Oh," Teddy replied.

Zoey turned to face Teddy full on. "Do you think I look sexy?"

Teddy threw his hands in the air, "I never heard of a fishing buddy looking sexy."

Zoey's face turned crimson red. Tears welled in her eyes. Furiously she jumped up and yelled at Teddy, "You can be so stupid. Stupid, stupid, stupid!" Zoey said, turning her back on him and stomping off toward home.

CƷ ℰꝺ

When Teddy reached home and came into the kitchen Sarah asked, "Teddy, I thought you and Zoey were fishing?"

Teddy plopped into a chair. "Not really."

"Did something happen, Honey?"

Teddy rested his chin on his hand and said, "Yeah, she didn't like what I said and went home calling me names."

"Well that's too bad. What did you say to upset her?"

Teddy looked at his mom. "She asked me if I thought she was sexy, and I told her I never heard of a fishing buddy looking sexy."

Sarah turned away quickly and giggled under her breath. "Do you want to talk about it?

"No, you're busy. Maybe I'll ask Wendy, she's got boobs."

Her eyes widened. "Whoa, just a minute young man. What was the word you just used? Maybe you should just stay here and talk to your mother."

Teddy got up and turned for the stairs. "Thanks Mom, but I'd rather talk to Wendy."

Raising her voice as he walked away, she told him, "If that doesn't work out, you can always come back."

She heard a faint, "Ok," as he climbed the stairs

ೞ ೲ

Sarah was making cheesecake muffins for the church bazaar when Teddy returned. Teddy walked up beside her as she slid a cookie sheet into the oven.

"Is that cheesecake, Mom?"

'Yes, in little muffins. Won't that be great?"

"Not this way they won't. You're doing it wrong."

Her jaw dropped. She looked at Teddy wide eyed. "Are you telling me I don't know how to bake?"

"No, Mom. I didn't say that. I'm saying you're not baking these right."

She stood with her arms folded and asked, "Well, just what am I doing wrong?"

Teddy took the muffin pan out of the oven. "Well, lots of stuff, actually. They're going to be undercooked and dry if we don't change a few things."

"Oh, really? And, I suppose you know how?"

"Actually, I do. Why don't you take a break and I'll help you?"

"Oh, great. My son's giving me baking lessons."

She sat in a chair and looked up at Teddy. "Speaking of learning, was Wendy able to help you out?"

"Naw. She didn't care. Thought I deserved to learn the hard way."

Catching Teddy's eye, she said, "Then you and I need to talk."

Lowering his head and looking at her out of the corner of his eye he asked, "Do we really need to talk about it, Mom?"

"Yes, we do. Sex education is a parent's responsibility, and we will talk about it."

Teddy gave in with a sigh. "Alright, why is Zoey to touchy and emotional? She never used to be."

"Well, quite simply… during puberty her body changes so she is capable of having babies. The result is her reproductive organs go through a monthly cycle that changes her body and her emotions."

As Teddy took a half-inch deep cookie sheet and filled it with water he said, "Mom, you need to put a water bath like this under the muffins so they don't dry out. So, what do Zoey's boobs have to do with it?"

"That's part of the change of her body, Teddy. If she ever has a baby, she will need to nurse. That's what breasts are for. There's a whole lot of things in a young girls life that are critical to her womanhood."

"Mom, you can't bake these muffins in half the time just because they're smaller. It has to be the full fifty-five minutes, just like a cake."

Annoyed that she was getting instructions from her son, Sarah let her attitude show when she asked, "Should I be writing this down?"

"Probably."

Sarah had her elbow on the table with her head in her hand, like an elementary school student. "So, how do you know all this? You don't make cheesecake at Wilma's."

"I've been studying to be a chef, and Wilma helps me with little tips she's learned along the way. This is one of 'em. Mom, let me ask you, why does Zoey get so emotional lately? A lot of times when I see her she's crying."

"She can't help it, Teddy. All girls become very sensitive and emotional as their bodies go through these changes. I suppose that's how Zoey felt today."

"Does that mean more stuff like this will be happening to her?"

"Probably, Honey."

"I have just one last question. Why is it important for Zoey to be sexy all of a sudden?"

"Teddy, this age is a romantic time for young girls. They read magazines and choose favorite actors, singers and things. They want to be attractive like the beautiful people."

"So, what's so bad about us guys around here?"

"Well, Honey, to tell the truth, you boys look like mules in a pasture compared to their idols."

"Well, that's pretty rude."

"I know, but it's true. You mules will start to look like stallions again in a few years as they grow out of their romantic fantasies."

Teddy turned and leaned against the counter. "Ok, Mom, you're all set. Your muffins should come out perfect."

She rose from her chair and hugged Teddy. "Oh, you two will get along just fine. It's just growing pains, Teddy. You'll go through it soon enough. And, thank you for helping with my muffins."

"You're welcome, Mom. I didn't mean to be rude. I just didn't want you to be disappointed at the church bazaar."

"How sweet of you," she said as she kissed the top of his head.

❃

Kent was reading in bed when Sarah entered the room.

"Did you have a good day, Honey?" She asked.

"Yeah, it was ok. How'd your church bazaar turn out?"

She spread her arms and twirled in front of him. "I'll have you know that I was the talk of the town."

He put his book down. "You?"

"Yes," she said with a big smile. "All the women thought my cheesecake muffins were magnificent."

Cocking his head he asked, "You? How'd you do that?"

She sat on the edge of the bed beside him. "I had a chef help me."

"You paid to have a chef help you bake for a church bazaar?"

"I did."

"Holy cow, what did that cost?"

She ruffled Kent's hair and kissed him. "Nothing, silly. He lives in our house."

"Teddy?"

"Yep, he's been studying cooking, and showed me some baking tips and viola, Mom's a hit with the ladies! Isn't that cool?"

"So now we've got a girl who wants to stand in manure working with horses and a boy who wants to over a stove and cook. Lucky we didn't have more kids."

Sarah poked his chest. "Oh, don't be that way. Give him a break; I think he's going to be really good."

He chuckled. "Of course you'd say that. He just saved your bacon. Oops, I mean muffins."

| CHAPTER 16

Friends and neighbors from miles around lined River Drive for the Fourth of July parade. An early morning drizzle didn't dampen spirits at all. The sky had cleared providing a bright sunny day for parade goers and vendors. The Bondi and Crodin families gathered along the curb to take in all the local custom cars, children and the high school band. In between two groups was a clown driving a souped up go-kart.

Kent turned to Teddy, standing beside him, and asked, "Isn't that your go-kart?"

Teddy was surprised, and stammered, "I don't think so, Dad."

Zoey heard his dad's question and knew Teddy was on thin ice. She couldn't let his dad find out the truth about that night at the airstrip. She stepped back quickly so his mom wouldn't see the look of fear on her face.

Teddy tried to avoid his Dad by looking the other way, but he could still hear his dad's question.

"Who's driving it, Son?"

"Looks like a clown, Dad."

Stepping behind Mr. Crodin, Zoey grabbed Teddy's hand and pulled him away. "Let's get that ice cream cone you promised me."

Kent looked over his shoulder as the two kids left.

"Where are they going?" Sarah asked.

"To get ice cream I guess," he replied as he turned back to watch the parade.

As they hustled away from his dad, Teddy let out a nervous sigh. "Whew Thanks, Zoe."

She looked back to see what his parents were doing. "Yeah, that was close."

"Dad's on to me, you know. I need to do something quick. If I don't replace that go-kart, he'll want to see the money."

Still holding hands and walking at a slower pace, she looked at Teddy. "What about that motorcycle Al Gunther traded for a boat at Norm's.

"Hey, that's an idea. We need to talk to Norm."

Walking up to the ice cream stand Teddy looked at Zoey sheepishly. "I don't have any money. Do you?"

"No, sorry. Dad said he'd take care of everything, so he didn't give me any."

"Well, I guess it's no big deal. At least we got away from my dad for a while. We could look on the ground to see if anyone dropped some change."

"Hey. Why are you two hanging around here? Aren't you gonna get some ice cream?"

Hearing that booming voice, there was no doubt in their minds that Norm had just walked up behind them

Teddy looked up at Norm. "Ahh, well, we were going to but we don't have any money. So, we're just hanging out."

"Well, ain't that a shame. Can't think of nothin' worse on the Fourth of July. Come with me. I'll buy you one."

Zoey couldn't believe their luck. They'd found Norm, and he was buying ice cream. She took his hand and smiled up at him, "Oh, Norm, you have such big heart."

Norm smiled with pride, and walked her along to the counter. He told the kids, "Now, order up. Whatcha' want?"

They decided to eat their ice cream at a picnic table, which gave Teddy a chance to approach Norm about the motorcycle idea.

"We're lucky we found you so quick, Norm. We were looking for you."

"Oh, yeah? What for?"

"I'm in big trouble with my dad since the go-kart is gone. I know he'll want to see the money or what I traded for."

"So, he doesn't know, yet?"

"No, and I need something right now. I was thinking maybe we could make a deal for that motorcycle you just took in."

"Let me guess, your dad saw your go-kart in the parade today, didn't he?"

Teddy lowered his head and mumbled, "Yeah. How'd you guess?"

"Come on kid, everybody knew it'd happen someday."

"But Norm, that's not the problem. I need something I can tell him I bartered for in return. The motorcycle would be perfect. We need to make a deal today."

"Teddy, I don't even know if it runs. Never ridden it yet."

"Don't worry, Norm, I can make it run."

Zoey joined in, "Come on, Norm, have a heart."

"Ok. We'll talk about it. Come down to the boat dock later after the festivities."

"Thanks, Norm. We'll be there."

As they got up to leave she smiled at Norm. "Thanks for the ice cream."

"You're welcome, kids."

Walking back to join their parents, the two were careful to stand by their mothers, away from Teddy's dad. Hoping the go-kart issue had passed, they focused on the youth groups performing as they walked down the street, and the high school marching band. A fire truck brought up the rear signaling the parade was over. Next was the tug-of-war competition between the Clayton and Garnavillo fire departments.

Kent turned to the Bondi family. "Well folks, you ready to head home or stay and watch the tug-of-war?"

As it turned out, the parents wanted to go and the kids wanted to stay. Zoey's father suggested that they let the kids stay for another hour, and one of the parents would come back to pick them up.

As they crossed the street, Sarah stopped. "Kent, would you mind if I stayed here for a while? I'd like to go by Adel's and see how she's doing."

"Sure, fine with me. I'll just tell Niki to pick you up when she comes for the kids. Ok?"

She gave him a peck on the cheek. "I'll see you later."

When Sarah reached Adel's house she was sitting on her porch swing taking in all the activity at the park. "Hello, Adel. Are you enjoying this grand day?"

"Oh, you'd better believe it," Adel answered. "Fine parade. One of the best."

"May I join you?"

"Of course. How's our girl, Wendy?"

"Adel, you won't believe it. Wendy has a boyfriend who likes horses just like she does. They're out trail riding so often."

"Hmmm, which boy would that be?"

Chuckling a little, she asked her, "Do you remember way back when Wendy got suspended from school for beating up a boy?"

"How could I forget?"

"Well, his name was Billy Goetz. Now they can't see enough of each other."

Shaking her head Adel said, "Never would have guessed."

"Guessed what?"

"Well, first off that she'd ever have a boyfriend for long, and second that it would be that Goetz boy."

"Now, Adel, she's always been unpredictable."

"Ain't that the truth?" Turning to her with a small grin, she asked, "What brings you here?"

"Now, what makes you think I have to have a reason to stop by and see you?"

"Nothin', dear, but you usually do."

"Ohhh. It's terrible to be so predictable. I was hoping you had some time for a frustrated mother."

Adel patted her leg. "What's on your mind?"

Looking at her feet as she rocked the swing, Sarah began. "Teddy. That boy frustrates me at every turn. I never know which boy I'm dealing with."

Looking up, Adel smiled. "How many are there?"

"Three that I know of."

"Really," Adel said. "I guess I haven't seen them all."

She turned her head and looked at Adel. "I'll bet you have. The most predictable one is when he's with Zoey. He's caring and protective, rather like a little gentleman."

"Oh, I've seen 'em together," Adel said, "but they're usually up to no good. Like that time they stole Doc's boat."

"Yes, they're mischievous, but he'd still give his life to protect Zoey."

Adel looked across the street at folks walking in the park. "So, that's only one."

Rocking the swing, Sarah continued. "Well, there's this cooking thing and his interest in Wilma's Café. It's such a feminine side. I don't know if I should worry about him or not?"

"Feminine you say?"

Sarah placed her hand on Adel's shoulder so she would look at her. "Adel, what would you think if your boy wanted to learn to cook, especially at his age?"

"Don't know, Honey, but he doesn't act strange to me."

"Then there's the other thing, Adel. He just has to build things that go fast. He's good at it, but it's so dangerous. "

"He sure is," Adel, replied. Even though he's a kid, I've never seen anybody that good in this town since Roy Cutler."

Sarah was surprised. "Really? Roy built fast cars?"

"Oh, yeah. Roy's specialty was painting, though, so every car he built had the most beautiful paint job on it. We all loved his cars and hot rods. Best in the county for sure." Patting Sarah's hand Adel said, "So, your Teddy's a talented boy. Why are you so frustrated?"

"Isn't it obvious? I never know which boy I'm dealing with."

Adel shook her head. "Oh, dear. Here I thought you'd grown out of it."

Sarah was aghast. "Me? Grown out of what?"

"That need of yours for achievement. You know… goals, plans, execution. The stuff you brought with you from Chicago."

"Adel, that's quite unfair. We're talking about Teddy, not me."

"One and the same, dear."

"You can't be serious."

Adel took her hand. "Just look at yourself, dear. What were you when you came to town?"

Sarah was somewhat perplexed. "I was an I.R.S. Examiner."

"Ok, after you married Kent. What did you do?"

"I taught your class in high school. You know that."

"I do." Adel continued. "Wendy was born and you became what?"

"A mother, of course."

"Then Kent opened the veterinary clinic. What did you do then?"

"I ran the towing business." Irritated, she put her hand on Adel's arm and shook it. "Adel, stop this. What's your point?"

Patting her hand, she chuckled. "Relax. Relax. I'm just trying to show you that you expect Teddy to be one thing so he's easier for you to manage. But, Sarah, Teddy's more like you than you think.

"I don't see that."

"Well, you're not one thing either. Look at all of your interests; your contributions to this community and all the different things you've been capable of doing. Look at me a second. Do you really want to kill that talent in Teddy just to make your life simpler?"

| CHAPTER 17

Zoey and Teddy smiled, said goodbye to their parents and headed toward the tug-of-war site.

She asked him, "How long should we wait here before we go to Norm's?"

"Ten minutes I figure, just in case my dad's watching"

"Ok."

But they were overanxious. Barely five minutes at the tug-of-war and they were gone, walking across the park to the boat dock. They looked around a bit, and found Norm.

"Ahh, want the motorcycle pretty bad I see."

Teddy nodded. "Can we see it?"

Following Norm to the back of his building, he opened the door and led them into his storage area. There, in the middle of the isle stood the motorcycle.

Teddy rushed to the motorcycle and eyeballed it as closely as he knew how. Besides the tires, he checked the chain, the control cables, wiring and the battery.

"Do you have the key, Norm?"

"Sure kid," Norm answered as he turned to a board by the door filled with key rings. "Here, see if it'll start."

Straddling the bike, Teddy inserted the key and listened to the motor pump a few times without starting.

Norm encouraged him. "Try'er again, Teddy. Been sitting here a while."

He tried to start the motorcycle again, and again, and the third time it started. It ran rough at first, and then smoothed out some. Good enough to ride anyway.

"This'll do, Norm. I can tune the engine at home."

"It'll take $500. Can't let'er go for less than that."

"Norm, he pleaded, I don't have that much money. What can I barter for it?"

"Barter, eh? Well, let me see. If you work every Sunday for $50 that'd be 10 weeks to pay it off. Guess I could do that. What do ya' say?"

"Yeah, Sunday's are perfect. That's my day off at Wilma's. Cool. You got a deal, Norm. Thanks."

"Ok, then. I'll give you a bill of sale for the sheriff's sake, but you don't get the title 'til you're done working it off. Understand?"

"Yeah. Yeah. Great. Can we take it now?"

"Sure, why not," Norm said over his shoulder as he went to his office for a bill of sale.

Teddy backed the motorcycle out of the shed, asked Zoey to wait for him, and drove the bike up the road and back.

"We'll do fine, Zoe. Put those pegs down for your feet and hop on."

Putting her foot on a peg, Zoey stepped up onto the seat, put her arms around him and said, "I'm ready."

Norm handed Teddy a bill of sale. "Good luck kid."

Off they went; Teddy was all smiles that he had a comeback for his dad and Zoey was thrilled to be holding him in her arms.

CB ED

Sheriff Norvus removed his clown mask so he could see to drive home in his go-kart. The railroad tracks were jolting his back something terrible as he crossed them, and saw Teddy flash by on a motorcycle.

"Now, I've got him," the Sheriff shouted as he hit the throttle and his go-kart leaped onto the highway, racing toward the motorcycle, reeling it in like a big fish. His polka dot clown suit flapped like a tent in a tornado. Pulling alongside Teddy, the sheriff waved him to the shoulder of the road, drove ahead and cut them off.

Crawling awkwardly out of the low slung go-kart, Sheriff Norvus unbuttoned his clown suit and pulled his ticket pad out of his back pocket as he walked back toward them.

"Just what the hell do you think you're doin?" he asked.

Teddy and Zoey were bent over laughing, which wasn't the answer he was looking for. "Teddy Crodin, I don't know where you got that motorcycle, but you're breaking the law."

"Oh, come on J.R. You can't give me a ticket dressed like a clown."

"I sure can. Even though I'm off duty, I'm still sheriff of this town. Did you steal that motorcycle?"

"No sir. I've got the bill of sale right here." Pulling it out of his pocket, Teddy handed it to the sheriff.

Sheriff Norvis looked at the bill of sale, and then began lecturing them about underage driving when Niki Bondi drove past to pick up the kids.

Zoey saw her mother first, nudged Teddy and they both experienced her stern look at the same time. Things were bad and getting worse.

"J.R.," Teddy said, "It's just transportation for work. From my house to Wilma's and back. I won't ride it anywhere else, I promise. Come on, give me a break."

"Well, I see your point, but what am I going to tell the other parents and kids in town who want to do the same. Pretty soon I'd have all you underage ragamuffins driving around town scaring hell outta people."

"J.R., let's make a deal then."

Sheriff Norvus just grinned. He got him again "Here's your deal," the sheriff said as he tore two tickets off his pad.

"What?" Teddy squealed. "You're giving me a ticket?"

"Actually two. Speeding and driving underage. Only way you're gonna' learn. A hundred and fifty bucks oughta' get your attention, eh?"

C３ ８０

Niki was waiting at the door when he dropped Zoey off at her house.

"Come with me young lady," Niki said as she let Zoey in.

Zoey's shoulders slumped and her head sagged as she followed her mother into the den. Niki closed the door behind her.

"Sit down. We need to have a talk."

But Zoey didn't sit down. She turned, walked up to her mother and pleaded.

"Mom, I don't care what you do to me, but please don't tell Teddy's parents that you saw the sheriff driving his go-cart."

He mother looked at her sternly. "You should know better. Sarah and I do not have secrets. And you children are not going to tell us what to do. "

"So you're going to tell her?"

"You're damned right I'm going to tell her. Right after I get done with you."

"You may not want to do that, Mom."

Niki was surprised. "And why wouldn't I?"

"Well, Mom, if you have to share one of my secrets then it's only fair that I share one of yours."

Niki regained her composure. "I don't have secrets. Not like you and Teddy, sneaking around together to your little hiding place, or whatever you call it."

"Yes, you do," she said, losing some fear of her mother.

"What in the world are you talking about?"

She put her hands in her pockets and looked at the floor. "Well, let me put it this way. Would it be inconvenient if I told Dad you're seeing a marriage counselor?"

Niki raised an eyebrow, "A marriage counselor? Where did you hear such a thing?"

Zoey sat on her dad's favorite chair and put a leg over the arm. "Didn't hear it. I saw you."

"When?" her mom asked, snapping at her.

"Oh, a while back I saw you go into Dr. Hoffman's office."

Niki waved it off and sat on the love seat. "Oh, for God's sake, I met his wife there and went to lunch."

"Never saw you come out," she said, kicking her foot in the air.

Zoey was making too big a deal about this, making Niki suspicious. She decided to give her as much rope as she wanted, and see where it led. "Just what does that mean?"

Looking up at her mom she said, "It means Dad wouldn't know that."

Niki acted disinterested. "You'd actually tell your father that, about me?"

"Only if you tell the Crodin's about the sheriff driving Teddy's go-cart."

"Why Zoey, that's blackmail."

"I think so."

"You wouldn't do it," Niki said as she leaned back and crossed her legs.

"I would too, Mom. And it would make you very uncomfortable and put you in a position where you'd have a lot of explaining to do. Wouldn't it?"

Niki got up and leaned into her face. "Zoey, I'm your mother."

"And, I'm your daughter. Isn't it possible for women to guard information to protect each other?"

Niki was not amused. "Yes, it is. But you're not a woman young lady, you're my daughter. And you live by our rules in this house, not the ones you make up."

The fact that her mom turned on her surprised Zoey. She thought she had everything under control.

Getting in her face, her mom told her, "The fact that you thought you could blackmail me gets you grounded for two weeks. Lying about my visit to Dr. Hoffman gets you another week, as well as a week for planning to lie to your father. "

"That's four weeks, Mom. That's not fair."

She stood beside Zoey. "Whether you think it's fair or not doesn't matter. For your information, grounded means you don't leave the yard except for school. Friends cannot visit you, and I want to know where you are at all times. Got it?"

"Mom. That's a whole month. I'm going to tell Dad. He won't let you do this to me."

"Really," Niki replied, "Be my guest. Just don't be surprised if your dad adds another week after I tell him about this blackmail trick you tried to pull."

CR&

After supper, Teddy was in the shed working on his motorcycle.

"Whatcha' doin', Teddy?"

Teddy turned and looked around. He didn't see anybody.

"Can you hear me?"

"Zoe, is that you?"

"Yeah."

Looking out the shed, he didn't see anything. "Well, where are you?"

"I'm on the bench outside. Mom says I can't see you anymore."

"I figured she would," he said as he shook his head.

"She's scared of motorcycles you know."

Teddy quit working and sat on the ground. "What'd she say?"

"She said that you're wild, dangerous and unpredictable. I'm also grounded for four weeks.

"Really, what happened?"

There was a pause before Zoey responded. "Let's just say I made a big mistake. As long as you have a motorcycle, I can't see you. She's afraid we'll sneak off for a ride."

He wrapped his arms around his knees. "Oh, come on."

"Teddy, you know we would."

"Well, what are we going to do, Zoey?"

"You've got to get rid of that motorcycle. My mom watches me harder than Sheriff Norvus watches you. She's gonna come looking for me any minute you know, and if she finds me with you I'm in trouble for life!"

"I know. You're right."

The porch light came on and he heard her run. Sarah hollered, "Teddy, come in the house. It's bedtime."

She held the door open for him. "What was that I saw scurry off the bench by your shop?"

Teddy looked away and kept walking. "Probably a chicken, Mom."

He tried to hurry up the stairs, but he still heard his mother, "Teddy, we don't have any chickens."

| CHAPTER 18

With a heavy heart, Teddy rode his motorcycle on the gravel roads to the feed plant, so the sheriff wouldn't catch him. He knew what he wanted, and he wanted it bad. Because he didn't know these people well, Roy coached him on how to handle the situation.

"What are you doing here, kid?" A man asked coming through the trusses holding up a circular storage tank.

"Ah, well, I heard someone down here wanted a motorcycle. I came to see if they had anything to barter for."

The man stood about ten feet away, eyeballing him. "I never heard anything about it. Who told you?"

"Roy, down at the barbershop. He said you might have an engine in a junk truck you'd like to get rid of."

"Now then, you'll have to speak to Big Ed about that. Follow me."

Teddy was led through the lunchroom of dirty unkempt men and didn't see a one who'd had a haircut recently. Continuing through an open office door Big Ed was at his desk, and blurted out, "Sit down, kid."

Teddy sat.

"Now, whatta you want?"

Describing his conversation with Roy, Teddy said that he had a car that wouldn't run. He needed a motor, and he'd like to barter his motorcycle for the motor in the old grain truck out back.

"And, what if I don't want a motorcycle, kid?"

"I guess you could sell it," he replied. "Looks like that motor's not doing you any good. If we'd swap, you'd have money from the sale and I'd have something to drive. What do ya' say?"

Getting up from his chair, Teddy thought Big Ed was six-foot-eight and weighed three hundred pounds. Teddy felt like a toddler when Big Ed scowled at him and said, "Let's take a look, kid." Walking around the bike, he showed some interest. "Well, your bike looks good enough; I guess I can take a chance on it. Let me pull that engine for ya'. I'll call when it's ready and you can bring this bike to me."

Teddy was excited. He'd made a deal. "Can you do one small thing for me, Mister Ed?"

"What, now?"

"Since you're not using the truck, can I have the dash instruments too?"

The man waved his arm in the air. "Oh, hell. Why not. We ain't going to use that old beast anyway. But you gotta' take'em out yourself, ya' hear."

CB ED

With a hook in the eyelet and the boom resting on the valve covers to hold the 409 Chevy V-8 steady, Kent drove Teddy and his new motor back home. A box strapped to the bed held the instruments he'd removed from the grain truck.

Kent glanced at Teddy. "You gonna tell me what you plan to do with this motor?"

"Sure, Dad. I'm going to put it in that old T-bucket over there," he said pointing to the rusty hot rod frame Kent took in on barter years ago.

Grinning playfully, Kent asked, "And who says you can have that old car?"

"Why would I ask, Dad? It's been my toy since I could walk. It's still mine, isn't it?"

Driving into the farmyard, Kent turned around and backed up so they could drop the motor in the shed. He got out and stood looking at the old rusty car. "Yeah. Just a pile of junk to me. Sorry I ever took it. If you think you can make something of it, be my guest."

"Would you hook it and drop it in the shed for me, Dad?"

Kent smiled and shook his head. "Why not. At least I'll know where you'll be for the next year."

☙❧

Roy coached Teddy through the building process. Holding to his promise that he wouldn't work on Teddy's car, he was generous in sharing his connections in the custom car business. Teddy learned that the integrity of the chassis was critical if he planned to drop that big block Chevy engine in. So off it went to Lou Green's shop for repair, cleaning and painting. Teddy would have to work some extra hours at Wilma's for enough money to pay for it.

While he was waiting for the chassis, Roy showed Teddy how to pound the dents out of the body. He was banging away after supper when Zoey showed up.

Standing in the doorway she asked, "How's it coming, Teddy?"

"Great, Zoe. When I finish this door, I'll only have one dent in the fender and I'm done. So, you must have finished your sentence and your mom let you out again?"

Zoey nonchalantly drug her hand across the metal on the other side of the body. "Yeah, man that felt like a lifetime. I think Mom made a mistake making it four weeks. We were really tired of each other. Say, can I help?"

Teddy stopped and looked at her. "Sure. See that black sandpaper over there?"

"Yeah."

"Well, take the roughest one and start sanding the rust off the body. I've got gloves for you, just your size."

"You bought gloves for me?"

"Yeah. I was hoping you'd help."

"Cool. Thanks."

Zoey began sanding a fender while Teddy finished pounding out dents. Then he started sanding too. It was slow tedious work, but the metal shined as the rust fell away.

"Zoe, did you hear that I asked Roy to paint the body for me?"

"Really? I thought you said that he wouldn't work on your car."

"I did. But, even though he won't say yes, I can see a glint in his eye whenever I talk about paint colors. I've still got time. I'm hoping I can get him to change his mind."

☙❧

The aisles of the hardware store were hard to navigate with all the merchandise Mr. Gliesen displayed. Zoey thought it looked more like a garage sale than a store. Standing in front of the paint, she looked for the ugliest color. When Mr. Gliesen walked up beside her he asked, "Need some paint, Zoey?"

"You know, I do Mr. Gliesen, but just for fifteen or twenty minutes. I need to show somebody the paint color first. If they like it, then I'll buy it. Would you let me take a gallon out for a few minutes?

"Well now, that ain't normal, Honey. Folks usually buy it before they leave."

"I know, but just this once." Zoey batted her eyes and smiled at Mr. Gliesen. "Please? Twenty minutes at the most. You can trust me."

Mr. Gliesen smiled at the teenager. "Yes, I trust you. Go ahead. But I'll be timing you. Twenty-one minutes and you're buying that paint. Understand?"

"Yes sir. I'll be back soon.

Zoey took a gallon of frog green paint and headed up the street to Roy's barbershop. She walked into the shop, greeted the men hanging out, and put the paint on the sink next to Roy's barber chair.

Roy stopped cutting hair and looked at her, bewildered. "Zoey, what are you doing here?"

"Got a question, Roy. Teddy says you know a lot about cars, so I wanted to ask your advice."

"About what."

Pointing to the gallon of paint, she said, "This paint. Do you think this would be a good color for Teddy's car?"

She could barely hear Roy for all the laughter in the shop. "Oh my God, girl. That is the absolutely worst paint color I've ever seen!"

Zoey remained focused and sober faced. "Really? It's supposed to be good paint, not showing any brush strokes or anything?"

Roy was appalled. "Brush strokes? Did you say brush strokes?"

"Yeah, Teddy doesn't have any other way to paint it, so we need a good paint like this."

Roy shook his head as he walked around the sink. "No, no, no. That'll ruin his car. That car is a classic. There is a heritage those T-buckets have to maintain. It has to be black, white, or red. And nobody in their right mind brushes paint on a car."

Roy turned to his audience seated around the shop. "Guys, have you ever heard of such a thing?"

Ben Samuels piped up, "Only you would know, Roy. You're the painter."

Pete Larkin agreed. "Roy, you'd better help him out, or we'll be looking at an ugly green car the rest of our lives."

Zoey stepped in. "Roy, you paint cars?"

"Well," Roy said reluctantly, "Yes, I used to paint custom hot rods."

"Oh, wow!" Zoey said excitedly. "Would you paint Teddy's?"

Pete spoke up. "All you gotta do is look at that ugly green paint, Roy."

Roy looked down at Zoey as if someone had just pulled his tooth. "Ok, ok. I'll paint his car. But on one condition, young lady."

Zoey tried not to look too excited. "What's that?"

"I get to pick the color. Otherwise, no deal."

Picking up the gallon of paint she smiled, "I'm sure Teddy won't mind. Can I tell him?"

"Yeah, you can tell him. Let me know a week before he wants it painted. But only this once. I'm not doing it for anybody else, you hear?"

Zoey boldly ran up to Roy kissing him on the cheek. "Thank you Roy, you're so sweet."

"Whoo whoo!" cheered the guys as Roy blushed. When she left the barbershop she looked at her watch. Three minutes was all she had. She ran down the sidewalk, past the café and Dave's Tavern to the hardware store. She threw the door open, dashed in and bumped into Mr. Gliesen looking at his watch.

"Oops! Sorry," she said.

"Forty-five seconds, young lady. You almost bought yourself a gallon of paint."

Panting and trying to catch her breath, Zoey managed to say, "I'm so sorry, but they wouldn't stop talking about it."

"I see. Well, did they, whoever that might be, like the color?"

Zoey walked past Mr. Gliesen and put the paint back on the shelf. "Oh, no sir. They refused to use it. Matter of fact, they already have chosen the paint they want to use. I'm so sorry, but thanks for letting me show it to them."

Mr. Gliesen blocked her exit. "Zoey, why do I get a funny feeling about all this?"

"I don't know," she said shrugging her shoulders, "maybe you're not used to selling paint to teenagers?"

Stepping aside to let Zoey leave, he commented, "Maybe."

ᘓᘔ

Zoey was sitting on the bench by the shed when Teddy came out after supper. It was a cool night with a light rain. The roof protected her, all except her feet.

Teddy pulled the hood of his sweatshirt over his head and dashed toward her. "Hey, Zoe. Ready to go to work?"

She hopped up and followed him into the shed. "Yeah, what are we doing tonight?"

Teddy loosened a rope from the cleat on the wall and let the rope run through the pulleys, lowering the engine.

"Well, this motor needs to be cleaned before I hook it up to the transmission. Pretty dirty job. Why don't you finish sanding the wheel wells while I do it?"

"No problem," she said as she walked over to her gloves and sand paper. "Boy, the body's looking pretty good, Teddy."

"Yeah, we'd better think about painting it."

Zoey turned her back to Teddy so he couldn't see her face. "I'll bet Roy will be surprised when you tell him it's ready to be painted."

Teddy stopped what he was doing and turned toward her. "Don't I wish. He hasn't said he'd do it yet."

Still not looking at him she said, "I'm surprised you haven't heard? He told the guys hanging out in his shop that he'd paint your car on one condition."

Teddy was beyond curious. "Really? He said he'd paint my car? Ok, ok! What's the condition?

Slowly Zoey turned to face Teddy. "He gets to pick the color."

"That's all?"

"That's what I heard. Something about tradition or heritage or something like that. He thinks this car is special and the paint has to be too."

Teddy rushed up to Zoey throwing his arms around her. "Well, ok then. Roy's painting my car. That's great! Really great! Man, I'm so happy."

| CHAPTER 19

"Dad," Teddy said at the supper table, "I need your help."

Kent set his drink down, and looked at Teddy. "Help doing what?"

Not looking directly at his dad, Teddy asked, "Well, I need to take the car body to Roy's place for painting and pick up the chassis and bring it home. I was hoping you'd haul them for me."

Kent thought for a few seconds. "I've done a lot to help you with that car, Son. But, I've got my own work to do. Why don't you take the flat bed and haul them yourself."

Teddy was shocked and excited at the same time. "Really, Dad. You'd let me do that?"

"Sure."

"You'd have to show me how. I've never driven it."

Kent looked at Teddy with a mischievous grin, "Are you sure, Son?"

CB&ED

Barroom—Blat, Blat, Blat! Barroom—Blat, Blat, Blat!

The loud rumbling sound startled Sarah so badly that she dropped a saucer into the sink and shattered it. *What has he done?*

Sarah burst out of the kitchen and ran to the shed holding her hands over her ears. As she approached, she saw Teddy and Zoey in red ear protectors smiling at each other. It didn't help her mood. She rushed up to Teddy, slapped him on the shoulder and gave him the cutthroat sign.

Teddy shut off the engine and took off his ear protectors. When he saw the look on his mom's face, he thought about putting them back on.

"Teddy Crodin, what have you done? Do you expect me to live with that awful noise every time you drive this thing?"

With his mother in his face and nowhere to go, Teddy had to think quickly.

"No, Mom. You've got it all wrong. It won't be this loud when I get the mufflers on. I was just testing it, that's all."

Sarah didn't budge from pinning Teddy against the car. "That noise is outrageous. If I hear it again I'll sell this car right out from under you, understand?"

"Geez, Mom. I didn't mean to upset you."

"Well, you did. And I don't want to hear this monster again until you have the mufflers on it. Is that clear?"

Teddy slid away from his mom and the car for some breathing room. "Ok, Mom. Ok. I'm sorry. It won't happen again."

Sarah whirled around and went back to the house.

Zoey looked across the car at Teddy, "That was scary."

"Well, there's one thing for sure."

Still petrified, Zoey asked, "What's that?"

"Mom won't be wanting a ride in my car."

CB EO

Roy walked across the street to Wilma's Café, passed through the dining room and peeked into the kitchen. "Hey, Teddy."

"Roy, what's up?"

"I finished your car last night. Needs to cure another day or two, but you can see it tonight if you want."

"Oh, man. How cool! " Teddy said as he took two burgers off the grill. Walking toward Roy he asked, "When can I move it?"

Roy chuckled, "Easy now. I said a couple days."

"I know, but I need to get it upholstered before I put it on the chassis."

Roy threw up his hands. "Oh, no. You'd ruin it! Put the body on, and then drive it to the upholstery shop."

"Ok. Makes sense. But, where should I go?"

"Dave Dietz, over in Dyersville. All he does is restorations and hot rods. He's done a dozen T-Buckets. I'll give him a call to let him know you're coming in a few days."

Teddy had lost all sense of reality until he smelled smoke from the grill. "Holy Cow!"

"Later," Roy said as he ducked out of the smoky kitchen.

Teddy was busy cleaning up two burnt chicken breasts when Wilma came out of the office. "What's going on? Is the building on fire?"

03 80

Kent and Sarah were enjoying a laid back Saturday morning finishing a cup of coffee when Teddy entered the kitchen. He got a bowl of cereal and sat with them, asking, "Would it be possible for one of you to take me to Dyersville today, to pick up my car?"

Sarah looked at Kent with a sparkle in her eye, and then addressed him, "Oh, Honey, that's such a long drive. I don't think I can make time today."

He didn't catch on. "What? Mom, it's only thirty minutes away."

Kent pitched in. "Son, you've got to realize that we're busy people, and can't cater to your every need"

Looking at them in disbelief he said, "I can't believe you guys. I need to pick up my hot rod. It'll only take an hour over and back."

Sarah placed her hand on Teddy's, "Oh, Honey, I'm so sorry."

He was ready to explode out of there when their laughter started. Not just giggles, but belly laughing. Teddy had been royally "had" by his own parents.

Popping out of his chair he screamed above their laughter, "How could you?" But they were laughing too hard to answer.

She got up and hugged Teddy. "I'm sorry, Honey; we knew you would be so excited we just had to pull your chain. I'm ready to go when you are. I wouldn't want you to miss a minute in your new hot rod."

Looking up at his mom Teddy asked, "Do you mind if Zoey rides along? She's helped so much I want her to be the first to ride in it?"

"Better call her now if she's going to be ready."

CB ℰℴ

Zoey ran her hand along the candy apple paint gazing at the white interior. "It's so beautiful."

Teddy smiled with pride, "It is, isn't it?"

Sarah hugged him. "You should be so proud, Honey."

He looked at his mom and smiled. "Wanna hear how it sounds, Mom?"

Putting up her hand and backing away she said, "No thanks, I'll leave that to you kids. Should I follow you home?"

"Naw, we'll be fine. Besides, this thing will make your truck look like a turtle."

While that made his mother smile, she also made a point of saying, "You do know that we're not paying your tickets or bailing you out of jail, don't you?"

"I know."

"Ok then. I'm off." Heading for the door Sarah said, "See you kids later."

"Ok, Mom. Zoe, why don't you hop in? Give me a minute to pay Mr. Dietz and we'll go."

As soon as they hit the road, they were surrounded by a symphony of sound. Engine whine and the whistling wind was joined by the bass rumble of the side pipes. Every head turned as they passed by. Some hollered. Others waved. Zoey waved back like a movie star.

Leaving Dyersville city limits onto the open highway Teddy asked, "Well, Zoe… you ready to see what this old bucket can do?"

"Yeah, let's go!"

Teddy pushed the throttle to the floor. The T-Bucket leaped forward, slamming their backs into the seats; at ninety miles an hour the wind pulled at their hair and deformed their faces. Zoey started bouncing up and down and waving her hands above the windshield; she was screaming for joy. Concerned she'd fall out, Teddy let off the gas and coasted back to the speed limit where he could be heard. "What do you think you're doing?"

"Oh, Teddy. This is so cool. It's exactly like we thought it would be when we were little, pretending to drive, racing down country roads. Our old toy has come alive. It's perfect."

C8 &0

When classes were over on Monday afternoon Zoey closed her locker and dashed out of the school building to find Teddy and ride home in their hot rod. Zoey was crushed when she saw him. Leaning back in the seat with his arms across the back and the door, Teddy looked like a movie actor at a photo shoot. Four of the prettiest girls in school surrounded him. Janelle, one of the girls with him noticed her, and shouted so all could hear. "Hey, Cinder-ella, your chariot's taken. Ride the bus home to do your moping and scrubbing."

Teddy wasn't pleased. "Hey, what's with the Cinderella bit?"

"Oh, Honey. Anyone as homely as Zoey deserves to be a housemaid."

It was too late to give Zoey a ride home, since the bus she got on was pulling away from the curb. "Well, I gotta' go, girls," he said as he started the engine.

Janelle opened the passenger door and slid in. Sweetly she asked, "Why don't you take me home, dude? The long way, please."

Teddy was annoyed. He nodded his head, popped the clutch and whipped her head back into the seat.

"Ouch! Hey, was that necessary?" Janelle complained.

"Sorry, this car can be hard to handle at times."

CR „

Janelle was right. Teddy had grown up to be tall and handsome like his dad. Zoey, on the other hand was flat chested with braces and glasses. Other boys thought she was homely and avoided her. But they were still buddies, and met at the fishing hole often. Teddy went to meet her after lunch on Saturday.

She was crying when Teddy arrived.

"Oh, go away, will ya?"

He stood beside her. "What's wrong, Zoe?"

In between sobs she said, "Leave me alone. Just leave."

"No. I'm not leaving. I've always been here for you, and I'm here for you now." Teddy sat down and crossed his legs, remaining silent as he gazed over the creek.

Zoey continued to cry. "It's all your fault, you know."

He didn't understand why, but continued to stare straight ahead, not moving.

"You're so damn handsome. Girl's swarm around you all the time. You think you're something special. And do you know what? Boys look at me like I'm a dumpster. Just plain and ordinary."

He didn't agree.

"Do you know how long it's been since a boy talked to me at school? Do ya? I counted the days. It was four days, six hours, and eleven minutes. Wanta' know what he said?"

Zoey leaped to her feet and walked away a few paces. "Would you pass me the salt?" she screamed at the creek.

Turning back toward Teddy she repeated, "Would you pass me the salt?" Get it. Nothing personal, just a salt shaker. Ya' hear that, Hercules? God's gift to the cheerleading squad!"

Zoey finally broke down and started crying heavily.

Teddy wished his mom was here. She'd know what to say. Without her help, he felt lost. He didn't know whether to hug Zoey, kiss her, say something or walk away. It seemed like the safest thing to do was to hug her.

Moving closer to her, Teddy put his arm around Zoey. With his hand, Teddy gently guided her head to his shoulder. He thought he could feel her anger melting away as she cuddled against him, sobbing softly.

Man, girls are weird. One minute she's ready to bite my head off, and now she's all soft and cuddly. No wonder I never know what to do!

137

Eventually Zoey spoke. "I'm sorry. It's not your fault. But, there's nothing I can do. I'm homely. I'm not sexy. I've never had a date like my friends. I'm just a nothing."

"Well, if you want to go on a date, I'll take you."

She looked up at him "Oh, big deal. We've spent our whole life together. So you think taking me to a movie would be special? Everybody in town expects that. I want something exciting."

He smiled at her. "Hmm, didn't know I wasn't exciting. I guess my go-kart and motorcycle and hot rod aren't exciting enough for you?"

"That's not what I mean." Pointing to her heart, she said, "Exciting in here."

"Zoe, I'm sure you'll find the excitement you're looking for someday. Until you do, I'll always be here for you." He pulled her closer and sat quietly, waiting for her emotions to quiet down.

| CHAPTER 20

Tony Ward had worked as a farrier for the Lexington Equine Surgery & Sports Medicine Clinic. He'd heard there was a new veterinary intern. A junior from the University of Kentucky named Wendy Crodin, that he hoped to meet soon. He was thinking about her while walking through the barn to shoe a horse when he saw her wrapping the cannon of a horse's leg.

Attracted by Wendy's blonde hair and sexy figure, Tony remembered people saying she could be pretty sassy. For fun he stepped up to the opening of the stall, set his toolbox down, put his hands in his pockets and leaned against the gatepost. Turning to wrap the horse's other cannon she noticed him. "Oh." She flinched with surprise. "Who are you?"

Casually he answered. "Tony Ward, at your service, ma'am."

Wendy turned her back on him, asking, "What are you doing here?"

He smiled mischievously. "I have an appreciation of thoroughbreds, and thought I'd stop by to admire one."

Wendy continued to wrap the second cannon. "Well, you're dumber than you look. This horse isn't a thoroughbred."

Folding his arms, Tony took a long look at Wendy. "I wasn't talking about the horse."

Wendy turned her head and glared at him. "Don't you have work to do?"

Tony didn't move. "Sure do."

Resting on one knee, she challenged Tony. "Well, why don't you go do it, and quit bothering me?"

Tony's chuckle irritated Wendy before he even spoke. "I would if I could."

Still annoyed with him, Wendy asked, "What does that mean? What's holding you up?"

"You are. I'm supposed to shoe this horse."

Wendy was astonished. Her jaw dropped. *This guy isn't going to leave?*

"You can't be serious?"

Enjoying his prank on Wendy, Tony maintained the smirk on his face, like he wasn't going to budge. "But, I am."

Wendy had to wrap the back legs of the horse as well, but wasn't in the mood to do it with Tony looking over her shoulder, if that's what he was looking at. Picking up her case, she stood and walked right up to him, nose to nose, catching him off guard.

"Liar."

Then she turned down the center aisle of the barn and walked away.

Tony couldn't help but watch her hips sway to and fro as she stomped off. She was right. He lied, but it bought him some time and attention that he doubted she'd give away easily.

೮೫ೞ

The next day, when Wendy finished her work with a horse named Sling Shot, she decided it was a good time to take a lunch break. All she had to do was get her lunch sack from her locker and she could sit at the picnic tables around the corner. But, as she rounded the corner and saw the picnic tables she felt awkward. Tony Ward was sitting at the end table eating his lunch and looking out on the landscape. Her movement attracted his attention.

I really don't want to sit with him.

Tony smiled at her. "Hey, Wendy. Won't you join me?"

She hesitated. "I'm not sure what to expect."

"Manners, my lady. Manners. Besides, I'm trying to be your friend."

Manners? I doubt he has any.

Wendy sat at his table, toward the middle so they weren't across from each other.

Tony watched Wendy as she started eating. "So, how's your day going, Doc?"

Wendy's face soured. "I'm not a doctor and you know it. I'm an intern."

He eyed her as he sipped a Coke. "Well, from what I've seen, you're the prettiest intern this place has ever seen."

She looked up from her sandwich. "Oh, give it up. If you're going' to flirt. get a new line."

Tony ignored the cheap shot. "Like a detective, I checked into your background, and I have evidence."

Wendy slammed her sandwich down. "You've been checking up on me? You've no right. And besides, I've done nothing wrong!"

"Oh, but I've got proof, or do you deny you're Queen of Clayton County?"

Wendy was outraged. "You got a picture of me and you didn't even ask?"

Tilting his head slightly he said, "Just a bit of computer time and this stunning young blonde's picture appeared."

Embarrassed, she felt violated. "You saw a picture of me?"

Happy to have Wendy on the defensive, Tony pressed on. "Yep. The Chicken Queen."

The image of that day caught her by surprise and she choked; quickly bowing her head, she covered her smile, as she remembered her smart-ass brother saying that at the fair.

Sitting up straight with his arms stretched out to the edge of the picnic table, Tony proclaimed, "Yep, you clean up good, Crodin."

Wendy looked down at herself, dressed in boots, jeans, a long sleeved work shirt with her hair pulled through the back of her cap.

How long has it been since I've worn a dress?

Giving Tony a determined look, she replied, "Any woman can for the right reason." Trying to change the conversation to something other than herself, Wendy asked. "What about you? What would I learn if I searched for information about you?"

"Well, you'll find a prankster who was lousy at school and good with animals. Especially horses."

With her elbows on the table, Wendy rested her chin on her hands. "So, you're a loser that was lucky to find a job?"

"Harsh. So harsh. My grades were good enough to get into veterinary school, like you."

"What? You can't be serious?"

"Oh, I am. Took one year to learn it was too much science for me. I need to be working with my hands, you know."

"So, now you're a drop-out."

Tony shook his head, finding Wendy very testy. "Hardly. I went from there to Meredith Manor Farrier School in West Virginia. I got my Equine Science Master, and here I am."

Nothing here to crow about. But he seems nice enough.

Wendy wadded up her lunch sack, and rose from her table. "Well, good for you. Listen, I've got to get back to work."

Tony left his lunch on the table as he jumped up with her. "Say, don't run off. You know, you said you'd dress up for the right reason."

Wendy was prepared to brush Tony off. "I said, sir, that any woman can for the right reason."

"That's my point. I'd like to give you a reason. One of my clients has invited me to attend a corporate reception he's having at his country club."

She stopped walking so the garbage barrel was between them.

"It would be my honor if you'll let me take you as my guest. No boy-girl thing. Just friends enjoying a fabulous dinner, wine and an evening out. Come on, what do you say?"

"No boy-girl, this is-a-date stuff?"

"Right."

"I don't think so, Tony. It'd look like a date, and we hardly know each other." Dropping her lunch sack into the barrel she turned and walked away.

Not willing to take this lying down, Tony rushed after Wendy and caught up with her as she was entering the barn.

Wendy was irritated, snarling at Tony. "What's the matter, you don't understand no?"

"Hey. Listen, I'm not asking you for me. I'm trying to do this for you."

She stopped. "Why me?"

Pleading, he said, "Because there are people you need to meet."

Leaning into his face with her hands on her hips, she challenged him. "Really, like who?"

"Like a lot of other vets, racehorse owners, and horse breeders. People who can help your career and medical practice when you graduate."

Wendy looked at Tony trying to size up his intentions. "When you put it that way, I suppose I should go."

Instantly his demeanor changed, and Wendy saw him smile from ear-to-ear.

Did he just trick me?

"Listen, Wendy, you won't regret it. "Friday at 7 p.m. Is that too early to pick you up?"

"That's fine."

Tony put his hands in his pockets, pulled his shoulders back and smiled. "Fine, seven it is.

Wendy walked off into the barn. What did I just agree to? Damn, he's persistent.

| CHAPTER 21

Wendy hadn't seen Tony all day, and knew he'd be worried, thinking she was sick, or maybe had an accident? But she had closeted herself in the office, a place Tony didn't frequent.

"Oh, Wendy, your hair looks beautiful," sales manager Sherrie North said to her as she walked through the office. "I love a curly hair style. The shoulder length fits you perfectly, girl. You should wear it like that more often."

"Thanks. Sherrie. I'm going to an event tonight and thought I should get my hair done for a change."

"Don't tell me. Are you going to Dr. Ambrosia's reception with Tony?"

"Ahh, how would you know that?"

"Because it's all he's been talking about."

"It's just a one-time deal. Nothing to get excited about."

"Maybe so, but mark my words. You couldn't find a finer man than Tony."

Wendy looked around the office before addressing Sherrie in a whisper. "Sherrie, don't say a word to anybody about my hair. I've spent all day in the office just so it'll be a surprise when I see Tony tonight. Don't ruin it for me. Please?"

"Something special for Tony, eh? Now, why would I want to ruin your fun?"

As Sherrie left her desk, Wendy thanked her and returned to her paperwork, finding Sherrie's remark about a 'finer man' quite a stretch. Learning that the whole clinic knew about their night out was disturbing. It was going to be hard to keep this as a one-and-done deal.

Charlie Wert, Wendy's supervisor, came up and sat on the corner of her desk.

"Aren't you supposed to be in the stables, young lady?"

"Oh, Hi, Charlie. Yes, but I've let all my reports pile up, and I need them done today. Just give me one office day, and I'll be done with them. Please?"

"I see. Well, up to now you seemed to get your reports done at the end of each day. Any special reason you let them stack up this week?"

Geez, even Charlie is pressing me about this dinner with Tony. What is it? Should I just put a banner over my shoulder, "Wendy's going to dinner with Tony." Damn it. I should have said No!

Wendy turned her chair around to face him. "Excuse me, sir, but are you trying to imply something? Because if you are, I don't understand."

He smiled and rose from her desk. "I've heard how important it is to be in the office today, and that's fine. But in the future, I prefer daily reports. Ok? Then he casually walked away.

ೞ⦆

Having seen Tony eyeing her figure closely, Wendy chose her outfit carefully. It was summer, so she picked a multi-colored sleeveless halter dress so there would be no cleavage showing, and a hemline that fell to her knees. The high heels made her feel like a different person, and brought back memories of the beauty pageant five years ago.

How sad. I don't even wear heels once a year.

Looking into the full-length mirror on the bathroom door, Wendy thought she was looking at another person, not herself.

Maybe it wasn't so bad that Tony asked me to come along. It appears as if I've been one dimensional for too long.

The ringing doorbell interrupted her thoughts. Wendy opened the door to greet Tony.

He stared awkwardly at Wendy, then came to his senses quickly, saying, "Excuse me, ma'am. I'm here to pick up Wendy Crodin. Does she still live here?"

"Tony, don't start that."

"Well, what should I say? You don't look like the Wendy I work with. You're gorgeous. I'm going to be so proud to be with you tonight. Bending his arm and holding it up for her, Tony asked, "May I escort you to your coach, Madam?"

Tony made Wendy feel special, and she couldn't help but giggle, and play along with his little charade. He was actually cute, and quite the gentleman.

છ80

Arriving at the country club, Tony held Wendy's arm closely as they passed from the valet to the dining room where every man they passed admired Wendy. Wendy couldn't believe the people Tony knew at the affair. He introduced her to doctors, lawyers, and almost every stable owner in town. And he was gracious.

"Dr. Shapiro, may I present my guest, Wendy Crodin. She's following in the footsteps of her father, a highly respected veterinarian and scientist in Iowa."

Wendy was surprised at the respect people showed for Tony. All who knew him revered the man she had called a 'drop out'. She listened carefully, but didn't learn why.

There is something about Tony Ward that is special, that's for sure. But, what is it?

Around ten-thirty Tony walked up beside Wendy while she was talking with a group of women. Standing close to her, he spoke quietly. "I think we should go before our chariot turns into a pumpkin."

Wendy chuckled at his silliness. "Yes, we should go now." She excused herself and they left the country club.

It seemed to please Tony when she took his hand as they left the dining room. She smiled at him and gave it a gentle squeeze. Walking to his car, he asked, "Would you like to have a nightcap?"

Wendy didn't know his intentions. "I don't think it would be appropriate, Tony?"

"Oh, come on. Starbucks is just a mile from here. Nice public place. Appropriate place for a lady with a gentleman, don't you think?"

Wendy sighed, glad it wasn't an awkward 'your place or my place' thing. "It does sound perfect, Tony. Yes, let's go there."

Wendy watched Tony with interest. He dropped his keys trying to open the car door for her, and drove out of the parking lot without his lights on, so she had to remind him.

Is he forgetful or nervous? I'd better check my purse in case he forgot money for coffee.

Wendy felt more comfortable with him than she ever expected. And Tony seemed more comfortable once they settled in at Starbucks. His clumsiness seemed to subside into his charming self again.

Starbucks wasn't all that busy at 11 p.m. so they had a private corner to themselves. After a period of quietly sipping their drinks, Wendy was the first to speak.

"Tony, I want to thank you for a wonderful night. You were a perfect gentleman."

"Surprised?"

She nodded as she stirred her drink. "A little. But that wasn't the most surprising thing."

"Really. That must be a good thing, right?"

"I think so. Just how did you earn the respect from those people I met? It was incredible?"

"Well, I know you don't think I have much of an education."

She interrupted quickly. "I never said that."

"Pretty close," Tony said as he nodded his head. "Anyway, what I didn't tell you is that I'm really good at diagnosing animal performance problems. Especially leg and hoof issues. The people you met hire me because, not only do I shoe their horses, but I make corrective shoes when their horses are lame, have tendinitis, strains and all."

Wendy sat up and exclaimed, "You can really do that?"

"I think I've saved a horse for each of the people you met tonight. I may not be as educated as you are, but I'm as good as you at caring for animals. Just in my own way."

So that's why. Pretty impressive.

Wendy reached across the table and placed her hand on Tony's. "Then let's help each other care for animals in our own way. No more bickering, ok?"

A big smile appeared on Tony's face as he turned his hand in Wendy's and held it. He took his eyes from their hands and looked at her. "Ok, no more bickering. Now, I'm not saying no pranks and stuff, 'cause that's just my nature."

Not to be outdone, Wendy leaned across the table. "Well, Mr. Ward, I don't believe you've seen me in action yet. I was pretty good in my day."

"Excellent, no more bickering then. Shake on it.

| CHAPTER 22

On Saturday morning, the day after graduation, Zoey was anxious to talk with Teddy. The sun was trying to burn off the humidity, and she knew it was going to be a scorcher. She wanted to meet this morning when it was cooler. But no one answered the door when she knocked. His dad's truck was in the farmyard, so she went to his clinic.

Entering the empty hallway, she called out, "Mr. Crodin. Are you here?"

A muffled voice came from somewhere in the clinic. "Yes, just a minute, please."

Zoey waited in the hallway. Things weren't going as she planned. It was important that she talk with Teddy before Monday, if she could find him.

"Yes, how can I help? Zoey? What a surprise," Teddy's dad said from the waiting room.

"Good morning, sir. I was hoping to see Teddy. Do you know where he is?"

"Why, young lady, I thought he was with you at the fishing hole. Only been gone a half hour or so."

She was relieved that she still had time. "Thank you, Mr. Crodin," Zoey said as she turned and dashed out the door.

❧

The grass was thick and damp as Zoey walked the little path to their secret place. She saw Teddy sitting cross-legged taking a hook out of a fish.

"Good morning."

Teddy looked over his shoulder at her. "Hey, Zoe. Fishing's good this morning. Did you bring your pole?"

"No, I just came to talk," she said sitting down beside him.

He smiled wide. "That's great; I've got news for you."

Although she wanted to tell him her news, she didn't act like it. "What's happened?"

"Just like Wilma said, as soon as I graduate I can be a full time cook. I start at ten today. Isn't that cool?"

She reached out to squeeze his hand. "Oh, Teddy. That's wonderful. You've worked so hard for it. Is this what you want for a career?"

"Don't know. Never thought about it like that."

Zoey took a deep breath, looked longingly at him and said, "Well, I've decided on a career."

"Really? A Career?"

"Well, yes. I've waited too long for something to happen here, so I'm taking things in my own hands."

Why? She's got everything she needs here, doesn't she? What's going on?

Casting his line into the creek, Teddy looked at her curiously. "What was supposed to happen here?"

She stared out at the creek." Romance. Excitement. A feeling that I'm important. But, I have few friends and the boy that I love doesn't love me."

"What boy?" Teddy asked." Who is he? Tell me and I'll kick his butt."

Now there's something I'd like to see. "No Teddy. That wouldn't accomplish anything. It's never going to happen. Let it be."

"Well, that's no reason to leave."

Zoey just shrugged. "Maybe not, but I have no future here. I'm going to start over and make a life for myself."

"I don't understand," Teddy said.

"I know. We've been so close. Maybe too close. It's like the old saying, 'You can't see the forest for the trees'."

"What's that got to do with anything?"

"Everything, Teddy."

"Come on. What can I do to convince you to stay?"

"Nothing. My mind's made up. I've already enrolled in a two-year associate's degree course in retail business management at Taylor University." Looking up at the pain on his face, she wanted to cry, but she promised herself she wouldn't. "Teddy, I leave Monday for Indianapolis. I don't expect to come back."

He rose to his knees, and grabbed her hands, thinking it would bring her back to reality. "I always thought you'd stay here in town with me. I don't understand why you're doing this so suddenly."

"Teddy, there's a lot of things you don't understand."

"Like what?" He asked, pleading for something he could hold on to.

"Like the fact that I want a new start. I want a life, Teddy. Here I'm nothing. I'm a nobody."

He pulled her hands to his chest and held them tight." Oh, come on. You're important to me."

"Am I?" Zoey asked.

"Of course. Look at all the things we do together."

Zoey ripped her hands away from his." Yeah, Teddy. Like a brother and sister."

"Well, what's wrong with that?" Teddy asked.

"Everything. You'll just never understand. I'm going Teddy and that's final."

"We'll see each other on holidays won't we?" Teddy asked.

"No, I'm not coming back. The twenty-four month course is intense. And I won't have money to travel home and back. This is it, Teddy. I won't be here anymore. I'm sorry."

Zoey kissed him on the cheek, rose and walked away. Teddy was totally confused, and sat holding his head in his hands. She didn't wipe her tears until she was far enough away that he wouldn't notice.

CB ED

Teddy felt a hole in his heart without Zoey, but with work, money, and the coolest hot rod in the County he kept busy. He had the attention of all the pretty girls in town, as well as Sheriff Norvus.

Showing off for the girls, he'd drive fast everywhere he went, which the sheriff was determined to stop. A cat and mouse game developed between them, but the sheriff won more often than Teddy. That's why he always scouted for the sheriff and then raced off in the other direction.

The game was on again one cool fall day when Teddy came to the intersection of the gravel road and highway 52. Off to the left he saw the sheriff's cruiser in the drive of Edgar's gas station, blocked by some trees. He turned right, eased out of town at exactly the speed limit and drove cautiously to the rest stop. As he passed, he hit the gas and drove the narrow river road at ninety miles an hour. It was a blast until he heard the siren.

Surprised, he looked back to see Sheriff Norvus chasing him with lights flashing. Teddy was mad. He'd been duped. The sheriff was not going to win this time.

He headed into the "S" curve.

The sheriff can't make this curve. He'll slide off the road and I'll be home free.

Cutting through the apex of the corner the rear of Teddy's car slid, caught the road again shooting him into the straight away toward the ninety-degree turn. He cut through the apex again, slid the rear again, and lost it. The rear end whipped around, pulling the car off the road, throwing dirt into the air as Teddy spun down the side of the ditch and slammed backwards into a grove of trees.

He was conscious but confused. He heard Zoey's voice in his head. Shook it. But it wouldn't leave. "Teddy, you can be so stupid. You coulda' died."

"Ah-ha. Gotcha right where I want ya."

He leaned back and looked up at J.R.'s scrawny face staring at him. "I thought your car was parked at Edgar's gas station."

With a grin as sly as the big bad wolf, J. R. leaned into Teddy's face. "Decoy, my boy. All hunters use'em."

CB&OD

The embarrassment never stopped. First his dad, who had to tow his car home. Then his mom, hysterical that he could have been killed. Plus the café, where every patron had something to say or questions to ask. And last but not least, Sheriff Norvus boasting that he was the great hunter that bagged his prey.

The real pain came in the courtroom. The bailiff announced the judge's entrance to start the proceedings. Judge Cornwall sat, looked quietly at some papers, then said "Teddy Crodin, please rise."

Standing before his parents and all the townsfolk that could fit in the courtroom, he watched the judge.

"Son, I'm glad that you weren't injured or killed in your accident. It was a blessing. However, in the process you've broken the speeding law, were driving recklessly, endangered other motorists on the road, failed to keep your vehicle under control, and tried to evade an officer of the law. Can you deny any of these charges?"

Teddy wanted to dissolve into a puddle, disappear, and be beamed up somewhere. But he couldn't.

"No, Your Honor, I can't deny them. But, Sheriff Norvus sure has been prejudiced against me, even trying to give me a ticket for riding my bike before I even had a driver's license. If he had treated me like everybody else, I don't think this would have happened."

The judge smiled at the sheriff, then looked at Teddy. "The evidence shows that the sheriff was doing his job. Very well, I might add. So, you need to understand, young man, that we've reached our limit. You've been in here far too often. You've attracted far too much of the sheriff's time. I'm fining you $250.00 for each of the five violations and I'm suspending your driver's license for one year. Maybe walking to work will give you ample time to think about changing your ways. Court's adjourned."

J.R. made sure he was in Teddy's path as he left the courtroom. "So, now what are you going to do, hotshot?"

He stopped and looked at J.R. with hatred welling up inside him. "I'm going to build a speed boat, damn it. You can't give me a ticket on the river, can ya'?"

J.R. just grinned, savoring his victory.

| CHAPTER 23

It was race day at Keeneland Race Park and both Wendy and Tony were assigned to the stables for the weekend. Wendy had a free moment, so she stopped at the stall where Tony was shoeing a horse. "Hey, it's time for a break, Shoe."

Tony commented while he kept working. "Find a spot and I'll be there in a couple minutes."

When Tony joined Wendy, she was sitting outside the barn on a bale of straw. She had a burger and Coke for him. Days at the track weren't all that complicated, but the pace was intense. Breaks were rare, so they were lucky to get one.

Opening his can of Coke, Tony took a sip. "Wendy."

"What?"

Leaning back against the barn, Tony glanced at her. "I've wanted to ask about your steeplechase riding lessons. How long have you been doing that?"

How does he find out these things about me? He's so spooky I want to cling to my clothes so I don't lose them.

Putting her Coke down she started opening her sandwich. "I've been steeple chasing a few months, now. I miss riding my horse, Ginger, and this was my only choice. I'm too tall and over the weight limit for thoroughbreds."

Giving her a surprised look, he said, "I didn't know you're a rider."

Oh, so now he doesn't know everything. Wasn't he the all-knowing detective once?

"I was a barrel racer back home."

"Ever win?"

Nodding, she told him, "Yes, eventually. Anyway, my steeplechase instructor entered me in some minor steeplechase events for practice. They worked out ok, so she's looking for an owner who will give me a ride in a local stakes race."

Tony was excited by the news. "I want to see you race."

Wendy turned her attention to her sandwich. "That would be nice. Let's see what she finds for me. "Ok?"

CB EO

As Wendy arrived at the Wind Gate stables, her instructor, Suzie Lane, was with a middle-aged man wearing a Stetson. Curious, she approached them with caution.

Suzie waved. "Wendy, please come and meet Gordon Weaver. He needs a jockey for next week's steeplechase event. It's your lucky day, girl."

"Really? I get to be in a stakes race?" Wendy was so happy she felt like jumping up and down and screaming as she did at her fifth birthday party. Instead, she politely shook Mr. Weaver's hand.

"Wendy," he said, "before we seal the deal, I want to see you ride. Would you do that for me?"

"Of course, sir." Turning quickly for the barn she said over her shoulder, "Just give me ten minutes."

Riding her training horse, Wendy entered the course. They knew each other well, and it seemed that her mare sensed her excitement, because she had extra spring in her legs. Blazing down the track at full gallop, they glided over the obstacles like a soaring Albatross. The better they jumped the more excited they became and the faster they ran. Wendy was thrilled. She knew they were making a great time, if not her best.

Wendy returned to the barn and pulling up next to Suzie and Mr. Weaver, she was pleased to see him smiling.

"Nice job. I think you're the rider for my new entry. I'll bring her over tomorrow so you can start training."

"Thank you, Mr. Weaver." Wendy said while dismounting and shaking his hand.

As Gordon Weaver drove away, Wendy turned to Suzie and threw her arms around her neck. "Oh Suzie, isn't this exciting? I get to be in a stakes race. I get to race."

"I'm so happy for you, Wendy. You've done well, and we've finally found a ride for you. Congratulations."

CB EO

Suzie got an uncomfortable feeling as she and Wendy watched her hired hands unload Star Bright. She couldn't put her finger on why, just that the horse didn't unload smoothly like a well-trained horse should. Not wanting to ruin Wendy's enthusiasm, Suzie kept her feelings to herself. She'd just watch Star Bright closely.

Wendy was bouncing like a child. "When do you think I can ride her?"

"Tomorrow. I want her to chill out in the pasture today. Let her rest some, Wendy. You can ride her tomorrow."

CB EO

Wendy wasn't having any problems riding Star Bright, and they were getting better times with each run. Suzie dispensed with her earlier feelings, and encouraged Wendy to push Star Bright harder.

While Wendy was out for her last run of the day, Suzie went to the house for some sandwiches and iced tea. Carrying them on a tray, she stepped out onto the porch, screamed and dropped everything. Star Bright was standing in the barnyard without Wendy.

Suzie left the mess on the porch and ran for the horse, calling her hired hands.

She and one of the men jumped into a Jeep and backtracked the course until they found Wendy walking toward them holding her wrist and crying.

Skidding to a stop, Suzie hopped out and ran up to her. "Wendy, are you all right? My God, what happened?"

"Star Bright balked. She straightened her front legs and dropped her head. I flew like a missile."

"Damn it, I had a bad feeling about that horse the first time I saw her. I shouldn't have let you ride her." Suzie reached for Wendy's arm. "What's wrong here?"

"I rolled when I hit the ground, and heard my wrist snap before I stopped."

Suzie looked for blood in her helmet, then her hair. "Did you hit your head?"

"Not hard. Oh, Suzie! I blew my chance. I've waited so long to get into a stakes race." Sobbing so hard her shoulders were shaking Wendy declared sadly, "I may never race."

CB EO

Word of Wendy's accident was known throughout the clinic the next morning. Tony heard about it the moment he reached the stable. His heart sank, knowing how much the race meant to Wendy. Where was she? How could he help? He had to find her.

All morning, he took time between jobs to look for her. Finding her was much more difficult than he expected. He wondered if maybe she hadn't come to work, so he asked around. He was assured Wendy was around somewhere. By lunch, he'd given up trying to find her. If she wanted to see him, she would have by now. He'd bet she didn't come to work. So he grabbed his lunch, sat at one of the picnic tables, and sank deep in thought about Wendy's dilemma.

Starring into space, worried and frustrated, Tony was surprised when Wendy quietly sat down across the table. Her eyes were red. Her cheeks puffy.

"Hey, I've been worried about you. I looked for you all morning. Where have you been?"

Wendy spoke softly. "Mostly in the ladies' room crying. I can't believe I was so close to riding in a stakes race. Two days." She looked up at him sadly, "Only two more days and I would've been riding."

Tony took her good hand in his. "I'm so sorry about what happened. How's your wrist feeling?"

"It's sore, and it throbs constantly. I'm supposed to have ice on it, but I haven't been very good at doing it."

"You probably shouldn't even be at work."

"I know, but what am I going to do? Sit at home and feel sorry for myself?"

Tony patted her hand. "Is there anything I can do for you? Besides go get the ice you need?"

She shook her head. "No, I'm so depressed. This racing thing is a lost cause. Mr. Weaver will have to scratch Star Bright and I'll have to give back the money he paid me to ride."

Tony reached out and lifted her chin gently. "Wendy, you can't do that. If that's on your record you'll never ride again. "

"I know. It's over before it started."

He got up and started pacing. She wanted to tell him it was making her nervous but couldn't find the energy. He stopped and turned to her excitedly.

"Wendy, this is not going to happen. I'm going to ride Star Bright Saturday. A rider getting replaced is no big deal, but if Star Bright is scratched it'll be a black mark on your record."

"Ha. You think you can do everything. What do you know about steeplechase?"

"Only that I've ridden in ten of'em. No wins, but I've done ok."

"Get real. You're an equestrian?"

"You'll see. I'm riding Star Bright for you. Take me with you to the stables after work, ya' hear."

| CHAPTER 24

When they arrived at Wind Gate stables Wendy was shocked to see Suzie approach Tony with open arms and a hug.

"What a surprise, Tony. What brings you two here?"

Wendy couldn't believe it. "Suzie, you know him?"

"Well, of course. Not only is he our farrier, but he's ridden for us, too."

Wendy looked at Tony in disbelief.

He chuckled. "Told ya'."

Wendy pointed to Star Bright. "Yeah, well, let's see you ride her, Hot Shot! If she doesn't throw you off, maybe then I'll believe you."

Suzie and Wendy sat on the porch steps while Tony was out on the course riding Star Bright.

"Wendy, how long have you known Tony?"

Wendy looked out across the paddocks. "About two months. Why?"

Suzie looked at her, lost in thought. "How much do you know about him, dear?"

She looked at Suzie. "Well, that's an interesting question. I'm finding I learn something surprising about him every day."

"Like what?"

She stared at the ground in front of her. "Well, at the country club he seemed to know everybody and they gave him the utmost respect because he's saved so many of their horses from leg injuries.

Here I learn that he's an equestrian. He's like an onion. Every day I see another layer."

Smiling, Suzie put her hand on Wendy's knee. "You should be grateful. At least he's not boring."

Wendy threw her head back and declared, "Oh geez! Boring he's not!"

"What do you think? Do you and Tony have a future?"

"Suzie! My, God! I've never thought of that. I don't even know if he can ride Bright Star."

Laughing, Suzie gave Wendy a hug. "Don't protest too loudly, my dear. You might just give away your intentions."

Their conversation was cut off by Tony's return to the stables. They both rushed to see how he had done. Suzie asked for his time, and smiled. "Pretty good." She looked toward Wendy. "Almost as good as your best time. Not bad for a first run, huh?"

"Gotcha covered, Ms. Crodin," Tony responded with enthusiasm. "Maybe I don't look as good as you, but I can ride as well. Tomorrow will be a breeze."

Wendy put on a fake smile just to mask what she was thinking. *I don't know whether to kiss you or kill you.*

಼ಸ಼

Saturday came and Tony was in the stable with the trainer saddling up Star Bright for the race. Wendy stood at the door watching them, wishing it were she getting ready to ride. Mr. Weaver and Suzie were talking, in a rather animated fashion, making Wendy wonder if Mr. Weaver wanted Tony to ride for him. When they came into the stable, Suzie walked over to Wendy.

"He's ok with Tony now. Took a little convincing though."

"He didn't want him to ride?" Wendy asked.

"Oh, he knows Tony can ride. It's just he wanted a lighter female rider. When I showed him your times were the same, he agreed to the change."

Wendy let out a sigh of relief. "Oh, thank God. I would have died if he didn't let Tony ride. This is all my fault and I want it to end as soon as possible."

CRWD

When Tony and Star Bright left the stable for the starting line, Wendy searched for a spot where she could see the most jumps. Star Bright leaped out of the gate and kept pace with the lead pack. She was proud of Tony. He looked like a real equestrian. Actually, she was learning that he could do almost anything he put his mind to. He continually impressed her. Then it happened, right before her eyes. At full speed, Star Bright balked at a jump sending Tony flying over the obstacle onto his head. He lay motionless.

"Tooonnnyyyyyyy!" Wendy screamed as she scrambled over the fence and jumped to the ground. She ran down the side of the course as the last horses cleared the obstacle. She was the first person to reach Tony. He was unconscious.

"Tony. Tony. Can you hear me?"

He didn't move. Wendy checked his pulse.

Thank God, he has one.

His eyes were dilated, but he was breathing normally. When he regained consciousness, Wendy asked, "Tony, Honey, are you all right?"

"I —I guess so."

"Step aside, please," commanded an EMT. "We'll take it from here. What's his name?"

Wendy stood up and backed away. "Tony Ward."

The EMT felt Tony's head, neck, arms, legs and ankles, finding no broken bones.

"Mr. Ward, you've got a bad bruise on your arm here." As he pressed the area he asked, "Is it painful?"

"No." Tony answered.

Looking up at his friend, with a curious look, he asked again, "Are you sure?"

"Yes."

"Let me check your hand," the EMT said as he pinched Tony's finger. "Does that hurt?"

Tony was confused. "Does what hurt?"

The EMT stood up and addressed his partner. "We could have a back injury here. We'll put him on the back board."

On the back board and gurney they started to move out. "Out of the way, ma'am," the EMT told her, "we've got to get him to the hospital."

Wendy jogged beside them as they wheeled him to the ambulance. She opened the door to enter the ambulance and was stopped.

"You can't go with us, miss."

Wendy resisted. "Why not? I'm responsible for this happening, and I'm not leaving him."

"Only next of kin can ride along. Sorry."

"I'm his wife, damn it." She shouted. "Now, get out of my way." Forcing herself into the ambulance Wendy sat in the passenger seat. While looking through the back window at Tony's motionless body tears began to run down her cheeks.

C8 80

Meanwhile, in Clayton, Teddy and Kent were already at work when the phone rang at the house. Sarah answered it, "Hello."

Sobbing and crying was all she heard. It has to be Wendy. "Wendy. Wendy. Is that you?"

"Uh-huh," followed by more sobbing and crying.

"What's the matter? Are you hurt, Honey?"

"No."

"Talk to me. Please. What's happened to you?"

"It's Tony, Mom."

She paced the kitchen. "What about Tony?"

"He's paralyzed, and it's all my fault. I want to kill myself. "

"Stop it," she scolded, "Don't talk like that. How did this happen?"

Leaning on the kitchen table, she listened to the story of Wendy's injury, Tony riding for her, then the accident on the course.

"I feel so responsible, Mom. I should never have agreed to him riding that horse for me. He did it to save my riding reputation at the track, and now look what's happened. How could I be so selfish?"

Sarah interrupted, "Honey, it is not your fault. That horse threw you, and it threw him. Now, let's get down to business. What have you done to notify his family?"

Wendy paused, "Mom, he doesn't have any family."

"He doesn't?"

"No," Wendy said softly, "His parents were dead before he was 12."

"So, he's alone?"

"Yes."

Her mind was filled with scenes of the tornado that hit Clayton over twenty years ago. She got lost, was stranded on the bluff looking into the eye of the tornado when Kent found her, threw her into a ditch and laid on top of her. When it was over his back was filled with glass shards. She sat by his side for days as he recovered from his injuries.

"Mom." Wendy cried, "Are your there?"

"Yes, Honey. I'm here. Now, I want you to listen and do exactly what I say, you hear?"

"Ok."

"Wendy, that boy needs someone by his side while he recovers, and you're all he's got."

Wendy was surprised, "But Mom, I've got a job. I can't do that."

"Are you saying that your job is more important than that young man?"

"Well… no."

Sarah was forceful. "You tell me, young lady, who's going to feed Tony if he's paralyzed? Who's going to get a nurse for him if he can't operate a call button. Wendy, the nurses can't be beside him 24 hours a day. Who's going to help him if not you?"

Wendy was silent for a while, and she didn't interrupt Sarah. Now was a good time for her to think.

Wendy responded meekly. "You think I can do all that, Mom?"

"I know you can. I did it for your dad."

"What. You did it for Dad? When? Why haven't I ever heard of this?"

She smiled. *There's actually something Wendy doesn't know.* "Wendy, I'll tell you next time we see each other, ok? Now, you just stay by Tony's side until he's released. You may still have to help after that. Just do it, Honey. You'll never regret it."

"I'll do my best, Mom. Thanks." The line went dead.

03 80

Wendy walked away from the phone dabbing her eyes with a Kleenex. She glanced at her reflection in the window outside Tony's room, checked her appearance, put on a smile and walked in.

"Hi, Tony. I'm so sorry."

Tony smiled. "Well, my angel-of-mercy." he said, "Aren't you going to kiss me?"

She couldn't believe him. "What?"

He grinned, "Well, don't most wives kiss their husbands when they're lying in a hospital bed?"

Plopping down in a chair she said, "You really did have a head injury. We're not married."

"Now, now. Not what you told the EMT's when you forced your way into the ambulance."

Wendy scowled at him. "Listen, I was upset, feared for your life, and would have done anything to be with you, even lie."

"I see," he grinned. "Anything to be with me?"

She ignored the remark. He didn't need encouragement. "Listen, if you're going to act like this, what are you doing in a hospital?"

Tony laid his head back and looked at the ceiling. "Interesting development, Crodin. I can't move."

| CHAPTER 25

Wendy was granted a temporary leave of absence after agreeing to work weekends to make up the time she missed caring for Tony. It was a great relief, and Sarah was pleased to hear she could stay by Tony's side. Her stomach was tied up in knots watching over Tony. He had no feeling below his neck, and couldn't move his arms or legs. All she could think of was the fun loving adventurous Tony laying in a bed the rest of his life. She left the room when she could so he didn't see her cry.

Wendy held his hand, dead to the touch, and relived their times together. Sure, he could be a smart ass, but she could be, too. He was a prankster, just like her. But he was thoughtful, responsible, supportive, and he had talent. Tony thought he could do anything. And he was so gracious at the country club, and considerate on their first date.

When the time is right, I should tell him how I feel.

Tony had made no progress at all for three days. Doctors and nurses were mum about his condition and his prospects. The quieter they got the more nervous she became.

As usual, Wendy sat in the chair beside Tony's bed, and held his hand whether he was awake or not. Holding his hand and laying her head on the mattress of his bed she felt Tony's thumb move. Wendy was startled and unsure of what had just happened. She sat up and stared at Tony's thumb... it jerked again.

"Nurse. Nurse. Please hurry," Wendy yelled.

A few seconds later, a nurse entered. "Is something wrong?"

"No. No. He moved. Tony moved."

The nurse asked Wendy to move aside, stepped in and held Tony's hand, observing his thumb. A minute later, it jerked in her hand. She looked over at Wendy, "I've got to get a doctor."

"When Dr. Knumb examined Tony he smiled at Wendy. "Well, young lady, we've got a chance here. If this is just a response to trauma, then I think we'll see a little more improvement every day. Pray that I'm right."

It was the fifth day when Tony could squeeze Wendy's hand.

"Does it hurt, Tony?" Wendy asked.

"Yeah."

"Want to stop?"

Tony smiled at Wendy with his mischievous eyes, "Are you kiddin' I've always wanted to hold your hand. Forever if you'll let me."

Wendy just rolled her eyes. "Tony, Tony, Tony. It's a miracle you haven't drowned, going overboard as much as you do."

On day six, Tony was moving his arm. Wendy made him do his exercises; she kept him busy squeezing, reaching, waving and pointing. Dr. Knumb ordered tests to compare with his entrance into the hospital. Everyone was pleased with his progress.

The stress and tension Wendy had been harboring rushed out of her when on the seventh day Tony could move his arms and legs. She almost collapsed.

"Hey, whataya' say, Crodin, want a hug?"

Wendy couldn't refuse. She had been so afraid of hurting him for days that she welcomed hugging Tony. It was beautiful. She was so happy, for herself as well as Tony. He was going to be all right. The worst was over.

"Excuse me, folks," Tony announced to the nurse and aide, "can we have some privacy please?"

Wendy watched them leave the room and close the door. "What's this all about?" she asked.

"I want to thank you privately for devoting all of your time to me this past week. I've just been given new life, and I never would have made it without you, Wendy."

What is he doing? He's leading up to something. Please don't Tony. Please, not now.

Wendy took his hand in hers. "I can appreciate your excitement and elation Tony, but you don't have to do anything special. You've already done that by surviving your injury."

Tony looked up at her. "But I couldn't have done it without you."

Nodding, Wendy smiled at him. "I know. I was glad to do it for you. I was terribly worried, and now I'm totally relieved. We did this together, Tony. Maybe today is the end for us, or maybe it's the first event in a life together. It's too early to tell, don't you think?"

Tony's chin sank to his chest. He squeezed Wendy's hand hard. "Well, the way you put it, the day I step out of this hospital is the day our relationship starts over."

"I think so. But remember, we've got a whole lot of good things from the past to bring with us. I know I do."

"Crodin, you're very special."

"You too, Shoe."

With a twinkle in his eye, Tony looked up at Wendy. "Will you kiss me?"

Wendy leaned forward, their lips touched, and Tony pulled her close. Wendy felt her lips tingle, thoughts left her in a rush, and she felt warmth in her body that startled her.

"Wow." Tony exclaimed. "We should do that again."

Wendy felt shaken. "I'm afraid that was your good bye kiss. I've gotta go."

Wendy slid off the bed and picked up her purse. Giving Tony's hand a squeeze she turned to leave. "I'll see you when they bring your supper."

Outside Tony's room Wendy stopped and leaned against the wall.

I've never felt that way before. Never. How can a kiss make me so distracted, and my body feel like it's on fire? I've gotta call Mom.

♋ ♋

"Hi, Mom."

"Wendy, dear. How nice of you to call. How are you? Is Tony better?"

"Yeah, Tony finally came out of the paralysis, seems fine and they might send him home tomorrow."

"Oh, how wonderful. I'm so glad you stayed to help him."

"He was a pretty good patient, Mom, until he started feeling better. He can be a handful."

"I'm so glad to hear it though. Means he's feeling good and getting some energy back. That had to be a scary experience for him."

"Me too, Mom. If it wasn't for me getting injured, he wouldn't have been on that horse."

"Now, now. You can't feel guilty about that. It was an accident, that's all. So, how did you come through it all?"

"Fine. I'll be a doctor you know, so being with an injured patient wasn't disturbing. But something happened that was very disturbing."

"What was it, Honey? Anything serious?"

"He kissed me."

"Ok, I would have expected that."

"But, Mom, it wasn't like a normal kiss."

"What are you trying to tell me, Wendy?"

"Mom, it was scary. My lips tingled, my mind went blank, and my body lit up like a stove. Has that ever happened to you?"

"Oh, my, yes! When I first kissed your father."

"Really. What did you do?"

"I got in my car and drove away fast, before I melted in his arms and let him carry me away."

"You didn't."

"Oh, yes. I was scared, just like you. I knew he was the man for me, and I didn't think I was ready for it. I had to think."

"You think Tony's the man for me, Mom? Is that what it means?"

"Let me put it this way, I wouldn't be surprised."

"Oh, Mom. I've only known Tony for a few weeks. "

"Time has nothing to do with it, dear. Love at first sight only takes a day you know."

"I don't think I'm ready for this, Mom."

"And when do you think you will be?"

"When I finish my degrees, have my own practice, some money in the bank. Then I'll have time to think about love."

"Wendy, Wendy, Wendy. Love doesn't work that way! Love comes in its own time, and I feel yours is now, Honey. Enjoy it. True love only comes once."

"I'm not ready, Mom. I'm scared."

"We all are, Honey. That's part of the thrill. So, I suspect you should be getting back to the hospital?"

"Yeah, I should. Thanks a lot, Mom."

"Relax, Honey. Just let things happen and enjoy the journey. Love you."

"Bye."

CA 80

Tony had just started eating supper when Wendy walked into his room. The few hours of separation had been good for Wendy. Tony didn't seem fazed at all.

"Hey, Doc. It's good to see you again."

"It's good to see you, too. How are you feeling?"

"Like I'm ready to get out of here. With you, of course." Taking Wendy's hand, Tony looked into her eyes and asked, "Will you be mine?"

Wendy pulled her hand away and sat in a chair. "Tony, please, this isn't the time or place."

She looked up with sad eyes. "Tony, I understand how you feel, and I'm very flattered. But it's too soon for this."

Tony looked very frustrated and disappointed. "So, now what should I do?"

"Give me time to understand my feelings."

Tony's heart was aching. "What feelings?"

"Tony, I need to know if I care for you just because I feel guilty about you getting hurt and being helpless, or because you're in my heart, and I can't live without you. The helpless part is almost over. The heart part will start soon. I hope you can understand."

"I suppose, but I don't want to," he said dejectedly.

Wendy moved from her chair to the bed and kissed him. "We'll be ok."

| CHAPTER 26

The deep snow outside made Christmas special for Wendy, sitting in the cozy living room with her mom and dad, drinking hot cocoa with a marshmallow gliding around her cup. Glancing out the living room window she saw Teddy trudging through the snow towards the Bondi's house carrying a package wrapped with Christmas paper. She looked over at her mom, "What's Teddy doing?"

"He's taking a Christmas present over for Zoey."

"Oh, cool. She's home for the holiday. I'd love to see her."

"It's not like that, honey. She hasn't been home for a year and a half."

"What? She's not home and he's taking a present to her. Is he nuts?"

"Heartbroken, is more like it. They've been so close for all his life, and he doesn't know what to do without her."

Wendy couldn't believe it. She looked at her dad. "For a year and a half?"

Kent nodded, and rose from his chair saying, "I'll let you two deal with this," as he left the room.

Her mom was nodding, too.

Wendy shook her head and looked pleadingly at her mother. "He needs a life, Mom."

"We know dear, but he's got to do it himself. I'm afraid we'd only make it worse if we said anything to him."

"Well, what about Niki? She's gotta know he's nuts. "

"We all know about it, Honey. Niki puts the presents he brings for Christmas and her birthday in a closet. Who knows if Zoey will ever open them? She told Niki she wanted a clean break from Clayton. She wants a new life, Dear, and didn't leave an address or phone number for anyone. Especially Teddy. Please, just let it be. Don't say anything to him."

Wendy slumped back into her chair. "That's going to be really hard, Mom."

"We've all done it. You can too. It's only a few more days before you go back to school. Now, let's talk about you. Tell me all about your life in Kentucky."

CR&CO

June came, schools let out, and tourists were beginning to visit Clayton. Business was picking up at Wilma's Café and Teddy opened the café at five AM, like he always did. He'd unlocked the front door and was doing the same at the back door when he heard someone come in. He turned and hollered, "Sorry, we don't open for another hour."

"Teddy?"

His heart stopped beating. He knew that voice. He cautiously stepped into the dining room and saw a beautiful redheaded woman. Her long flowing hair covered her shoulders. She wore a sleeveless dress hemmed above her knees, showing off her beautiful legs. She was carrying a folder.

Heels at five in the morning?

He was thrilled to see her. He asked, "Zoe ,is it really you?"

She smiled. "Yes, Teddy, it's me."

Teddy rushed across the dining room and threw his arms around Zoey and hugged her. "Zoe, You're gorgeous."

Hugging him back, she smiled, "Thank you, Teddy."

"I missed having you around, Zoe"

"I know. Thanks for the presents."

Teddy released her and held her at arms-length. "No glasses?"

"I wear contacts, now."

"No braces?"

"Well, of course not, silly. I outgrew those."

"I see you got the sexy boobs you wanted."

Zoey's smile faded. In a hushed voice she said, "Teddy, you don't say that to a woman."

Teddy was surprised. "Why not? You're the one who told me they wouldn't grow."

Shaking her head, she threw her shoulders back and stood tall. "That was when we were kids. We're adults now."

"Ok, I like your adults, then."

She shoved Teddy's shoulder as she walked past him, "Will you ever grow up?"

As she went through the kitchen Teddy heard Wilma say, "Zoey, dear, you're right on time. Please come in."

Teddy looked at his watch. Ten after five.

What the hell do they have to talk about at ten after five in the morning?

After warming up the grill he began prepping for the breakfast crowd. As the two women came out of her office, Teddy was surprised to hear Wilma say, "Teddy, welcome our new employee."

"New employee?" Teddy said, freezing in place.

"Yep, Zoey's my new business manager. She's going to manage the restaurant and my investment properties. Isn't that great?"

Looking at Zoey's broad smile, Teddy was confused. "I thought you weren't ever coming back. Now you're going to work here?"

"Of course, Teddy. I studied retail management in school. I can work here and live at home. Best of both worlds, don't you think?"

"Sure is," Teddy replied as he went back to cooking. He didn't understand. *How did Wilma get Zoey to come home?*

| CHAPTER 27

Teddy was anxious to show Zoey the boat he had built for them, but wasn't sure when to do it. So, he waited until the mid-afternoon break to mention it. He opened the office door a little. "Hey, have you got a minute to talk?"

Zoey stopped what she was doing and turned her chair toward the door. "Sure. What's up?"

"Well, I made something for you while you were gone, and I want to show it to you when you have time."

Zoey hopped out of her chair. "You made something for me? Where is it?"

"Ahh, down at the river."

Looking at her watch she asked, "We still have a half hour before the lunch crowd. Let's go see it now!"

She walked briskly toward the boat dock while Teddy lagged behind, a little unsure how this was going to work out. As they approached the dock, Zoey saw a long red and white cigarette speedboat and ran toward it.

"Wow! Look at this boat Teddy. I've never seen one like it around here, ever. That motor is huge. How fast do you think it goes?"

Teddy smiled at her reaction. "It goes between ninety and a hundred miles an hour on a smooth day."

"Whose is it?"

"Guess you'll have to come back here to find out?"

Unsure what he was up to, she went along with him to the back of the boat, and was surprised beyond belief. 'Miss Zoey' was painted on the transom. "Miss Zoey? Teddy, what have you done?"

"I built her for you."

Taking his hands in hers Zoey looked up at him. "You did this while I was gone?"

"Yeah, it took most of two years. No one else has ridden in it. I saved the maiden voyage just for you, always hoping you'd come back home."

She released his hands and skipped up the dock looking at the beautiful boat.

He called out to her. "We don't work Sunday afternoon. Want to take her for a spin then?"

She jumped for joy, just like she used to. "Oh, yes, yes! I want to ride in it."

CB ᘓ

After church Sunday, Zoey picked up Teddy and they headed to the boat dock to take out the new boat. Getting into the boat, she had to watch her step. "What's that tool box doing in here?"

"I forgot it when I cleaned up. Must've been interrupted or something. It won't bother us."

Ok, Miss Zoey. Get ready for one helluva ride!

When that big 409 Chevy engine fired up Zoey ducked and covered her ears. "Hey, is it supposed to be that loud?" she yelled.

"Yeah." Teddy yelled back. "The vibration of a big V-8 is a thrill every man longs for. Some say it's better than sex."

The noise garbled his words. "What did you just say?" Zoey asked.

"Don't worry; it's quieter at higher speed."

True to his word, the speed and the wind made the motor quieter as they raced up and down the river. A barge choked the channel so Teddy had to steer down river and behind the barge to go across. Motoring slowly up the east bank they saw a large slough branching off the river.

"Teddy," Zoey asked pointing toward the slough. "What's down there?"

"Don't know, never been in there before."

"Well, it looks big. Let's go and see."

"Ok."

Protected by trees, there was no wind in the slough. The surface was calm and smooth as glass. Just tempting enough that Teddy opened up the motor to see how fast they could go. It was heaven. The boat sliced the glassy surface like a knife. The wind blew her hair into a rooster tail, and Zoey laughed at the thrill.

WHAM!

The motor whined as the boat died in the water, and coasted.

"Damn," groaned Teddy.

"What did we hit?" Zoey asked, looking over the mirror like water for an obstacle.

"Must have been a sunken log, Zoe."

"What broke?"

"Probably the bolt that holds the propeller."

All they could see were trees and water. Who knew how far away the main river was. This was not a place to be stranded.

"I need to get it on that sand bar over there and try to fix it. I hope there's a pin in my tool box."

Before losing all speed, he steered for and landed the bow on the sand bar.

"Come on, we need to pull it up some more so it won't move when I'm working on it."

Opening the toolbox, Teddy rummaged around and got the screwdriver and pliers he wanted, and then stepped over the transom into the water.

"Can I do anything to help?" Zoey asked.

"Maybe later. Not now."

"Ok, I'm going to swim then."

She took off her T-Shirt revealing a black bikini that accentuated a figure no one from Clayton High School would have ever believed. Slipping out of the boat into the water Zoey breast stroked for a while, then back stroked, all the time making sure Teddy could see her and her new figure.

"How's it going?" she asked.

"Slow. I'm having a helluva time getting the broken bolt out."

While he was working Zoey asked, "So tell me, are you dating anyone?"

"What?"

"You know what I mean. Is there a special girl in your life now?"

"What kind of question is that?"

"Well, I just wondered. I would think a man your age would have a woman in his life."

Teddy shook his head. "I haven't had a date since I wrecked my hot rod."

"What! You wrecked it?"

"Yeah. J.R. set up a decoy so I thought he couldn't catch me speeding down Highway 52. When he started chasing me I went through the 'S' curve and slid off the road into some trees." Teddy pointed to the boat motor, "This motor is all that's left."

"Oh, Teddy. I'm so sorry. Were you hurt?"

"No, but all the girls that hung around vanished the day I wrecked it. Guess they liked the car more than me. How about you? As beautiful as you are you must have a special man in your life."

Zoey was evasive. "Oh, you know, when our studies were over a bunch of us would go out. No one special though."

"So I guess we're two twenty-one-year-olds still hanging on the vine waiting to be picked."

She giggled at his remark. "That's one way of putting it."

"Yeah. Damn!"

"Are you ok?" she asked nervously.

"Look, he said pointing to the west. Storms coming. It's starting to rain. We have to get out of the water before any lightning strikes. Out Zoe, now."

"Ok, ok." Zoey swam to the side of the boat, pulled herself up and swung over the side. Teddy got into the boat, too.

"Well," Zoey asked, now what do we do. Aren't we kinda' sittin' ducks here?"

"Maybe. We can't run for those trees, and only the top of the sand bar is dry." Teddy crawled under the steering wheel and looked into the bow of the boat. There was room if he got rid of all the life jackets.

"I'm going to hand these out; throw them to the back of the boat."

"Ok."

When all the life jackets were cleared out Teddy said to her, "Now, crawl in there. You'll be safe from the lightening."

"Are you kidding? I'm not going in there."

A clap of thunder and a bolt of lightning changed her mind. Zoey hurried into the opening under the bow.

"Now, let's see if there's room for me."

Zoey could feel Teddy wiggling into the remaining space under the bow. His warm breath brushed her legs; his chest brushed her abdomen and her breasts as he crawled up into the bow. It's the closest she had ever been to him, and she loved it.

"Alright. Damn it's tight. Hope we don't have to be in here long."

"I agree," Zoey lied as she enjoyed their closeness.

Suddenly it sounded like an bullets were hitting the boat. The pounding on the fiberglass could only be caused by hail.

"Thank God we got under here," he said.

"Ouch, it's hurting my feet!" Zoey screamed.

"Let me turn over so you can bend your legs."

He rolled away from her and bent his legs. Zoey pressed her hips against his and bent her legs so they were in a spoon position.

"Is that better?"

"Yes," Zoey replied as she smiled, "Much better."

"What a nightmare. I still have to put that propeller together when this storm is done. Hope we can get it together before dark."

"I agree," she said still smiling, "But, I'm getting cold."

"Well, put your arms around me and squeeze closer. Maybe we can keep each other warm."

"Oh, that's better," she said as she snuggled against him.

A half-hour later, still cramped and spooned under the fiberglass bow, the storm blew on down the river.

"Well, I think it's safe to get out now."

"You don't think we should wait a little longer?" Zoey asked dejectedly.

"No, I've gotta get this boat fixed. You're smaller, so why don't you crawl out first."

It was as much fun for her to wiggle down his back, hips and legs, as it was when he did it. Only, he couldn't watch her like she watched him. Teddy followed her out and immediately got back into the water.

"Stay in the boat, will ya'. I'm going to need your help in a minute."

Forcing the propeller off its shaft, Teddy pulled out that last small bit of the broken bolt and replaced the propeller.

"Now, in the tool box should be a bolt that's shiny except for a few threads on the end. Can you find it and hand it to me. I'm almost done here."

Looking in the toolbox, she asked, "Which one do you want? One's bigger than the other."

Teddy put his hand over the transom. "Zoe, it should be the size of my little finger."

"Ok, is this it?" She said holding the bold over the transom.

"Yeah, thanks. Now, there should be a nut to fit it with plastic in the middle. Can you find that?"

"I think I found it," she said.

"Good, hand me the bolt first."

Teddy inserted the bolt, then used his channel locks to tighten the bolt to the propeller.

Reaching his hand in the air for a 'high-five' Teddy said, "Way to go, partner."

Zoey liked the idea of being Teddy's partner, so she slapped his hand and returned the favor, "Nice job, partner."

It was getting dusk by now, and chilly. They pushed the boat out into the slough, and Teddy turned the key to start the motor. "Let's hope this works."

| CHAPTER 28

Wilma emptied a tub of dishes into the sink, and then walked over to Teddy. "I need to meet with Zoey for a minute. Will you be ok on your own for a while?"

"Sure, I'll be fine."

Entering the office, Wilma closed the door and sat down.

Zoey turned and watching her carefully said, "Wilma, is something wrong?"

"No, nothing like that. We need to talk, Honey." Pointing at Teddy she said, "It's time to shake that apple off the tree."

Looking at him, then Wilma, Zoey looked confused. "I don't understand what that means."

"It means it's time for you to take control of this situation between you two."

She slouched back into her chair. "What can I do Wilma? He just seems so dense. Do I have to just grab him and throw him to the floor and sit on him until he says he loves me?"

"No, Honey, I've got a better idea. Just listen to me for a minute and see what you think."

Cʒ ᵭჂ

Teddy noticed Zoey leaving work early Friday and wondered why. When she returned at six-thirty, he became even more curious.

Zoey walked into the café with a new hairstyle, and a black thigh-high spaghetti-strap dress showing just enough cleavage to get a man to notice.

"Wow," he said. "You look great. Where are you goin'?"

Zoey walked to him, stood close, and said, "I'm going out to dinner tonight."

He couldn't keep his eyes off her. "Where are you going dressed like that?"

She tossed her head. "Well, not the Pink Elephant, that's for sure."

Teddy was dying to know about her date. "Who you going with?"

She smiled and pressed her chest up against his and looked into his eyes. "Why, you, of course."

"Me?" The shock of what she said, and her body against his, left him breathless. He grabbed the prep counter to hold himself up.

"Yes, you're taking me out to dinner tonight."

"In this?" He said, looking down at his baggy black chef's pants.

"No, I've got your clothes with me."

Now he was uncomfortable. "What? How'd you do that?"

"I stopped by your house, and your mom picked them out for me. You can change upstairs."

Looking for a way out, he turned to Wilma.

She gave him thumbs up. "I've gotcha covered. Go have fun."

He was trapped.

Looking back at Zoey again, Teddy asked, "Why am I taking you out to dinner?"

Before answering his question, she folded her arms under her breasts, and lifted them a bit, in case he hadn't noticed them already. "Well, let's see. We've been out on your go-kart, motorcycle, hot rod and boat. We've been fishing and hiking together. I think it's time you treated me like a woman. So, tonight is lady's night. You're taking me to dinner."

"You once told me I wasn't exciting. Now you're telling me I don't treat you like a woman?"

"Well, you don't. You treat me like the tomboy I used to be. Tonight I want to be your woman, and you're gonna be my man. So, Wilma, I think it's time for him to get dressed. Don't you?"

With hands on her hips and a wide grin, Wilma chuckled. "Absolutely."

Zoey headed for the back door. "Wait here, I'll get your clothes."

Feeling he was being treated like a child, Teddy asked sarcastically, "Did you bring my toothbrush too?"

Zoey stopped at the door. "Yes. I did, and your mother even gave me your favorite teddy bear."

Teddy's head sank to his chest as he blushed. Wilma giggled and said, "How you feeling now, big boy?"

CB   80

Zoey drove her car out to the highway and headed south.

Teddy looks so uncomfortable. I hope this works like Wilma said. If he won't say he loves me when he is comfortable, how in the world can I get him to say it now? Come on Zoey, relax. Just play it like we planned it.

"Where are we going?" Teddy asked.

Teddy's question brought her back to reality. "To Maquoketa. We're going to an Italian restaurant for dinner."

"Why there?"

"Simple, it's a different type of cuisine. You don't want to eat the same old thing every day, do you?"

"Guess not," he said.

Zoey watched him out of the corner of her eye as she drove. He sat back, folded his arms, and appeared deep in thought.

Come on! Come on! I've got to get us to the restaurant quick, or I'll lose him. Wilma, this isn't going to work. I told you he's too sensitive to be strong-armed like this. Damn! Hang in there Teddy, Please. For me.

They avoided talking about their relationship during the thirty-minute drive. Once he came out of his shell, Teddy did ask some questions about her experience at school, which she answered evasively. It was a little awkward, and Zoey was relieved to reach the restaurant.

"Welcome to Pitrini's, Teddy. It's supposed to be a great restaurant."

"If it's so great, why haven't I heard of it?"

Zoey parked and got out of the car. "Probably because you haven't been out of Wilma's kitchen in years. Tonight, I'm going to open your eyes."

Teddy wasn't totally inept when it came to women. He met Zoey at the front of the car and offered her his arm. It made Zoey smile with pleasure as she took his arm, squeezed it, and walked into the restaurant with him.

Once seated at a table, she asked, "Do you drink wine?"

"Can't say that I have, Zoe."

The waiter appeared at that moment and asked, "Would you like wine, Sir."

Before Teddy could say a word, she motioned to him, "I'll get this." Looking at the waiter, she said, "Yes, we'd like a bottle of Semi-sweet Merlot, please."

"Coming right up, madam."

"How did you know that?" he asked.

"Well, I didn't just sit in a closet the past two years, you know. And since you haven't had wine before, I thought I'd get one that wasn't too dry or too sweet."

"Oh, I forgot. You're a woman of the world now. So, since I'm the village idiot, do you have any idea what I should order?"

Oh no! This isn't going well at all. If he feels like an idiot, we'll never make any progress. This was supposed to be romantic, and he keeps feeling worse.

Hiding her disappointment behind her menu Zoey said, "Don't worry about a thing. I think we both should have the five course Italian dinner. That way we can sample lots of things."

Teddy layed his menu down. "Five courses, that sounds like a lot of work."

Zoey took his menu, put it with hers and layed them on the table. "Listen, you're not a chef tonight, you're a customer. Try to relax and let someone else do the work. Ok?"

When the waiter poured their wine, Teddy sipped his and understood why his mother liked it. It was nice. He was surprised to find the first course had a variety of tastes, and it wasn't all that filling. While they were eating he asked, "So, be straight with me Zoe. Why is it so important for you to take me out of town for dinner?"

"Well, you know how we always met at our 'secret spot' to talk about how we felt about things?"

"Yeah."

"It seems kind of childish now that we're twenty-one years old, so I thought getting out of town in a romantic setting might be nice for a change."

"It is nice, but does that mean there's something you want to talk about?"

"Just you and me, that's all."

Teddy thought about her statement. "After all these years, is there anything we don't know about each other? So, what do you want to know that you don't know already?"

"Well, I've been wondering about that girl you said you loved while you were fixing my car. Do you still love her?"

"Yes."

"Then, why don't I see you two together at the movie, or out in your boat?"

"Just you never mind, I see her. Almost every day."

Who does he think he's kidding? I'm the only woman he sees every day. There's no mystery woman. He just can't say what he means to me. Maybe if I push him a little.

"You do? I don't know anybody that's seen her."

"Listen, I said I love her but she doesn't know it yet. I just feel awkward spilling my guts to a woman. What if she doesn't love me? Then I look like an ass. I'm not ready to take the risk."

Now what do I do? I know he loves me, but he just won't say it to me. I don't think getting him drunk is going to do a damn bit of good. Help!

"Oh, that's too bad. I hope she doesn't find another man before you tell her."

Teddy circled his plate with a fork, "Yeah, me too."

The waiter brought another course and refilled their glasses. "How does the wine suit you, ma'am."

"Oh, just fine, thanks."

Leaning toward the center of the table, Zoey said, "Teddy, my friend, you've got to learn how to express your feelings."

"Really?" Teddy sat his wine down and leaned back. "You've known me all my life. Don't you know when I do?"

"I'm not sure what you mean."

"All right, you want feelings; remember when I built the go-kart?"

"Of course."

"Why do you think I bought one with two seats? I built that go-kart for you."

"Yes, I can see that, and it was very thoughtful."

"Plus, when you wanted to drive it on the airstrip, didn't I break all sorts of rules and laws just so we could do it together? And, I lost my go-cart, too."

Placing her hand on his to comfort him, she said, "Yes, I know it was heartbreaking."

"Well, what about the motorcycle. I loved that bike, but it was no fun without you. Remember, I sold it so your mom would let us see each other again?"

"Uh-huh. I knew you loved it. It was so sad when you sold it. You've always been loyal."

Leaning toward the table Teddy added, "And the hot rod. Red with white interior, just like you pretended when you drove the old junk car. That was for you."

"I knew it when I saw it at the upholstery shop. I was so pleased. You were so considerate."

"And I missed you so much when you left. I thought of you all the time I was building that boat, hoping you'd come home so you could see it."

I know Teddy. I've known it for years. But, can't you just say it so I know for sure?

"That's all very sweet, Teddy. What's your point?"

"My point? I guess I'm not like other guys. When I care for somebody, I do things to make them happy instead of talking about it. Dad's the same way, you know. All action and not much talk."

I'd marry his dad anytime. Actually, that's what I'm trying to do with his son.

Zoey was glad the waiter interrupted again with their final course.

"Teddy, there's nothing wrong with you. I think it might be that in addition to the wonderful things you do, and have done for me, a woman likes to hear a man share his feelings. I love you, twelve times a day loses its meaning, but saying it to a woman once or twice a week can make her feel warm and wonderful. It makes her feel appreciated."

Teddy sat back in his chair and looked at Zoey. "Is that what you think I should do?"

"All I can say is if it were me, that's what I would want."

Teddy finished his wine, and put his napkin on the table. "Well, are we done here?"

So close! Damn it, Teddy.

Driving home, Teddy shared a thought with Zoey. "You know, I liked this experience. It's a nice restaurant, and I might come back again."

Well, good for you. It wasn't as nice as I hoped it would be. Next time I take, you out we're going to the dentist where I can pay him to pull it out of you.

They were each deep in thought on the way home. Their conversation focused on the realities around them, not each other. When Zoey turned into the driveway to her house, she parked halfway up the drive so the motion light wouldn't shine on them. She shifted to park, turned off the engine, and asked, "Teddy, do you remember that time at the fishing hole when I asked you to kiss me."

"Yeah, that was a little awkward."

"Well my friend, tonight you're going to kiss a woman. Let's see if you can tell the difference."

Zoey placed her hand on his chin, turned him toward her and pressed her lips against his. Then she placed her other arm around him and squeezed him to ensure he felt the firmness of her breasts and understood that love is a contact sport.

When he came up for air, Teddy's eyes were wide and he seemed a little breathless.

"Ready for another?" Zoey asked.

"I only get one more?" he asked. "Wow, you sure know how to make it hard on a guy."

She giggled and kissed him again. After twenty minutes, their emotions were high and the windows were steaming up. Teddy lifted her head off his shoulder, looked at her and said, "Zoe, we have to stop this."

"Oh, Teddy. Why now?"

"I'm not going to do what I feel like doing in front of your parent's house. We'd never live it down. I gotta' go."

As Teddy opened the car door, Zoey reached out to him, "Oh, Teddy, don't be so sensitive. They won't know."

Looking into the car he said, "Not taking the chance, Zoe."

She picked up the bear on the floor and said, "Don't forget this."

He took it and smiled at Zoey, "Could've done without it."

After a few minutes to get her emotions under control, Zoey fluffed her hair, and on her way to the house, she straightened her dress.

| CHAPTER 29

When Teddy came into the house he saw his mother in the living room watching television. She muted the sound as he entered the room and asked, "How's my boy?"

"I'm fine, Mom," he said walking to the foot of the stairs.

Smiling pleasantly she commented, "I heard you went out to dinner. Did you have a good time?"

Teddy looked at her closely for any hidden meaning. "Yeah, it was nice. Think I could've cooked the meal better though. I'm going up to change. Is Dad around?"

"Yes, he's in the lab. Do you need something?"

"I've just got to see him for a minute."

Halfway up the stairs he stopped. "Oh, Mom."

Sarah looked up over her shoulder at him. "Yes, dear?"

Teddy shook his teddy bear at her, "Was this teddy bear necessary?"

"Oh, that. Just a little reminder from your mother that you're not a boy anymore."

Giving her a sour look, he asked, "Could've just told me, ya' know."

She couldn't help but giggle. "Yes, but you wouldn't have remembered it."

Leaning on the railing, he looked down on her, "So you think I'm acting like a baby?"

"Absolutely not. But you do need to start acting like a man."

"And I'm not?"

She raised her eyebrows and smiled wryly, "You could do better, Honey."

CR EO

Peeking into the lab Teddy asked, "Dad, do you have time to talk?"

"Sure. Come on in. What's on your mind?"

"Will you tell me what I need to know about women."

"Why do you ask?"

"I'm not sure, Dad. It's just that everyone is telling me I need to understand women. I haven't a clue how to do that."

Kent sat in his office chair, leaned back and put his feet on the table. "Are we talking about Zoey here, Son?"

"Yeah, she's back in town you know, and has really changed."

"Yes, I've noticed myself."

"She's beautiful and much more sophisticated than I am. She wants me to do things I don't know how to do."

"Any idea why she left?"

"Yeah, said something about feeling like a homely nobody here. Boys ignored her and stuff. But let me tell you, Dad, she isn't homely anymore."

"Any idea why she came back?"

Teddy pulled up a chair, turned it backwards and leaned on the back of it. "No. Not really. Unless it was because Wilma offered her a job."

"Have you heard the story about your mother running away from me?"

Teddy sat straight up, shocked by the revelation. "Holy cow! Mom ran away?"

"Yep. I proposed the day she was leaving Clayton. She couldn't imagine staying in this small farm community, so she said she couldn't marry me and drove off to Chicago."

Cocking his head, he looked at his dad. "How did you get married if she ran away?"

Kent waved his hand. "Needed time to think I guess. She came back after a few days."

"Kinda like Zoey going to away to school?"

Kent smiled. "Possibly."

Looking at the floor he said, "We had a dinner date last night, you know."

"Yeah, your mother told me. Kind of a setup, huh?"

"But the message was clear, Dad. She said, 'There's more where that came from when you learn to treat me like a grown woman."

Kent laughed. "Whoa, sounds like an invitation to me."

He looked sadly at his dad. "Maybe so Dad, but nothing's going to happen 'til I learn how to do that?"

"Just be yourself, Son."

The frustration showed as he sat up. "Come on, Dad. I've been doing that with her for years. Obviously it isn't working. She wants me to be something else. I just don't know what."

Putting his chin on the back of the chair, he looked defeated.

Kent shook his head. "Let me ask you… do you still see her as your childhood buddy? Or is she a part of your life that you can't live without?"

"Both. She's been a part of my life forever, Dad."

"Ok, if Zoey died tomorrow, how would that affect you? Would you be sad? Or, would your life be changed forever?"

He sat up and spread his arms. "Dad. Why say something like that. It'd tear my heart out. A part of me would be missing forever"

Kent got out of his chair and walked to the refrigerator. "Do you want something to drink?"

"Yes, please."

"So tell me, does Zoey know you feel that way?"

"Are you kidding? I've never told her that."

"Why not?"

"What do you mean, why not? I don't know how to say that to her."

Kent handed him a Coke and sat down. "My advice, Son, is if you want her to be a part of your life, you'd better start telling her how you feel. You're not kids anymore. She's a bright woman looking for a future, and a man she can count on to provide the security she needs to raise a family."

Teddy thought about all that for a minute. Turning to his dad he asked, "Isn't that a lot to ask of one man?"

"No. I did it with your mother. There's a time in a man's life when he has to put away childish things; quit thinking about himself. Make a commitment. Obviously, Zoey's ready. The question is, are you?"

Throwing his hands in the air he said, "Dad, that's why I'm here. I don't know what to do!"

Kent leaned toward Teddy with his elbows on his knees. "Son, you need to let her into your heart and soul. If she wants you, then she'll light up your life like you've never imagined, and you'll be the happiest man in the world."

"You're saying I don't?"

"My guess is that you're treating her like the buddy you grew up with, not the woman she is now."

Frowning, he mumbled, "Maybe."

A woman wants a man for all seasons. To be proud of. To be proud of her. To think she's special and beautiful. To appreciate her acts of love and kindness. To support her when she's not at her best. To cheer her when she is at her best. Could you do that for Zoey?"

"Well, sure I can. She's my best friend. I've always protected her."

Kent put his feet back up on the table and took a sip of his Coke. "Again, does she know it?"

Teddy sank his head back onto the chair. "Probably not. I don't say those things, Dad. They're pretty personal you know."

"Son, I've looked at my relationship with your mother as if we're in a foxhole during a war. Back to back, we support and defend each other to the death. There's no other woman I would do that for. And there's no other woman I'd trust to do that for me. So the question is, does Zoey fit into that picture for you?"

"Well, yeah, Dad. I could do that. There's nobody else I'd want in that foxhole but Zoe."

"Then you'd better find a way to let her know how you feel, Son. The ball's in your court. You've gotta' run with it and see if you can win her heart? Or, are you gonna fumble the ball and lose?"

Watching him slouch on his chair, lost in thought. Kent said no more. Sipping his Coke, he let the boy think. After a few minutes, Teddy stood up. Shaking his dad's hand he said, "Thanks, Dad. This really helped."

Leaving the lab Teddy walked slowly back to the house.

Dad makes a lot of sense. But I need to learn how to do it.

C3 EO

When Zoey came to work the next day Wilma couldn't wait to see her. "Well, did it work?"

She was sullen when she answered, "I don't know if I did the right thing or not. He would get so down on himself, then up and thoughtful, then defensive. I felt like a psychologist to tell the truth. And Teddy talks about me as the other girl, just so he doesn't have to say things directly to me.

"I'm so sorry, Honey. I thought for sure it would work."

"I did too, Wilma. But he just doesn't like that kind of pressure. I feel like things are even worse now."

| CHAPTER 30

A week later Zoey and her dad returned home from the church's Father/Daughter dinner, and she saw the light was still on in the Crodins' shed.

"Daddy, Teddy is still working on my car. Would you mind if I go over and see how it's coming?"

"Not at all dear. I'll let your mother know you'll be a while."

She walked across the field, just as she did when they were kids, and saw him working at his bench.

"Hi, Teddy. How's my car coming along?"

"Hey, Zoe. You sure look nice. Be careful when you sit. I have a jacket here. You can sit on this so you don't mess up your skirt."

"Well, thank you sir. That's very considerate."

"You're welcome."

"So what is that thing you're working on?"

"It's your gas tank. The fuel pump burned out and I put in a new one."

"Well, wasn't it heavy to get up there?"

"It's empty. Your gas is in those cans over there. I can't work on it if it's full of gas, you know."

"Oh, I guess not."

"I don't mean to keep you up. I'll be finished in half an hour or so. Is that alright?"

"I'll just sit and wait. Ok?"

"Sure. Kinda like old times when we were kids, huh?"

"It really is."

She watched him work as her mind flashed back to those days when she'd sit right here and watch him build his go-kart, repair his motorcycle, then it was the hot rod they'd race around in. She knew he was an amazing man. Creative. Mechanical. And he was a good chef too. He interrupted her quiet thoughts.

"Hey, Zoe, you ever been in love?"

"Why do you ask?"

"Just curious."

"Well, that's not easy to answer, Teddy. I do love a man, but I don't think he knows it. So I guess not."

"Sorry to hear that."

"Why do you want to know? Are you in love?"

"Oh, I loved a girl, but she left. Nearly broke my heart."

"Oh, I'm so sorry to hear that. Is that the only time you've been in love?"

"Yeah, never been anyone else like her," he said as he slid the gas tank under Zoey's car and crawled underneath with it.

"What does that mean?"

"Oh, I don't know. I'm trying to understand women, like you said, but it's hard."

"What's hard about us?"

"Well, remember that night you said I needed to learn how to treat you the way a woman wants to be treated?"

"Yes. I do."

"Well, I talked with my dad about it. Man, it's complicated."

"How so, Teddy?"

"Well, for example, when a man and a woman have a baby."

"Hey, we just went from love to pregnancy. What happened to the wedding?"

"That's not important. I'm trying to make a point here. What I wanted to say is that when the man finds out his wife is pregnant, he makes a big announcement, buys everyone a drink, and he's done."

"Is that how it happens?"

"Yeah, for the guy. Then when the baby's born, he passes out cigars, names the baby, takes the mother home, and he's done again."

"Where are you going with this?"

"It's just an example of how a man communicates. In brief summaries. Not a lot of details and stuff. However, you see the rest of the story is that it takes nine months for the woman to deliver the baby. In the process, her hormones change, then her body changes, then her emotions change, then she gets big and clumsy, and finally the pain of delivering the baby."

"Teddy, what's that got to do with the way a woman communicates?"

"Everything Zoe. Every time a woman talks she has to start at the beginning, describe all the steps of the pregnancy in order to get to the labor pains."

"So you're trying to tell me that a man's story is short and a woman's story is long. Why didn't you just say that?"

"Oh, I don't know. Zoe, I think there are four screws on my bench with hex heads. Can you hand them to me please?"

She got up and went to the bench, saw the screws he wanted, picked them up and walked to the back of the car.

"They are in my hand here, Teddy."

He reached out under the bumper, found her hand, and felt her warm soft skin on his as she rolled her hand to drop the screws into his. It was quite distracting.

"Let me try again. Let's say I'm at the Cozy with a friend. The conversation goes like this. "Hey Joe, guess what, I went hunting yesterday and shot a deer." So Joe says, "Hey that's great, Teddy. Congratulations, let me buy you a beer." End of conversation. Get it?"

"Yeah, short, and sweet."

"So Zoe, if I went home to my mom and told her the same story, what do you think the difference would be?"

"Well, if it was my mom, she'd have a lot of questions."

"Exactly my point. Mom would want to know where I was, who I was with, when I saw the deer, how I shot the deer, what I did with the deer, and so on. Zoe, it's just so hard for a man to talk to a woman. I don't know how my dad does it."

"Women are just different. I'm glad you know that now. But I don't know what this has to do with love that we were talking about before."

"It's got everything to do with it, Zoe. When a man's in love with a woman, he wants everything to be perfect. If he can't talk to a woman in the right way, he'll always be miserable."

"Do you think you have to be perfect to love a woman?"

"Yes I do. If a man loves a woman, and he makes a mistake it really hurts."

"I didn't know that."

"Well it does. Then he doesn't know if he should try to fix it, or just go on and try something else, or what. It's really confusing."

"Sounds like you are in love again, Teddy."

"Yeah, I am. Kinda."

"Well, either you are or you are not. Which is it?"

"It's like you said earlier. I'm in love with a person, but she doesn't really know it."

"Why not?"

" 'Cause I haven't told her yet."

"Oh, come on, why not?"

"I guess I'm afraid to."

"Well what's she like? Tell me. I might know her. Is she pretty?"

"I think she's beautiful."

"Well, that weeds out 85% of the girls in town. Is she talented?"

"Yes, very."

"Have you known her a long time?"

"Yes."

"What color is her hair?"

"Well, Zoe," he said as he crawled out from under her car. "Your fuel pump is fixed. You can take it home."

"Great. So, what color is her hair?"

"Give it up, Zoe. If I'm uncomfortable telling her how I feel, I'm certainly not going to tell you everything about her."

"Oh, alright." She smiled to herself, and then said, "I just thought I could narrow it down to maybe two or three girls in town, that's all."

Teddy started Zoey's car and drove it out of the shed. He left the door open when he got out and met her. She took both his hands, looked at him, and said, "You are my sweet Teddy Bear. Thank you so much." Pulling him toward her, she kissed his cheek.

"Hey," he said, "That's not a real kiss."

"Ha, ha, you remember, don't you?"

"I sure do, and for a big job like this was, I want a real kiss."

She put her hands around his neck, pulled his lips toward her, and gave him longest hottest kiss she could. Leaving him breathless, Zoey got in her car and closed the door.

"Hey, you didn't tell me who you love."

Smiling, she gave him a little finger wave. "Bye, Teddy. Thanks."

ෆ৪০

The next morning Zoey walked through the kitchen toward the office.

"Good morning, Teddy. Thanks so much for fixing my car. That was sweet of you."

"No problem. Thanks for coming over. I was getting really frustrated, and I'm glad you were there so I could talk through it."

"Anytime you need someone to listen, call on me. I'm always here for you."

Zoey's smile reflected the warmth and pleasure she still felt from the time she spent with him the night before. He was no longer a boy, and was becoming so much like his father. It was wonderful.

As Zoey walked into her office, Wilma greeted her. "So, did you get your car fixed?"

"Oh, yes, Teddy finished it last night about 9:30. It's perfect."

"So, he must be a pretty handy guy."

"He is. He wanted to talk last night, so I heard a lot about how he feels and what he's thinking."

"But did he say he loves you?"

"No. He still won't say it. He's like a baby chick that can't figure out how to break the shell. It makes me so mad I just want to smash it for him."

| CHAPTER 31

Sarah came out of the laundry room carrying a basket of clothes humming and moving to the beat of the tune on her kitchen radio. As she lifted the basket onto the table, she saw movement at the door and gasped.

"Wendy? You scared me to death. What are you doing here?" She rushed to the door to let her in.

Wendy stepped in, threw her arms around her mom's neck and bawled.

"Wendy, Honey. What's happened?"

More bawling.

Oh Lord, give me wisdom... and please hurry.

She pulled herself away from Wendy's grip and held her at arm's length so she could see her. "Wendy, are you all right?"

"No."

"What's happened to you?"

Wendy threw her arms around Sarah and broke into tears again. "I'm pregnant."

Sarah let out a sigh of relief.

Oh, thank God. I thought it was something serious.

"Come with me, Honey. Make yourself comfortable. I'll make some tea."

When Sarah brought the tea into the living room she saw Wendy stretched out on the love seat, her legs propped up with pillows and a box of Kleenex on her stomach.

"Here you go, dear. Nobody is home but us, so this is a good time to talk."

Wendy was still upset. "Mom, this will ruin everything; School… my career… everything."

"Now, now. One thing at a time. Who's the father?"

"Tony."

"Why aren't you with him?"

"Cause the bastard took off as soon as I told him I was pregnant. The coward."

"Oh, dear. That's unfortunate."

"Unfortunate, hell. It's a disaster. I can't nurse a baby in a classroom, or change diapers in a stable. Damn it. It's not fair. One and done, then he gets to have all the fun. My career's ruined."

"Are you two in love, Honey?"

"Are you kidding me? How could I love a man who abandoned me?" She was so agitated she spilled tea on her shirt.

"Settle down. Calm yourself. Before you knew you were pregnant, did you love Tony?"

"Well, yes. We were madly in love. I was such a fool. I thought he was the only man for me, sent from heaven by an angel. But he showed his true colors as soon as the chips were down."

"Does Tony love you?"

"Well, he acted like it, until this happened."

"Would you marry him to give the baby a good home?"

"Mom! No! I don't ever want to see him again."

"Ok, ok. These are just important questions you need to consider, dear. All the choices are yours. What can we do to help you?"

"I just want to be away from him and have a quiet place to think. There's no way I can salvage my career. I need to find a way to deal with this."

Sarah got up from the couch and took Wendy's hand, helping her up. Hugging her she said, "You can stay as long as you like. Why don't you go up to your room and rest?"

CB&O

Wanting her conversation with Kent to be private, she called his office. "Hi, this is Sarah. Can Kent come to the phone for a minute?"

After a few seconds Kent answered, "Hey, why a phone call?"

"We've got a crisis on our hands. Wendy's up in her bedroom right now, she's pregnant, and very upset. Is there any way you can make yourself scarce after work. I need some time alone with her."

"Nothing can make me scarcer than a pregnant woman. Why don't I hide out at Oly's, and you can call when the coast is clear."

"Good idea. Sorry."

CB&O

A couple of hours later Wendy came down the stairs and joined her mother in the kitchen. She looked to be in a better frame of mind. "Are you feeling better, Sweetie?" Sarah asked.

Wendy rubbed her eyes. "Yeah, a little."

"Listen, I know pregnant women aren't supposed to drink wine, but honestly, I think you need one. Come out on the porch with me."

Wendy held the door so her mom could carry two glasses of wine to the porch swing. Turning sideways on the swing and folding one leg under her, Sarah asked Wendy, "Did you know that on this very swing I told your dad I was pregnant?"

"That's kinda romantic, Mom. How long were you married?"

"Three weeks."

Wendy almost spilled her wine. "Mom. You were pregnant before you were married?"

"Yes. And the baby was you."

"How did that happen?"

"Well, we were so passionate for each other that every time we were together we broke down another barrier. We tried not to, but in a split second, we were christening our new bed and couldn't stop. Bingo. I'm pregnant."

Wendy bowed her head and stared at her wine glass. "I can relate to that. I guess we were the same way. But, I didn't think we should get married because of school. So, we tried to put it off. The mental part worked ok, but holding off the physical part was almost impossible. We blew it."

"Honey, I just want you to know that everything will turn out alright. Your dad and I have had a wonderful life together, and you can too. A baby is just a baby. Not a death sentence."

| CHAPTER 32

The next day a service truck with a horseshoe on the door drove into the farmyard. Wendy jumped off the couch, looked out the window and ran for the stairs. "Mom, that's him. Damn it, he followed me. I am not here, understand? I don't want to see him." Her bedroom door slammed before Sarah could get out of the living room.

The young man stepped onto the porch.

Sarah noticed that he was thin, good looking, and walked with purpose in cowboy boots. Kind of a skinny John Wayne. "Hello. Can I help you?"

Tony fidgeted, looked at the ground and said, "Excuse me, ma'am, but I'm looking for the Crodin farm. I'm told it's in this area."

She found his awkwardness charming. And he didn't look like an S.O.B. or a coward, either.

"Your search is over, Son; you've found the Crodin place. Would you like something to drink?"

"Yes ma'am. I'd appreciate that."

"Ok, then. Sit yourself on the porch there and I'll be right out."

When Sarah came out of the house she handed Tony a glass of iced tea and sat down. "From what I hear, your name must be Tony."

"Yes ma'am, I'm Tony Ward."

Bent forward staring at the floor Sarah thought he was really taking this issue with Wendy seriously. "And, I guess you're here to see Wendy."

"I am."

"So you won't be surprised to hear she doesn't want to see you."

Tony turned his head to address her, "I guessed that, but I don't understand why."

"Well, you ran from her when she told you she was pregnant. I can't think of anything more rude and frightening than that. To abandon her at that moment is suicide for any relationship."

Tony set his glass down and stood. Pacing the porch, he tried to explain. "Mrs. Crodin, with all due respect, I did not abandon Wendy. She abandoned me. You see, we talked about getting married and postponed it because of her schooling. But when she said she was pregnant, I thought we should get married right away."

She interrupted. "Whoa now, did she know that?"

"No ma'am. I left for the jewelry store that had the ring she liked. They weren't open yet, so I had to wait an hour. When I got back home, she was gone."

Thoughtfully sipping her tea she asked, "So, you're telling me you wanted to marry her."

Tony stopped pacing in front of her. "Still do, if she'll have me."

Sarah sat back, looked out over the farm, then said, "Hmmm. Tony, would you excuse me. Make yourself comfortable. I'll be back in a minute."

She walked to Kent's clinic and went to the reception desk. She asked the receptionist for a pen and paper to leave Kent a note.

— Kent, Wendy's boyfriend is on the porch and she's in her room. I can't do this alone. I need you NOW! —

When Kent arrived, she introduced him to Tony and then told him, "These kids need to eat something." Why don't you two go to the barn and take care of Ginger and the other animals while I make supper."

The men walked away toward the barn, giving her time to approach Wendy. Knocking on her door she announced, "Wendy, I'm making dinner. You want to come down?"

In a booming voice that vibrated the door Wendy shouted, "No! I'm not leaving this room as long as he's here. I'll starve to death first."

Hmmm. She's bull headed and he's persistent. What do we do now?

| CHAPTER 33

Tony ran his hand down Ginger's nose. "This is a beautiful horse, Mr. Crodin."

"Wendy thinks so. She's had her for a few years now. Barrel raced with her, you know."

Tony smiled. "Yeah, she said she was a barrel racer. Was she any good?"

Kent sat Ginger's water bucket down by her. "She placed a number of times, but I think she was a little intimidated by the older girls. Once she got over that, she won a few. Gutsy little girl."

Tony frowned. "Did you say little?"

Kent nodded. "Yep, started when she was thirteen."

"Holy cow, she is good, isn't she!"

Kent smiled at Tony, "Son, she can do anything she puts her mind to. Sometimes it gets her into trouble."

Tony remembered she had mentioned to him that she pulled pranks when she was a kid. He wondered what kind. "So, Mr. Crodin, Wendy's been in trouble?"

Kent sat on a bale of hay and motioned for Tony to join him. "You mean she hasn't told you?"

Shaking his head Toney replied, "No sir. I've told her about the mischief and pranks I've pulled, but she's been mum about hers."

"So she didn't tell you about orchestrating the raising of the flag upside down at the Memorial Day celebration to embarrass the Mayor?"

"No sir."

"And she didn't tell you about the leaf-raking enterprise she created that got three of her friends jailed when her plan didn't work?"

"No, sir. I'd like to hear more about that one."

Kent looked over at Tony. "She'll have to tell you. All I saw was three boys in prison shirts doing community service."

Kent put his hand on Tony's shoulder, firmly. "Listen, son, I need some questions answered. My daughter is sitting in her room distraught over this pregnancy thing. What do you intend to do about it?"

Tony stood so he could look at Mr. Crodin. "I intend to marry her, sir. Always have."

"Do you love her?"

"With all my heart. She's the best thing that's ever happened to me, and all I want to do is be with her and make her happy."

Kent stood, put one foot on the bale and asked, "Well, now. Do you know how difficult she is to live with?"

He smiled as he thought about her. "Well, sir, I know she's stubborn as a mule, independent as a mustang, physical as any man, and mischievous enough to make me never lose sight of her."

"And you think those are her lovable traits?"

"No sir, she's also warm, loving, passionate about animals, and soft and fragile under her protective shell. I learned just how loyal she can be when I was in the hospital paralyzed."

"How do you feel about all that, Son?"

"Actually, I'm a lot that way, too. I like her spunk. I don't worry about her when she's on her own. She can take care of herself when she has to.

"Just how do you intend to finance the two of you and a new baby?"

Her parents were not bashful and Tony suspected this question was coming. "Mr. Crodin, I have my own business as a farrier. I'm connected with all of the best horse owners and trainers in Kentucky. Even if Wendy wasn't a vet, we could live comfortably on my income."

Kent looked him in the eye. "Does Wendy know this?"

"Yes, sir."

"Ok, tell me what you would do to help her finish her veterinary degree?"

Her father's stare was intimidating. Tony turned away and paced a bit. "My business is such, Mr. Crodin, that I could schedule my work early morning and late evening. Whatever is needed so I could watch the baby while she is in class. Let me say this, Wendy is number one in my life. Our baby would be number two, and my business number three."

Kent nodded. "Pretty commendable intentions, Son."

"Don't expect me to be perfect, sir. But you can expect me to love your daughter more than any other man in this world could."

Kent walked out of the stall. "Come on, Son. Let's see if dinner is ready."

After dinner, Kent took Tony down the hall and showed him an extra bedroom he could use for the night. Tony took his overnight bag with him and wasn't seen again 'til morning.

ରେ ଉ

Sarah and Kent stayed out on the porch swing for a little solitude. She laid her head on his shoulder and sighed.

"What are we going to do, Honey? These two kids are so bull-headed, and persistent I see no way to help them."

"You just leave it to me. Tomorrow morning we'll meet this issue head on.

She sat up straight, "You're not going to do something to hurt Wendy are you?"

Kent put his arm around her to calm her. "Honey, don't you worry about a thing. Both of them are going to hurt before this is done. I'm going to lead. All you need to do is follow. Everything will be alright."

Closing her eyes, Sarah gritted her teeth.

Now I'm as uncomfortable as the kids are.

ೞ ೲ

In the morning after breakfast, Kent was directing Sarah. "Put that chair here and the other chair there."

She looked at him from the corner of her eye. "Really? It looks like a conference."

He nodded. "It will be. Now, you go get Tony and put him on the swing there. I'll get Wendy."

Standing in front of Kent she said, "Oh, no. She'll never do this."

"Look, I said I'll get Wendy. Now, please go get Tony."

Kent climbed the stairs and knocked on Wendy's door. "Wendy, its Dad. Please come out. Now."

As expected, Wendy resisted. "Is Tony still here? If he is, I'm not coming out."

"Wendy Jo Crodin, this is your father, and I just told you to get out here. Now, do you want to do that voluntarily or do you want me to come in and get you?"

"Daddy, you wouldn't do that."

Kent used a key to unlock the door, opened it and stood tall in front of his daughter sitting on her bed. "How do you want to do this young lady, on your feet or over my shoulder?"

Wendy was astonished. Her dad had never been so demanding. It scared her. "Ok, ok, on my feet, please."

"After you young lady."

They walked down the stairs and out onto the porch. When Wendy saw Tony sitting on the swing she balked. "Daddy, I don't want to be here."

Kent directed her toward the swing. "I don't care where you want to be, you're going to sit there."

Wendy was unnerved. Her dad was angry, like she'd done something wrong. And Mom wasn't saying a word.

So, the four of them sat. Wendy and Tony on the swing, Kent and Sarah in separate chairs. It was obvious her dad was in charge.

"Ok, here's the deal. You two kids are going to listen to each other. First Wendy will tell her story. Then Tony will tell his. I want no interruptions, understand?"

Both Wendy and Tony nodded, out of either fear or respect.

Kent pointed to Wendy. "You go first."

Wendy told her story of cowardice and abandonment. It obviously hurt Tony's feelings, but he didn't say a word, like her dad said.

Kent pointed to Tony. "Now, let's hear your story."

Tony told his story of commitment to marry, buying a wedding ring, planning his proposal and Wendy's disappearance. His lost business while searching for her, and traveling to her home in Iowa.

It was obvious that Wendy didn't want to hear it. But she did. She didn't want to admit she was wrong, but she was.

When Tony finished Kent stood up and motioned for Sarah to do the same. "Ok, this is all your mother and I can do. Seek the truth. What you two do with it is your business. Wendy, I have only one thing to say. Tony and I have had a chance to talk. If you decide you want to marry him, you have our blessing. Now, you can kiss each other or kill each other. It's your life. Do what you want to with it. Come along, Honey," and Kent and Sarah went into the house.

ങ്ങ

Tony looked over at Wendy. "Boy, you really pissed off your dad."

Wendy wrinkled her nose. "Yeah, I guess so. I've never seen him so mad."

"Is he that way a lot?"

Wendy looked at Tony, "Never. And it's the first time in my life my mother has not said a word.

"Man, if she's quiet, then your Dad was really mad."

Tony leaned back on the swing. "They think we made a mistake, don't they?"

"No doubt."

"What do you think?"

Wendy put her hand on top of Tony's. "I think we missed each other at the crossroads trying to do the right thing."

"Can you ever forgive me?" He pleaded.

She kissed him on the cheek. "You know, there's nothing to forgive. Obviously I jumped to conclusions, caused my parents a lot of trauma and you all that heartache and effort to find me. I'm truly sorry."

Tony stood, reached into his pocket and kneeled before Wendy. "Wendy Jo Crodin, I love you very much and wish to marry you. Will you be my bride and live with me forever?"

Wendy brought her hands together in a prayerful position as tears welled up in her eyes. There was only one man she could love and he was on his knees before her. She was so grateful. Putting her left hand out for him, Tony placed the ring on her finger. When it was in place, she leaned down, threw her arms around him and cried.

They both stood and kissed. Wendy let the emotions flow out of her, smiled at Tony and said. "Well, I suppose Dad is going to want to know what happened."

"Not a problem. Let me handle this. I'm not afraid of him."

Wendy grinned and kissed Tony on the cheek, whispering in his ear, "Liar."

ଔ ଓ

The consensus was to get married as soon as possible, which happened the next day at the local Justice of the Peace. Sarah and Kent stood up with them. The day after they packed their things in Tony's truck and left for Kentucky.

Standing in the farmyard watching their truck turn onto the gravel road Kent said, "You know what surprises me?"

"I have no idea," Sarah answered.

"You're not a bit upset about all this?"

"You know, Honey," she told him, "I'm not. I see myself driving down that road to run away from you. I was able to get my life together, and I'm confident she will too. Wendy is more like me than I ever imagined. She'll be alright.

| CHAPTER 34

It was a beautiful Saturday morning in Clayton. People enjoying the summer were already stopping by the café for breakfast before going to the Scout Park farmer's market. The café was buzzing when Wilma heard a knock on the back screen door. She didn't recognize the woman standing outside, who looked to be thirtyish.

"May I help you?"

"I hope so," she said. "Teddy said to meet him here at nine o'clock." She smiled sweetly. "He does work here doesn't he?"

Wilma didn't answer. A strange woman at her door, asking for Teddy, smelled like trouble to her. She turned and hollered toward the kitchen. "Teddy. You expecting a visitor?"

Zoey heard her too, and showed up at the door the same time as Teddy. She couldn't believe what she was seeing. A sexy blond woman stood outside in flip flops, white shorts and a loose red tank top that didn't cover all of the things Zoey thought it should. Watching Teddy greet the woman with a huge smile didn't help things.

Why is he doing this to me?

His back turned to Zoey, Teddy poked Wilma on the shoulder. "Well, Wilma, thanks for the day off. See you in the morning."

Zoey walked to the window and watched them get into a new red Camaro convertible, parked at the curb. The woman smiled at Teddy and patted his shoulder before she started the car and drove off. Zoey was furious; making fists, she threw them down to her side as she stomped her foot, "Wilma. What went wrong?"

Wilma gave her a hug and a box of Kleenex for her tears.

Cଃ 80

After work, sitting alone in her room, Zoey couldn't stand it any longer. She had to know what Teddy was doing with the blond woman. So she dressed in black jeans, a black T-shirt and black tennis shoes. She put a black scarf around her neck and headed for the front door of her house.

"Zoey, what are you up to, Honey?" Niki asked.

"I'm just going for a walk, Mom. Don't know how long I'll be gone, but don't worry, I won't be far away."

Dressed in black, not going far away, Zoey's mother was no fool. Something was up. She waited until Zoey left the porch and turned toward the Crodins' house. That's when Niki stood in the shadow of the porch and watched her daughter cross the field like she'd done thousands of times before to meet Teddy. Zoey stopped in the dark shadows of the barn and sat on the ground.

Niki trusted her daughter and usually gave her a lot of leash, knowing she usually steered away from trouble. But the mood tonight didn't feel good. She decided to intervene.

Zoey jumped when her mom sat beside her. It took a moment to catch her breath before she whispered, "Mom, what are you doing here? You scared me to death."

"I came to ask you the same question."

"Well, ahh."

"Why are you spying on Teddy?"

"I'm not spying."

"Look at you. Dressed so he can't see you. Hiding in the shadows. If you're not researching a mystery novel, then you're spying. Why?"

"Oh Mom, I thought I had him so close to saying he loved me, but he just won't say it. Then this blond woman shows up and takes him away for the day. While he was with her, he sent me flowers. Can you believe it? Does he think I'm a blind fool?"

"Was there a card with the flowers?"

"Yes."

"What did it say, Honey?"

"Something about missing me. Some sappy crap."

"I thought sappy crap is what you wanted. What do you expect to see tonight?"

"He's either going to take her out, or bring her home. Either way, I want to see what he does."

"What do you plan to do?"

"Well, if he hugs and kisses her, I'm going to be fuming mad. If he takes her into the house, we're done. No questions asked."

"Honey, I'm sorry you feel this way, but I have to tell you, this is all your fault."

Zoey turned on her mother burning with anger. "How can you say that, Mom? I've done everything to make him admit that he loves me, and he just won't."

"That's my point, dear. You manipulate things to come out the way you want them. It's a gift, and a curse. In matters of the heart, I think it's more of a curse. You can't manipulate someone's heart, Dear."

"So, you think I'm trying to manipulate Teddy's heart?"

"Yes, I do. That's why you're not getting what you want."

"Well, Mom, I've given him every chance. I've told him what he has to do but he hasn't done it. What's left?"

"You told him what? My God, what did you say to him?"

"Well, I kinda did, I . . ."

"You shouldn't have done it, should you?"

"All I said to him was that when he learned to treat me like a grown woman wants to be treated, there was more where that came from."

"And just what did you expect him to do?"

"Quit treating me like a kid, I'm a twenty-one-year-old woman, Mom."

"I see. So you fell in love with a man because of the way he is, then you told him he had to be different. Right?"

"I didn't mean that."

"But how do you know what he heard?"

"You think that's why all this is happening?"

"Zoey, why would Teddy want a woman who doesn't like him the way he is?"

"Oh, no, Mom! Do you think I lost him?"

"You will if you don't show faith in him. You've got to let Teddy lead, Dear."

Zoey laid her head on her knees. "But he doesn't go anywhere."

"No, what you mean is he doesn't go where you want him to go. Big difference."

"Stop it, Mom."

"Listen. If a man loves you and cares for you, he wants to protect you. That means he wants to lead, and have you follow, so he can face life's ups and downs first and be able to protect you."

Zoey was aghast. "Mom, you couldn't be more archaic."

"It's basic man and woman. The only man you're going to attract with your 'I'm going to tell you where to go and how to do it' attitude will be some wimpy guy who will carry your bags, lick your boots, and follow you anywhere. Is that what you want?"

Covering her head with her hands, she squealed. "Mom. Get Real!"

"That's what I thought. You've known him all your life. You two love each other. You know it. Maybe he doesn't yet. Or, maybe he just hasn't figured out how to tell his fishing buddy that he thinks you're sexy, and he wants to marry you. Ever think of that?"

"Well, why doesn't he just come out and say it then?"

"Well, maybe you'll just have to take him back to the fishing hole, like the old days. Huh?" Niki felt she'd said enough, and Zoey needed time alone. As her mother got up to leave Zoey felt a gentle pat on the head, leaving her with nothing but her own confusing thoughts. She sat in the shadows, scarf over her head, staring at the Crodin's house. She thought about the times at their 'secret spot' where she'd shared so many good times with him. They had talked about everything in their young lives in that place. School, their first kiss, puberty, work, everything. So, why did he feel so comfortable talking there, but not when they were together other places?

Only minutes later lights shown on the lane to the Crodin's house, and a red convertible pulled in. Zoey watched as Teddy get out of the car, and was relieved the blond woman was only dropping him off. Her worst fears seemed foolish, now. Her relief was short lived though, as he walked around the car and in a rare act of chivalry opened the driver's door for the blond woman. She smiled sweetly at him, took his arm as he led her toward the house.

No! No! I can't let this happen.

Leaping to her feet and running out of the shadows, she screamed "Teddy Crodin, don't you dare take that woman into the house!"

Stunned by the voice screaming from the darkness, the couple stopped, turned, and looked in shock at someone dressed in black racing toward them. Before Teddy could say anything Zoey had ripped their arms apart, turned her back to the woman and stood nose to nose with him. "Why are you doing this to me? After all this time we're trying to tell each other we're in love, you go off with this slut? What an insult. It's supposed to be me, you idiot!"

Zoey gasped for air, giving Teddy his first chance to say something. "Zoe, you're all wrong. It's not like that."

Getting in his face, she challenged him. "So, now you think I'm blind? I suppose all I have to do is show some T & A and you'll love me too?"

"Zoe, stop it!"

The blond woman smiled at Zoey, touched Teddy's arm and said, "I think I'd better go now."

Even this slightest show of affection annoyed Zoey. "That's got to be the smartest thing you've said today, sister."

Teddy looked from one woman to the other wondering what to do. His attempt to speak was interrupted again, this time by his blond companion. "Good luck. Don't forget all the things you've learned."

Are you kidding me?

Zoey turned her gaze from the unwanted woman to Teddy. She shoved Teddy in the chest with both hands, throwing him backward. "You're taking lessons from a hooker?" She shoved him again and got in his face. "What kind of man are you? Not the man I fell in love with, that's for sure. She shoved him hard. "Are you trying to make a fool out of me? Is this what I came back home for? If I wanted to be treated this way, I could have stayed in the city. Pounding his chest with her fists she cried, "I hate you, Teddy! Hate you. Hate you. Hate you."

As she collapsed against him and started to cry Teddy threw, his arms around her and held tight. Letting her head rest on his chest he asked, "Are you done now?"

"I'm done with you."

He looked down on her and said, "Just shut up and listen, will ya'?"

Zoey tried to shake her head in the little space Teddy's strong arms gave her. "I don't want to know about her."

"It's not about Sheila. It's about us."

"I don't want to know her name."

"Sheila is a relationship counselor. I hired her about a month ago."

Zoey broke out of Teddy's arms. "So, that's what they call hookers now?"

Teddy pulled her back against his chest and held her tight. "Will you give it up? Sheila's a coach to help me learn how to be the husband you want."

Zoey struggled to pull away. Teddy didn't let her.

"Let go of me," she said, still struggling.

"No. You had your say, now you're going to listen to me."

Zoey gave up the struggle and collapsed against him. "Auugh!"

Light washed over them as Sarah turned on the porch light. Opening the door she asked, "Are you kids alright? I heard yelling and was worried."

Teddy squinted as he looked into the bright light. Seeing only the shadow of his mom, he said to her, "We're fine, Mom."

"Do you want me to leave the light on for you?"

Teddy shook his, said "No, thanks anyway," and lowered his sight from the glaring light.

| CHAPTER 35

As the dark of night surrounded them again, Teddy felt Zoey's body was no longer tense and her crying had quieted. "Zoe, I've loved you all my life. But since you returned from school I didn't feel like I fit into your life anymore."

Zoey felt tired and didn't move when she asked, "Why didn't you say something?"

"I didn't know how." He shrugged his shoulders. "You are always so far ahead of me, so much more sophisticated in the ways of the world. It was as if you were riding a thoroughbred and I was on a donkey. I had a lot of stuff to learn."

Putting her arms around his waist she said, "I just wanted you to say you loved me."

Loosening his hold, he looked down into her eyes. "Not the impression I got, Zoe. When you told me I had to learn how to treat you like a grown woman wants to be treated, I felt inferior. I couldn't understand why I was ok with you before you went to school, and then you demanded I do so much when you returned. I missed you so much. I loved you so much. But you were telling me I'm the wrong kind of guy for you. I really needed help."

She sighed, "What did you do?"

"Well, I got a lot of help from my dad, but Sheila was the biggest help."

Talking through her gritted teeth and turned up lip she snapped, "Stop it. I don't want to hear her name again. Ever. I can't understand how spending time with another woman is supposed to please me?"

"It's obvious. You want a perfect husband, and I don't want to be a disappointment to my wife."

Zoey put her hands on his shoulders. "Teddy, why are you doing all this when you've never even told me that you love me?"

He just shrugged. "You know it. You have for a long time."

Zoey gasped. Her eyes widened as she pulled away and looked directly at Teddy. "Did you say wife? You said wife, didn't you? I heard you say it."

"Yes I did. Zoe, you're my reason for living. You put the beat in my heart. I want you to marry me and make my life complete?"

Zoey collapsed into his chest again. "Oh, Teddy. Is this how you want me to remember our engagement the rest of my life? Standing in a farmyard after a fight?"

"I don't know. What did you expect?"

"Oh, a gondola in Venice would be so romantic, or maybe dinner in an exclusive restaurant with the ring hidden in the flowers. Something like that."

Teddy kissed the top of her head. "I'm not that guy and you know it. We're standing right where we were raised. We're in the arms of someone we love. This is who we are. Do you want to be my wife or not?"

Zoey released her arms, placed her hands on the sides of Teddy's face and kissed him. "Of course I do. I can't imagine my life without you. Wrapping her arms around his neck she purred, "I love you so much, Teddy."

When he released his arms around her, Zoey took his hand and led him the porch and the swing. She sat with her legs over his and her arms around his neck. "Oh Teddy, I'm so happy. It took us so long. I'm glad it's over."

"Yeah, me too."

Teddy, you won't believe how many times I've planned our wedding. It's going to be beautiful. You'll wear a white tux. I know which dress I'm going to wear. And I've pick such beautiful flowers."

Cぬ

Sarah quietly left the living room window, climbed the stairs and got into bed.

"What took you so long?" Kent asked. "I thought you were just closing the windows."

"All but one. I had a chance to do some eaves dropping on the way."

"You shouldn't have."

"Oh, but you won't believe what I learned. Teddy and Zoey are out on the porch swing planning their wedding. Can you believe it? Teddy must have proposed tonight."

"Will wonders never cease," Kent replied.

"I'm so excited for them. It's taken them so long. Oh, I can't wait. Reaching for the phone on her nightstand she said, "I've got to go call Niki. I hope she's still up."

Kent quickly grabbed her arm, "Whoa, there. You'll do no such thing."

"But Kent."

"No but's about it. You two busybodies are going to stay out of this until Teddy tells us and Zoey tells Niki and Oly. And, I expect you to act surprised when he does."

Sarah gave Kent a pouting look and slid under the covers.

Cぬ

Teddy enjoyed Zoey's excitement, but had a practical matter to think of first. "Easy now. Let's not get ahead of ourselves. This isn't when I planned to propose to you. It just happened. So, I don't have a ring yet."

Looking into his eyes she said, "It'd be fun to shop for one together. The Café isn't usually that busy on Mondays, so maybe Wilma will give us a few hours off tomorrow. What do ya' say?"

"Good deal. Why don't you talk with her? Well, it's been an exciting night. Come on, I'll walk you home."

"You don't need to, Teddy. I'll be fine."

"Zoe, it's what a man does for his fiancé. I'm walking you home."

They kissed at the front door of her house. "I love you, Teddy," Zoey whispered.

"I love you too. See you tomorrow."

೮೩೮೨

Entering the house and walking quietly toward the kitchen Zoey was surprised to see her mother at the table with finger nail polish, remover, and emery boards. A cup of tea, or coffee sat beside her.

"Mom, why are you up so late?"

"Well, I saw that red car pull into Teddy's driveway, and began to worry about you."

Giving her mother the eye she said, "You had to be spying to know about a red car pulling into Teddy's driveway?"

Niki held out her hand and looked at her nails as she replied, "How absurd. What do I care? Pull up a chair and tell me what happened."

"Nothing happened, Mom. The woman dropped Teddy off at his house. We talked a little, and I came home."

Niki filed her fingernail slowly, looked up at Zoey and said, "Has anybody told you you're a lousy liar?"

"Mom, I'm not lying."

"Technically, you're right. But you just left out all the information I really want to know. Now, try again, from the beginning."

Zoey plopped into a chair. "Well, things didn't go as planned."

Niki continued to file her fingernail, "I'm not surprised."

"Mom. What's with you? If you're so damned smart, why don't you tell me?"

Niki layed her emery board down, and smiled at Zoey. "Ok, I will. When I heard all that yelling going on I figured your emotions got the best of you and you confronted Teddy. Right?"

"Uh-huh."

"Alright, then I see a car go down the road about eleven-thirty, which never happens around here. That told me Teddy's blond friend kissed him goodbye and left. How am I doin'?"

"You think you're so smart, she didn't kiss him."

"Really? Did you have something to do with that? Anyway, it has been almost an hour since she left. Everything has been quiet. And, you come home with a grin I'd expect to see on a three-year-old girl who got her first doll. Now how could that happen to you, only moments after you attacked Teddy and his friend? Care to enlighten me?"

"I was wrong, Mom. She wasn't what I thought she was."

Niki pushed her chair back and stood. "Would you like me to get you something to drink, so it's easier to swallow your pride?"

"You're so thoughtful."

Niki got her a glass of water anyway, sat it in front of Zoey and sat back in her chair. "You've got so much to learn about love, girl."

I know. I've been wrong about Teddy. I tried to make him fit my fantasy and almost lost him. He asked me to marry him tonight, Mom, standing right there in the dark in his farmyard where we've been thousands of times. Kind of stupid, not very romantic, but it's who we are. He and I. He's my Teddy, Mom, and I'll never try to change him again."

Niki let out a sigh of relief. "I'm glad to finally hear you say that, Dear. I hope you can keep your promise. Now, it's extremely important that we keep this news to ourselves. Your dad has to find out about this on-his-own."

"Why do you say that?"

"Well, he and almost everyone in town have bet on a calendar date at the barbershop. As soon as they hear you and Teddy are engaged someone is going to come out of there with a fist full of money. I'm sure your Dad thinks he'll win."

Zoey was aghast. "What? People are betting on when we'll get engaged?"

"Oh, Zoey, you should know better. Everyone in town has been watching you two. Don't act so surprised."

"Mom, that's awful! You mean our relationship was public, and people were betting on us?"

Niki grinned and shrugged her shoulders. "Honey, it's Clayton."

෬ඏ

If there were any residents of Clayton that hadn't heard of the engagement, they did when Harvey Chalmers came out of the barber shop whooping and hollering with a fist full of money. He'd won the engagement pool. "Bless you Teddy and Zoey. You're my heroes."

Of course, Oly, Zoey's father, was especially disappointed, since the day he bet on had long passed. He blamed his loss on Teddy for dragging his feet so long.

CR&

Wilma offered to run the restaurant while they were away for their wedding and honeymoon. But, Teddy and Zoey knew it wasn't practical. They decided on a small wedding so they could have a big reception with all their friends in town. They got married at the local church with only family attending and had their reception in the street at River Drive between Wilma's Café and Roy's barber shop. Wilma served the food and Roy served the drinks. Of course, Norm's Bait and Tackle Choir provided the music.

"Oh, Niki," Sarah said to her, "this is perfect. It's just what they wanted."

"I know, and just think of the volunteers that are helping Wilma and Roy. It's awesome."

Zoey had ditched her heels long ago and was dancing in slippers. She looked so beautiful every young man in town wanted a dance with the girl they had ignored in high school, but Teddy didn't let her get too far away. Sarah attracted her share of attention from the men in town, and of course everyone that had a crush on Kent in high school vied for a dance with him as well. Zoey's dad insisted on monitoring activity at the beer tent to ensure nothing went awry with the revelers, and his beer mug never ran dry.

About that time when dancers were getting tired and some folks showed signs of drinking too much, a black Ford truck drove down River Drive parting the crowd. Scribbled in white with signs and sayings and cans clanking behind. The newlyweds chariot awaited them. Teddy and Zoey kissed their parents goodbye, thanked Wilma and Roy, then drove off for two nights at the hotel and spa in Bluffton as Mr. and Mrs. Theodore Crodin.

 Cঙৎঠ

When the newlyweds returned they moved into Wilma's apartment above the restaurant. She used the rent money for a small one-story rental house that didn't have stairs to climb. Wilma knew her knees were wearing out and they were painful at the end of the day. "Let the kids run those stairs, not me," she told her friends.

| CHAPTER 36

Zoey was cleaning tables and setting up for the dinner crowd when Wilma entered the dining room. Zoey looked her way and smiled. "You here to help do setups?"

"No child," Wilma answered, "I need to see you and Teddy when you're finished. Come to the office."

When she finished setups and entered the kitchen Teddy was prepping for dinner. "Did Wilma talk to you, too," she asked?

"Yeah, go ahead. I'll be in when I finish this."

Wilma was not a meeting kind of person so Teddy and Zoey felt awkward. Teddy couldn't seem to find a comfortable spot to sit in his chair, and fidgeted. Zoey was wringing her hands and glancing between Wilma and Teddy, constantly looking for clues.

Wilma broke the awkwardness. "Well, I've got good news and bad news for you. Let me share the bad news first, and get it out of the way."

Zoey gasped, thinking Wilma was seriously ill or something. Teddy looked down at his hands, trying to hide from his suspicion that Wilma was going to close the restaurant.

"My sister's illness is terminal."

Zoey was immediately relieved. "Oh, Wilma. I'm so sorry."

"Thank you, dear. Well, it means that I need to care for her in her home. She's got nobody else. I leave Sunday and I won't be back."

Teddy was surprised. "What about the café, Wilma? What are you going to do about it?"

"That's the good news. I want the two of you to run it for me. I'll give each of you ten percent of the profits, over and above your pay, if you'll do this for me. Run it like you own it. Don't ask my permission for anything, because I won't have time to be bothered. As long as the income matches the previous year I'll be happy."

Teddy was instantly relieved and sighed heavily. He looked at Zoey who was smiling and nodding. Turning to Wilma he said, "Yes, we'll do it. And don't worry about a thing. We won't let anybody notice a change in management."

CB ᘓ

It only took three months for Teddy to break his promise. "Zoe, can you join me? I need to talk with you."

Sitting at a dining room table was totally out of character for Teddy. She sat and eyed him for clues about what he was thinking. "Ok, what's up?"

"Do you remember the night you took me to that Italian restaurant in Maquoketa?"

Zoey giggled. "Of course. What about it?"

"I want to do that here."

"You can't," she blurted out, "You promised Wilma people wouldn't notice a change."

"Settle down," he said. "Just listen. I want to create a special event. Once a month. A five course Italian dinner, preset with only tossed salad or eggplant as menu choices."

"Once a month?" She asked.

"Yeah. I'd fill the dining room twice… requiring a reservation for every seat at six o'clock and eight o'clock dinner times."

"You'd restrict the number of diners?"

"Yes, that's what will make it a special event. Can you imagine? A place to take your wife or date for a special dinner. Only thirty reservations. Different Italian dishes every month. I think it would be fun."

Zoe had been looking around the dining room as Teddy talked. "This place doesn't look very Italian to me."

"I know. That's where you come in. I want you to go shopping and get the stuff to decorate it. Linen table clothes, red and green napkins, just whatever you need to create the atmosphere. Will you do it?"

"This is a first," she said. "The only time I've known you to be creative was when you were building something. It's an intriguing idea. I like it. I can see it working. And, if it doesn't, well, it's only one night a month that we could stop anytime. Let's try it, Teddy. "

Teddy grabbed her hand and kissed it. "Thanks, Zoe. Now, here's what we're going to do...'

CB ♥ BD

The table included Oly and Niki Bondi, Sarah and Kent. Their server, Zoey Crodin, looked cute with her green apron over black slacks and shirt. She poured the wine all around, and one for her, and set the bottles on the table.

Out of the kitchen came a man dressed in all white except for a red and green scarf tied around his neck. It was noticeable only after his tall bulbous chef's hat. He raised his glass and proclaimed, "Ladies and gentlemen, welcome to Italian night. Salute."

Teddy's family cheered, laughed as they clinked their glasses and sipped wine. It was amazing to them that Teddy had created such an event. No one had ever imagined him doing such a thing. And, their surprises weren't over, as each course came out with the appropriate wine served graciously by Zoey.

Sarah looked to Niki and said, "My goodness, what a team."

"I know," she answered. "Aren't they beautiful? "I always wondered if he was lazy, hanging around here all the time. But this is an outstanding idea. He'll blow this town away. "

Kent agreed, "Yeah, and the food's perfect."

"Don't you wonder how he learned to do this?" Oly asked.

After five different courses and six wines, everyone at the table was pleased and content. Their chatter was interrupted when Teddy came out from the kitchen. He motioned for Zoey to join him, placed his arm around her waist and presented themselves to their families. "Well, what do you think of the idea?"

Everyone applauded and shared accolades. Sarah stood. "Teddy, I have never seen anything so elegant and professional in Clayton. It rivals those I've seen in Chicago. Offering this only once a month makes it extremely special. It's brilliant." She raised her glass of wine, "I'm so proud of you."

Again, applause, toasts and laughter filled the room. Zoey kissed Teddy and he held her tight.

I wonder if Wilma would ever sell this restaurant to me.

CR &

About two-thirty the next afternoon, Teddy stepped out the back door of the café for a breath of fresh air. There was a nice breeze off the river, and he was enjoying the view. As he scanned the riverfront, he was shocked to see a body lying on the sidewalk.

He quickly dialed 911 on his cell phone and ran down the sidewalk. Kneeling down and looking into the woman's face, he saw that it was Adel Parker. Sirens blared louder and louder as the fire department approached.

Hearing the fire truck pass by the café, Zoey rushed to the door to see what was happening. When she saw Teddy down the street, she ran to see what had happened.

"Teddy," she said as she caught up with him, "is it Adel?"

He looked up at her. "Yes, maybe she passed out or something. I don't know."

The firemen and EMT's took over, began treating Adel and rushed her away to the hospital.

Teddy and Zoey walked back slowly, disturbed by Adel's fate. "What can we do for her, Teddy?"

"I don't know, Zoe, but one thing you could do is go to the hospital and be with her. I can hold things together until you return."

"Yeah, somebody should. I'll get my purse and go now."

ಃಝ

Zoey called to inform Sarah, who relieved her before suppertime at the café. They alternated keeping Adel company until her family could arrive.

Doctor's confirmed that Adel had suffered a mild stroke. She was released the third day with orders to be in her wheelchair unless she was in bed. Zoey was concerned, and approached Teddy with a proposition.

"Teddy, you know Adel won't be able to cook in her wheelchair. If somebody doesn't help her with her meals, you know she's going to try, and could burn her house down."

"Now, that's not gonna happen."

"Maybe not so bad, but it's going to be tough for her to feed herself. Why don't we take her meals to her? It's only six houses down. You could make'em, and I'll take them to her."

"Mmmm, that wouldn't take much."

"No, and if I take something like a shake or smoothie along with breakfast she could put that in the refrigerator to have for lunch. Then I'd only have to return with supper. Come on, where's your heart?"

"Hey, you know I have no problem helping her. Sounds like it'll work. I'll make supper for her and you talk to her when you deliver it. Ok?"

As Zoey walked up the porch steps, she heard a voice from inside the house, "Come on in child. What are you carrying?"

"Why, Adel, Teddy made supper for you."

"How sweet. You married a good man, Zoey. Worth the chase wasn't it?"

"Yes. I'm very lucky to have him. Now, I've got a proposition for your health and safety."

"Oh, my. Sounds ominous."

"It isn't. We'd like to help with your meals so you don't get in trouble trying to cook and feed yourself."

"How in the world are you going to do that?" Adel asked.

"With your permission, of course, we'd like to bring you breakfast and supper from the café. I can also bring something like a shake with your breakfast that you could refrigerate and have for lunch. All on us, if you'll let us help."

"Oh, that would be wonderful. I was afraid to try to use my stove anyway. You kids are so thoughtful. You tell Teddy thanks for doing this for me, ya' hear?"

"He'll be pleased you accepted. So, here's your supper. What time should I come in the morning?"

"Hate to say it, but I'm an early riser, dear. Is six-thirty a problem?"

"Not at all, Adel. I'll see you tomorrow at six-thirty. You sleep well, now."

Zoey left pleased that it hadn't been a problem seeking Adel's acceptance. Apparently she was worried enough about it herself that she couldn't resist.

As Zoey entered the Café and passed through the kitchen Teddy asked, "Well, how'd it go?"

"No problem. She liked the idea. We need to take her breakfast at six-thirty in the morning."

| CHAPTER 37

A month later, the evenings were cooling off quickly, like they all did in the fall. The air was fresh and the night sky aglow with moonlight. Sitting on the porch swing together, Sarah wrapped in a wool blanket and Kent a suede jacket, she said to him, "There's so much happening here, Honey, but I have a feeling I need to be with Wendy."

"You want to go to Kentucky?"

She leaned on his shoulder. "I have tried to talk myself out of it, but I can't help but feel a mother has her place. It's Wendy's first baby. I need to be there for her."

He smiled, put his arm around her waist and hugged her. "Plus, you can be the first to see the baby."

"Of course."

"Go on ahead. I can survive on pizza, burgers and beer. Make your plans to fly out of Bluffton. We'll get you to the airport."

"Well, that's silly. Just go to Wilma's and Teddy will cook for you."

"Guess I'm not used to thinking that way."

"Well, when will you? What do you think? Will a couple weeks be ok?"

He kissed her forehead. "Of course, three if need be."

"Ok, I'll get a one-way ticket."

CB EO

Wendy was so pleased her mother was with her. Tony said she wasn't as anxious after her arrival. As future grandmother, Sarah experienced everything. The three of them traveling to the hospital as Wendy screamed through her labor pains; Tony running out of the delivery room with a smile as big as a barn; and that heart warming scene of Wendy holding little Katie for the first time.

Then the work began. Sarah's days were filled with babysitting while Wendy slept, doing laundry, changing diapers and cooking. Wendy took nights so she could get used to Katie's sleep pattern. Tony took to diapering as well as any man.

During a quiet time, Wendy and Sarah relaxed in the living room while Tony was at work. "Mom, I'm so glad you're here. There's so much I need to know, I can't thank you enough for helping me."

"Don't forget your dad, too, dear. He and Teddy are surviving without me, just so I can be here with you."

Holding her close to her bosom she asked, "What do you think of little Katie, Mom?"

"She's beautiful. A little fussy now and then, but well-behaved overall. She looked at Wendy and grinned."

"What, Mom?"

"I was wondering who you think she'll be like. You or Tony."

"Well, me of course," Wendy said wrinkling her nose and smiling. "Who else?"

"You wanted to be like your father for so long, Honey, we thought you'd never become a lady!"

"And now look at me. I feel like I'm living in your footsteps."

"That makes me so proud. You know the old saying, "No matter how hard you try to resist, you will become your parents."

"I'm beginning to understand that, and am so glad to be like you. You've set a great example."

"I'm sure you'll do the same for Katie, who, by-the-way will be like you and Tony."

"Ooooh, that could mean trouble, huh?"

"Just considering the genes of her father and mother, this little girl may make your childhoods seem tame."

"I think Tony was…" The phone ringing interrupted Wendy. Sarah told her to relax and answered the phone.

"Hello."

"Is that you, Mom?"

"Teddy, how nice to hear from you. How's your dad?"

She turned and whispered to Wendy, "Teddy."

"Well, that's why I'm calling, Mom. He's had a serious accident…"

"Oh, no!" Sarah fainted, collapsing to the floor. Wendy screamed and ran to her side.

"Wendy. Wendy!" Teddy's voice came faintly from the phone. She picked it up off the floor.

"Teddy, Mom just fainted. What's wrong."

"Dad was in an accident. We're at the hospital. He has a bad leg injury and is in serious condition. Mom needs to get home ASAP."

After hanging up the phone, Wendy put the baby down, ran cold water on a towel and placed it on Sarah's forehead. She was sitting on the floor with her mom's head resting on her leg. Both were upset about the news.

"Oh, Honey, I should have been there. I stayed too long. He needs me."

"Mom, forget it. You couldn't have prevented the accident. We just need to get to him, fast."

Sarah looked up at Wendy. "No, Honey, you stay here. I'll go."

"I should be able to take Katie, shouldn't I?"

"No, no. I don't want you to do that?"

"But I can, can't I? Come on, get up and rest on the couch. I'm looking for airline tickets, now."

CB &0

"Clayton County Hospital, how can I help you?" answered the receptionist.

"Hello, my name is Wendy Ward and I need to speak with my brother, Teddy Crodin. My dad, Kent, is a patient."

"Oh, Wendy. How are you? This is Melanie. It's been so long since I've heard from you."

"Yes, Melanie, I know. My call is urgent, is there a way you can get Teddy to the phone?"

"Oh, yes, yes. Just a second."

"Hello, this is second floor nurse's station; he'll be here in a moment."

"Hello."

"Teddy, it's Wendy. How's Dad?"

"He's coming out of the trauma ok, I guess. His leg's busted up pretty bad. Doc says they won't know anything for sure 'til the swelling goes down."

"It's not life threatening?"

"Naw, nothing like that. Still, it's pretty bad."

"Well, are you ever going to tell us what happened?"

"Oh, yeah. Guess I didn't. Well, he had some time on his hands and a service call came in for an abandoned car on the highway. Seemed like a pick and drop run so he didn't call a driver and did it himself. When he was pulling the cable to hook up the abandoned car, some idiot hit the back corner of the car and shoved it into the tow truck."

"Oh, my God. Where was Dad?"

"Between the car and truck. He'd have been dead if he hadn't jumped onto the hood. As it is, his lower leg and ankle were shoved into the truck bed supports. In a way, he was lucky."

"Teddy, that's horrible. All these years and now this has to happen."

"I know. Feel the same way. Listen, are you coming?"

"Oh, yes, I almost forgot. We leave here early tomorrow morning and arrive in Bluffton at ten thirty AM. Can you arrange to pick us up? I'm sorry, but we'll need room for all of Katie's baby stuff.

"If it was just you, you'd be on your own, but for Katie, we'll do everything we can."

Teddy's little dig brought a smile to her face. He seemed to like his role as an uncle.

CB&

Carl Mueller answered his phone, held the receiver an arm's length away, then spoke toward the mouthpiece. "Norm, damn it. Use your inside voice, will ya'. What are you so excited about?"

"Carl, I want to swap trucks. I need a quad cab real bad for a trip to Bluffton."

Shaking his head and almost laughing at Norm's idea he said, "You know I can't do that. It's a one year contract that isn't finished. What's the urgency?"

"Sarah, Wendy, the baby and her husband are arriving tomorrow morning. Nobody I know has a truck big enough for'em all."

"Well, let me think on it a while. If I come up with something and call you."

"Alrighty. Later."

Carl left his office and went out on the lot. The vans were sold, so he couldn't use them. The crew cab had an offer that wasn't signed. He didn't want to lose that deal. "Hmmm." He walked to the service bays where he saw Joe Meyer's Ford crew cab. The service manager was close by. "Gene, what's the deal with Joe's truck?"

"We did fuel injector service," he answered.

"When does he plan to pick it up?"

Gene shrugged. "Didn't say. He's driving his wife's truck right now."

Carl walked toward the shop office. "Will you get his phone number for me."

Joe answered the call, "Hey, what's up, Carl."

"Joe, I need a favor. We need to pick up Kent's family in Bluffton tomorrow morning, and only a crew cab will do. What do ya' say you loan me yours for a day."

"Suits me fine, Carl. But, I'd feel a lot better about it if you'd nip a little off my bill."

"I'll do that, Joe. How's fifteen percent sound?"

"Ya got yourself a deal. Go get'er done," he said. "And tell Sarah how sorry I am about Kent's accident."

Carl got Joe's keys from Gene and drove his truck out front to the sales lot. When he reached his office, the first thing he did was call Norm.

"Norm's Bait and Boat Shop, Norm speakin'."

"Carl here, I found a truck."

"Alright! You are the man. "

"Thank Joe Meyer, not me. It's his truck."

"You're my hero anyway, no matter what they say about you."

"All right, so tell me when their flight lands in Bluffton?"

"Yes, sir. Ten thirty AM."

"Ok. Since Joe's truck is still a part of my dealership's liability, I'll have to drive it to pick up the family. Will you let Teddy know what we're up to?"

"Sure thing. Thanks a bunch."

"You're welcome."

| CHAPTER 38

Sarah was so concerned about Kent she was very distracted. Wendy or Tony had to make sure she had her purse, her ticket, her boarding pass. Wendy had never seen her Mom so helpless. But, they understood why, and kept helping her along.

When Carl picked them up at the airport Sarah latched onto him like a leech. She wanted to know everything that was said, heard or done. Wendy was grateful to be in the back seat nursing and caring for Katie. Her Mom was just too intense for her.

As Carl drove up to the hospital he asked, "Tony, would you want me to drive you up to the farm so you can get another vehicle for you all?"

Tony looked at Wendy and shrugged his shoulders. "What do you think?"

"Yeah, good idea," She said. "I don't know what Teddy's driving, so bring Dad's truck. Keys are hanging in the kitchen. His has a yellow tag."

"Ok, Carl. Let me get these ladies settled and I'll be right back."

ೞ෨

Sarah entered Kent's hospital room, went straight to his bedside and looked at his swollen purple and yellow leg. She gasped, covered her mouth and started crying. Wendy pulled the curtain around her dad's bed to give them some privacy, looked at Teddy and motioned toward the door.

When they sat, Wendy said to Teddy, "This has been brewing from the moment she heard he was injured. She's been clueless, distracted, and so out of it. I've never seen her this way."

"That's really odd. Dad's been cool, calm and collected. Knows what the doctors are doing, knows what to expect. Didn't even panic when they said they may have to amputate his foot."

Wendy almost screamed. "No! Oh, No! They can't. They won't, will they?" She grabbed Teddy's leg and squeezed it hard as fear engulfed her. "You can't tell Mom. Don't you dare tell Mom. Teddy, what are we going to do?"

Teddy motioned down the hall as Tony approached them. Wendy took a deep breath and tried to compose herself. "Hi, Honey. I guess you found the keys?"

"Yeah, no problem. How's your Dad?"

Wrestling with the news Teddy shared, she focused her attention on Katie, resting in her arms. "Mom's with him now."

"Wendy, Honey, your dad wants to see you."

They all looked as Sarah came out of his room. Her face was pink, but she seemed composed.

"You alright, Mom?" Teddy asked.

"Yes, I'm alright. Tony, why don't you go, too." She said, sitting in the chair that Wendy vacated.

Wendy's dad was alert and smiling. "Hey there. I want to see my granddaughter. Can I hold her?"

Wendy was surprised at his attitude. "Sure, Dad. She made a special trip to see you." Laying Katie on his chest she said, "Introducing Miss Katie Ward. Katie, say hello to Grandpa."

He held Katie while they talked. After a while, he motioned to the portable tray. "Want to grab that phone for me?" he asked.

Wendy retrieved the phone. "What do you need, Dad?"

"Honey, a lot of folks have called needing a vet. I was wondering if you could help out the worst ones."

"Well… I'd love to help, but I've got Katie to take care of. I can't imagine how to do it."

"Have Teddy call Zoey. Maybe she could babysit while you made a run or two for me?"

"I guess I could try." Looking at the phone she asked, "Do you know what's on here?"

Kent handed Katie back to Wendy and laid his head back. "Floyd's got a horse whose leg's cut and bleeding, and Herman is going to lose a dozen piglets if the sow doesn't start nursing. There's others on there, but you may not have time. Just do what you can. I'd appreciate it, Honey."

She looked at Tony and rolled her eyes. He just shrugged. "I've never done this while minding a baby, Dad. I'll try, but no guarantees. Understand?"

"I understand, Honey," Kent said as he closed his eyes.

C3 &0

Teddy and Sarah stayed with Kent while Tony and Wendy headed home with Katie. Zoey was sitting on the porch when they arrived. She rushed down the steps to greet them.

"Oh, Wendy, it's so good to see you. Is this Katie? She's so beautiful. She's going to be just like you." Making a sour face, she recanted, "Oops, maybe not, exactly?"

Wendy burst into laughter as Tony looked on curiously. "Zoey, I wasn't that bad, was I?"

"I don't know. People in town still talk about you from time to time."

Tony interrupted, "Excuse me, but who is this lovely lady?"

"Oh, sorry, Honey, this is my brother's wife, Zoey. They manage a restaurant in town. Her parents live on the farm over there," she said as she pointed across the open field.

Holding out her left hand to show off her wedding ring Zoey said, "Finally."

Seeing her rings cheered up Wendy. "Zoey, I'm so happy for you. Please forgive me for not making the wedding. My doctor simply wouldn't let me travel. I'm so sorry."

"I know Wendy. We all missed you, but understood why you couldn't be here." She smiled and rubbed Katie's cheek. "This little bundle of joy makes up for it all."

Tony set up a bed for Katie while she held Katie and Wendy used her breast pump to leave milk behind in case she wasn't back for the next feeding. In the process, they gave Tony the abbreviated version of Teddy and Zoey's relationship.

"So, you see," Wendy said, "Born only hours apart and growing up almost like brother and sister Teddy never saw Zoey as anything other than his buddy."

"And," Zoey said, "Having fallen in love with him I could not find a way for him to see me as a woman."

"Must have been frustrating," Tony remarked.

"You think? One day I might write a book about it, and Teddy's going to be the first. I want him to see what he put me through."

Tony chuckled as he looked over at Wendy. "You ready? We should get goin'."

Putting baby bottles in the refrigerator, Wendy kissed Katie and picked up her dad's medical bag.

"Here's our cell number, Zoey. Please call anytime you need me. I hope we aren't long."

| CHAPTER 39

Wendy asked Tony to drive her dad's truck while she listened to the messages on his cell phone. In the process she said to Tony, "'Take a left up here. We'll look at the horse on the auction lot first."

Following her hand signals, Tony came upon the auction lot, and then asked, "Ok. Where to?"

"Behind those pens over there."

As they parked and got out of the truck Tony asked Wendy what was on the messages she'd listened to.

"A lot of nickel and dime stuff that can wait," she replied.

Wendy hustled ahead and headed toward the owner, Floyd Thompson. As she approached Floyd, she had to smile. The old fart hasn't changed a bit.

He wore the same old dusty black cowboy hat he had when she was eight years old. Standing six foot four his belly made him three feet thick, and his fringed vest had no chance of meeting up in the middle.

"Hello, darling," Floyd said as he put his arm around her.

"Hello Floyd," she said as he squeezed her to his chest. "You haven't changed a bit."

"Well, thank you."

"Tell me," Wendy asked as she patted his belly, "how do you find shirts long enough to tuck in over this belly?"

"Now then, that's a mighty personal question."

"Tell you what Floyd; if you'll get rid of this I'll kiss you."

Floyd laughed. "You will? That there is a good reason to start a diet."

"It's a promise. Now, where's this horse that's injured?"

Floyd pointed across the corral at a mare haltered and tied to a fence rail. She was agitated and jumpy as the other horses milled about.

"Floyd, I need a pen or a stall where I can settle her down and work on her."

"Don't have one of those, Wendy."

"Well, ok." She looked around the pen, then at the farmers hanging around, a dozen at a quick count. "Floyd, can you get these men in the pen to make a wall shoulder to shoulder to cut off a corner from the other horses. Maybe I can make that work."

"Alrighty. Hey, listen up you guys, come with me. We need to help the Doc. Hurry up now."

Wendy motioned for Tony to follow her. "What do you want, Honey?"

"Tony, while he's doing that, I need you to calm down that mare. Can you do it for me?"

"Sure, give me a couple minutes. I'll do what I can."

Wendy directed her attention to the men cutting off the corner of the corral. She pulled them in so they were shoulder to shoulder from fence to fence. She had them turn their backs to the other horses so they wouldn't be spooked while she was working. It gave her about fifteen feet across the corner of the pen.

"Thanks, guys. Now, if everyone stays quiet we can keep this mare calm enough to fix her leg."

When she turned toward the mare Tony nodded his head, and she saw the mare was standing quietly. She approached her front leg and knelt to assess the bleeding cut above the fetlock. Lifting her hoof off the ground, Wendy cleaned the wound. Half of the four inch cut needed stitches.

"Tony?"

"Yeah."

"I've got to stitch this. I think it would be better if I held her leg up like you shoe a horse. How do you do that?"

"First get under her belly and back into her leg."

"Like this?"

"Yes. Now, push up with your legs to take the pressure off her leg."

"Ok."

"That's it. Lift her hoof off the ground, squeeze it between your legs and get busy."

Wendy reached into her bag for needle and thread, lifted the mare's leg and held her breath. To her amazement, the mare was calm as could be. She wasn't though, her legs were straining already.

Finishing the stitching and wrapping the wound, Wendy let the leg down and crawled from under the horse. Looking at Tony she exclaimed, "Whew. Is that what you do all day?"

"Pretty much," he replied.

"I just gained a lot more respect for what you do. That's not easy."

Wendy turned to the men forming her fence line. "Gentlemen, I can't thank you enough. That was perfect."

As they dispersed, Floyd approached her. "Great job, Wendy. Thanks for coming, darling. What do I owe you?"

"You can call me Dr. Ward, Floyd. I am a doctor now, you know. And I'll have Dad send you a bill when he can. Ok?"

"Yes, yes. That's fine. But I think Doc Jr. fits you better."

As they walked to their truck, Wendy checked the time. Tony started the truck and asked, "Where to?"

"Let's head home, we need to get Katie."

"Ok."

As he drove, Wendy rummaged through her dad's bag. Tony would glance at her now and then, but she never said what she was doing.

"Found it," she exclaimed.

"Found what?" he asked.

"Dad has a special ointment a friend of ours makes. It's for bee stings and skin rashes. It's perfect for Herman's sow. She looked around to get oriented. "There should be a left turn ahead about a mile. Take it, and we'll go to Herman's farm. We won't be there more than fifteen minutes now that I have this ointment."

The smell of the hog pen slapped Tony in the face as soon as he opened his door. Nothing like horses. This was a completely new odor for his senses. Wendy noticed as she rounded the rear of the truck and smiled. "Having trouble with this fresh farm air, Honey? Come on, see how we coax a mother to nurse."

With only the ointment in her hand, she followed Herman to the pen and his new mother sow. Wendy knelt beside her and examined her nipples. "Tony, can you see the dry cracking skin here," she said pointing to the skin above the nipples.

"Yeah, what about it?"

"It hurts the sow, so she won't let her piglets suckle. Dad uses this ointment to clear it up. Like this."

Wendy rubbed the ointment on the sow's skin rashes then squeezed each teat until she saw milk squirting out. "Well, Herman," she said, "I think you can let the piglets nurse now. She should be more comfortable.

Tony jumped back as a dozen piglets rushed toward the sow squeaking and squealing like little alarm clocks. As soon as the first piglet latched onto a nipple the sow layed quietly on her side. The lucky ones drank their fill as those left out crawled on top of 'em squealing for their turn.

Herman put his arm across her shoulders and hugged her. "Thank you, Wendy. I'd hate to see them little buggers die on me. I'm sorry about your Dad, but you saved me a lot of money by coming out here."

"I'm only doing what Dad would do, Herman."

"And, I appreciate it. What do I owe you?"

"Whatever Dad usually charges. I can have him send a bill."

"How about two turkeys, Honey. Usually pleases your Dad. Come along with me."

Tony was still dealing with the smell when he looked in amusement at Wendy following Herman to be paid. When they reached a pen full of turkeys, he reached over the fence and grabbed one in each hand. Before Tony knew it, he was holding them by the neck as they shook and flapped their wings so vigorously he was being beaten up.

Herman smiled at Tony as Wendy laughed. "I don't think we'll get them home like this Herman. Maybe later?"

Herman didn't answer. He took one turkey out of Tony's hand, spun it around by the neck and it was dead still, literally. Taking the other he spun it's neck the same way and it was dead too. He held them out, saying, "This oughta be easier."

Tony's eyes were bulging out of his head as Wendy chuckled at his reaction. She grabbed the turkeys, thanked Hermann for them and led Tony back to their truck. She tossed both birds into the back of the truck and got in.

Herman's parting words were, "Don't forget to clean'em soon as you get home."

Driving out the lane Tony regained his composure, "I can't believe what I just saw. He killed those turkeys with his bare hands, and that's how you get paid?"

Still getting a kick out of Tony's reaction she said, "Yeah, welcome to my world."

When they arrived home, it was mid-afternoon. Zoey was swinging Katie on the porch, and Wendy rushed up to see them.

"Was she good for you?"

"Oh, sure. We got along just fine. How'd you do?"

"We took care of two of Dad's worse cases. Picked up a problem along the way though."

"Really? What's that?"

"Do you remember Herman, the hog farmer?"

"I do."

"Well, he bartered two turkeys for my services. They're in the truck and need to be cleaned. I really want to see Dad first. Could you help?"

"Of course. But, better yet, why don't I take them home and Mom and I'll do it for you. You just go on ahead, and pick them up later."

"Really? Zoey, that would be so helpful. Thank you so much."

Tony took Katie from Zoey so she could follow Wendy to the truck. Holding a turkey in each hand, Zoey hiked across the field towards home.

Wendy turned toward the house and saw Tony staring at Zoey "What are you doing?"

"Look at her, Tony replied. Those turkeys could be fifteen pounds each. I have never been in a place where women naturally do things that men would do, and think nothing of it."

"Well, there are two oars on a boat, Honey. If only one person pulls, you'll end up going in circles. We have to pull together if we're going to survive out here."

Tony looked at her curiously. "Your Dad's words?"

She walked towards the truck. "No, mine. Let's go. I'll drive."

| CHAPTER 40

When they walked into Kent's hospital room Wendy sat beside him and Tony stood at the end of his bed holding Katie. She took his hand, "Daddy, how are you?"

"I'm comfortable, Honey. I'm scheduled for surgery early tomorrow morning."

Wendy was so glad to hear they could operate and not amputate his foot. "That's such good news. Is there anything we can do?"

He smiled at her and Tony. "You've already helped. Tony, thanks for going with her."

"It was a pleasure, sir."

"Son, I'd like to have a word alone with Wendy. Do you mind?"

"No, sir."

Kent pulled his hospital gown off his shoulder. "Young man, do you see any stripes on my arm, or bars on my shoulder?"

Tony stopped in mid-stride. "No, sir."

"Then will you please stop calling me, sir?"

Tony was at a loss, then replied, "Yes, Mr. Crodin."

Shaking his head, Kent knew Tony was uncomfortable. "Dad will do just fine."

Wendy's mouth dropped open in surprise. She looked at Tony, and then broke into a wide smile.

"Ah, ok, Dad, Katie and I will be in the waiting room. Let me know when the time is right to return." He turned away and left the room.

"Oh, Daddy, that was so sweet. It'll mean a lot to him."

Looking at her, he squeezed her hand. "He's part of the family now, he might as well act like it, don't you think?"

"Oh, yes. Yes I do."

"Just one thing, I don't ever want to see you crying on my doorstep again. You stick right with him and iron out your problems face to face. If you're going to be his wife, I expect you to be a good one."

"I promise, Daddy. It won't happen again."

Looking into her eyes Kent said, "Good. Listen, Honey, you've grown into a strong young lady and a good vet."

She was a little embarrassed. "It's all because of you, Daddy. You taught me"

"I don't believe a word of it, he said. You know, years ago I knew a blacksmith who said there was no way to make a sharp plow if you didn't have the right material. You are your mother... smart and strong willed. I just did the sharpening so you could be what you wanted to be."

Wendy started to shed a tear. "I'm so sorry I made it difficult," and kissed his forehead.

"Well now," he said as he cleared his throat, "getting down to business—my days as a vet are over."

She jumped out of her chair. "No! Don't say that. "

"It true. They're going to put plates in my ankle so I can walk, but that's all I'll be able to do. Doc says I won't have the stamina to stand in the clinic very long, or the flexibility to walk in fields or barnyards."

Wendy sat again, grabbed a box of Kleenex and tried to wipe the tears that wouldn't stop. "What'll you do?"

"Well, Dr. Steinhouse at Iowa State suggested I be a visiting professor some time ago. I think now's the time to take him up on it. Kind of a retirement plan."

"Really?"

"What? Don't you think Dad can teach?"

"Of course you can." She said blushing. "I'm sure you'd be good at it."

"Well, anyway, I've got to sell the clinic. I've already talked to Steinhouse, and he's sending a graduate over for an interview when I'm out of the hospital. If he's the right person, I'll offer to sell it to him. If he can't raise the money, I may just hire him to run it until he can."

She was stunned, scared, and heartbroken all at once. Her head fell on Kent's chest, and he put his hand on her head. "Daddy, no. You can't do this. That clinic is your life. It's been part of our family my whole life. No. Please don't, Daddy."

σև

Tony was concerned. Wendy had been crying since she left her dad's hospital room and was now driving home like a zombie. Katie was hungry and crying to be fed; Wendy ignored her. Remaining silent he gave her all the room she wanted until Katie was fed and she got into bed.

"Are you going to tell me what happened with your father?"

"I don't want to talk about it," she said, turning away and covering her head with a pillow.

"Yes, you do. There's nobody else here you can confide in."

Wendy growled from under her pillow, "How could you possibly know that?"

"Who else can you talk to about your dad going out of business?"

"What!" She roared as she threw her pillow at Tony and got into his face. "You were listening, weren't you? How rude. You were supposed to leave the room."

"Listen," he said. "I didn't have to hear a word. The only thing that could crush you like this is if he told you his injury was going to force him out of business. True or not?"

Wendy collapsed into his arms and started crying again. Neither said a word as he comforted her.

CB&O

When Wendy walked into the kitchen the next morning, Tony and her mom were talking. Mom's back was turned as she poured cups of coffee. Without hesitation Wendy slipped her dad's key ring off the hook and put it in her pocket as she sat down. Tony noticed, looked at her curiously, then let it pass when he got no response from Wendy. After breakfast, she made an announcement. "Mom, Tony and I are going for a walk. Can you watch Katie while we're gone?"

"Sure. Go, enjoy your walk. It looks like a great day for it."

Tony followed Wendy down the lane and up the road until there were out of sight from the house. Then she led him across the parking lot to the front door of her dad's clinic. She opened the door and let him in.

"Holy cow, this is his clinic?"

"Yep, built it from the ground up."

Tony looked at her and asked, "So, why are we sneaking around here?"

Wendy's head hung as she replied, "Well, I guess I just wanted you to see it without explaining why to Mom."

"It's awesome." He wandered the hallway, reception desk area, and waiting room. "Who would ever expect something like this in such a small town?" When he faced the entrance, again Wendy was kneeling next to a cage. "What's up, Honey?"

"Oh, I was just reminiscing about Lucky."

"Who was he?"

"A badly burned dog that dad thought would die." She looked up and smiled. "I would sneak out of bed when everyone was asleep, snitch mom's baster from the kitchen and come in to feed Lucky every night. Fooled Dad for a while."

"Where is Lucky?"

"He didn't have the strength to make it."

"I'm sorry. So this was his cage?"

"Uh-hum. First animal I helped that died." She got back on her feet without the melancholy. "So, there's more to see. Follow me."

"Wow, your dad has two operating rooms. That's not normal is it?"

"Not at all. But Dad figured it would be more efficient when one room could be sterilized while he's working in the other." Wendy placed her hands on the operating table and bowed slightly over it.

After a moment of silence Tony asked, "Another memory?"

She smiled, "Yes. I was suspended from school three days for beating up a boy named Billy Goetz. Dad made me work here all three days. The very next day Billy and his dad came in with his cat, and Dad euthanized it."

"Wow, that must have been awkward."

"It was, and it was the first time I'd seen Dad kill an animal on purpose."

"What'd you do?"

Wendy laughed at herself. "I ran out screaming that Dad was a killer. I must have embarrassed him something awful."

When they stopped laughing, Tony sobered up. "Wendy, why are we here?"

"It just breaks my heart to see all this go away. There is so much good here, and so many memories. Dad's built a legacy that I don't want him to throw away."

Tony guided her to a chair in the waiting room. He sat beside her. "Wendy, don't let it go. You can carry it on for him, and the family."

"I know. I've thought about it. But it means I'd have to give up everything I've worked so hard for."

"For instance," Tony asked.

"Well, I haven't finished my degree, and I have to do that."

"I hear your dad has connections at Iowa State. Maybe he could help you finish up there?"

"He probably could, but then how could I do that with baby Katie?"

"You've got me. And I'm sure Grandma wouldn't mind chipping in now and then."

"Tony, I couldn't ask you to do that."

"You didn't, I volunteered."

Wendy got up, went to the reception counter and absentmindedly rubbed the top. "Where would we live?"

Tony joined her. "You know, I've been thinking about that."

Surprised, she looked up at him. "Really?"

"Oh, yeah. Listen, your dad can't live in their house anymore because there's no way he can climb stairs."

"So?"

"So, what I'd do is make him an offer to buy the clinic, and the house, so they can build a one level ranch house. Best of both worlds for everyone."

Wendy walked away. "But Tony, we'd need a lot of money to do that."

"And, that's what banks are for. If you want to stay here, I say we need to talk to a banker."

Wendy walked back to him and put her hands on his shoulders, "Do you want to stay?"

Tony kissed her. "I do. This is the most interesting and crazy place I've ever seen. I don't know how we could ever be bored here. And you?"

"I've never wanted to live here. But it would be a good place for Katie to grow up. I just don't see how it can happen."

"Let's try. Come on, we need to call a banker."

| CHAPTER 41

Business at Wilma's Café was steady. Teddy and Zoey were earning a comfortable income and Wilma was pleased.

Although surprised that Teddy started the monthly Italian Dinner night, Wilma couldn't argue with the fact that reservations were booked three months in advance and her café was becoming the talk-of-the-town. Her sister's health was slowly declining, requiring all of Wilma's time. Being away from the restaurant gave her time to think, and that's when she decided to meet with her young managers.

Zoey tapped on the window of the office to get Teddy's attention. When he looked over, she motioned for him to come in.

He opened the door and peeked in. "What's up, Zoe?"

"Come in for a minute."

When Teddy was seated she said, "Wilma just called. She wants us to meet with her Sunday afternoon."

"Why?"

"She wants to talk about the business, and asked me to bring the P & L report."

"Is something wrong?"

Zoey shook her head. "Hey, don't go thinking the worst. It's her restaurant. She has the right to meet us and talk about it. It'll be fine. I promise."

"Ok, then. What time?"

"She said two."

⚬⚬

Wilma met them at the door Sunday afternoon and invited them in. When they were comfortably seated in the living room Teddy and Zoey quietly waited for Wilma to speak.

"Zoey, dear," Wilma said, "Will you tell me what the year-to-date profits are compared with last year?"

"Sure," she said as she thumbed through the pages. "After six months, we're fifteen percent better than last year."

"I kind of expected that. You two have done a fine job. Thank you."

"You're welcome," Teddy replied.

"Well, that leads me to the reason you are here. Being away from the Café has given me time to think. And, I can't see myself going back after my sister passes. So, I've decided to sell it."

Zoey took the news calmly, but Teddy reacted emotionally. "Wilma, please don't sell it. We're happy here. Where would we go?"

Wilma chuckled, looked at Zoey and smiled. "Is he always this way?"

"I'm afraid so," she replied, "When it involved the café. It's like his baby, Wilma."

"That's what I thought. And it's why I'm offering to sell it to you first. If you can swing it, I'd like you to be the new owners."

Teddy sat back and sighed, "Wilma, we just got married, and don't have any money. How could we possibly buy the café?"

"I've got a plan, young man. Hear me out before you go off the deep end. Please take notes Zoey so Teddy here doesn't have to remember everything."

"Ok, I will." She answered as she opened to a new page of her ledger.

Wilma stood and walked slowly around the room as she spoke. "Ok, to begin I want $20,000 as a down payment. For that amount I'll give you kids twenty percent ownership to start. That means twenty percent of the profits." Then, at the end of each fiscal year, you can buy another ten percent for $20,000. In eight years you'll own it."

Zoey was the first one to speak. "Wilma, are you saying that you'll carry this loan on a contract for us. We won't have to go to a bank?"

"Yes, dear. I doubt you could get a loan anyway, right?"

They both nodded.

"All you kids have to do is come up with the down payment. If you continue to run the café as well as you have, I see no reason you won't be able to make the yearly payments. I've made it as easy as I can for you. It's up to you to make it happen."

When Teddy and Zoey left Wilma's, he drove to their apartment, parked and took Zoey's hand as she got out of the car.

Where are we going, Teddy?"

"I want to find a park bench where it's quiet and I can think."

When they were seated by the river's edge she asked, "What are you thinking? I thought you always wanted to buy the café. Have you changed your mind?"

"I'm just not sure we can do it, Zoe. A hundred and eighty thousand dollars is a lot of money."

"Sure it is, Honey, but it's over eight years. We won't swallow the whole thing at once, just a little bite each year."

"Yeah, I guess. But where are we gonna get twenty thousand dollars. I don't feel good about asking my dad. Then we'd just have two loans to pay."

"Teddy, we have twenty thousand dollars. It's just in equity."

"Oh, yeah, where?"

"The boat you built."

Teddy's reaction was predictable. He left the park bench taking a few steps toward the river. A few seconds later, he turned to Zoey. "No. I've put my heart and soul into that boat. I built it for you. I won't do it."

She didn't say a word, and let Teddy wrestle with his thoughts. When he calmed down and sat on the bench again she said, "That was when you were a boy. Now you're a man."

"I know."

"If your boyish toy can buy you something you've always wanted, and security for our family, why not use it to take the next step?"

"It's special. I spent two years building it for you. It means a lot to me."

Zoey took his hand in hers. "Teddy, we don't have to own Miss Zoey for me to be remember what you did for me, and the wonderful times we've had with her. What do you want, Teddy, the fastest boat on the river or a future?" Zoey kissed him on the cheek, rose and left him alone.

Teddy was quiet when he returned home, and all through the next day. About three in the afternoon, he told Zoey he had an errand to run and would be back in an hour. She waited until the door closed before she looked out and watched him walking away. Wherever he was going and whatever he was doing was going to be hard on him. She steeled herself for some unexpected news.

As he approached Norm's Boat and Bait shop, Teddy looked around for Norm and found him in his office, of all places.

Norm was at the copy machine when Teddy entered. "Hey, what brings you down here?"

"I need your help, Norm."

Norm laid his copies down and offered Teddy a seat.

"So, how can I help?"

"I want you to sell my boat."

The shocked look on Norm's face told the story. "Are you kidding me? I thought you'd never sell that boat. Are you sure?"

"Yes, I'm sure. I want you to sell it for $25,000."

Norm sat up and leaned over his desk. "You've crazy. A 31 ft. Bullet boat is worth twice that much."

"I know, Norm. But I need the money now. It's tourist season and I want a quick sale. Add your commission if you want to, but I want a check for twenty-five thousand as soon as possible."

CHAPTER 42

Wendy and Tony arrived at the bank for their appointment. "Follow me," the receptionist said as she took them to the loan officer's office. As they began to enter, Wendy stopped abruptly.

"Billy. Oh, my God. You're a banker?"

"Hello, Wendy. Yes, I'm your friendly loan officer. Come in and have a seat."

As Tony looked from one to the other, trying to remember where he'd heard this name, Wendy introduced him.

"Billy, I'd like you to meet my husband, Tony Ward. Tony, meet Billy Goetz."

"Ah-hum, I go by William these days. A little more professional I think. But I know I'll always be Billy to you."

Tony stepped forward to shake his hand. He looked toward Wendy and began to speak.

Billy interrupted him. "Yes it is, Tony. Wendy and I go back a long way. But that was a lifetime ago. No need to rehash it, right Wendy?"

"Right."

"So, let's get down to business. I assume you're here to talk about buying your dad's clinic, Wendy. Is that right?"

"Oh, Lord." Wendy said as she shook her head. "Everybody knows?"

"Afraid so." Billy said. "Started at the hospital I suppose."

"Ok. Well, our plan is to buy the clinic and the house. That way Mom and Dad can build a one story ranch house without stairs for Dad."

"Do you know how much you need?" Billy asked.

"Not exactly. I was hoping you would have some information about their assessed values."

Billy opened a folder in front of him. "Fortunately, having an idea what you wanted helped a lot. I've checked our records and the county property assessments. Your dad's clinic is valued at $250,000, and the contents are insured for $140,000."

"How much for the house?" Tony asked.

Billy thumbed through some papers and pulled out the house assessment. "The house, Tony, is valued at $160,000. That brings the total for both properties to $550,000."

Wendy's head sank to her chest in despair. Tony leaned forward on the desk and asked, "We could make these two different loans couldn't we?"

"We would," Billy answered. "The house would be a mortgage loan, of course. It would require a down payment, then a mortgage of thirty years if you wish."

"How about the clinic?" Tony asked.

Wendy was glad Tony was talking with Billy. She only saw doom and gloom. She saw no way to keep the clinic.

"Well," Billy said, "We've got property, a building and contents to consider. If I were to accept it all as collateral, what it would need is enough money out of your stream of income to pay the $390,000 loan. From what I see in her dad's account, that looks feasible. Of course, I'll need $40,000 down on the loan. Plus, even though we know each other, Wendy, I'll still need your Dad to cosign the loan."

"Can you have the loans drawn up for us?" Tony asked. "Then we can work with the actual numbers and payments."

"Sure, make yourselves comfortable while I do that for you."

After Billy had left the room, Wendy put her hand on Tony's knee. "This is impossible, Tony. There's no way we can afford to do this. We can't even come up with the down payments? It's a lost cause."

"We're not done yet, Honey. We'll just work through it. Be patient."

A tear crawled slowly down Wendy's cheek. "You must see something I don't."

CR&O

Zoey had the phone in her hand when she opened the office door and told Teddy, "Norm's on the line. He wants to see you."

"I'm too busy. Tell him to come here, ok?"

"Sure," she said, closing the door.

It wasn't long before a booming voice came through the back screen door. "Hey, Teddy!"

Without looking Teddy replied, "Yeah, come on in Norm. There's a chair back here."

Norm looked excited when he came in and sat down.

"So, what's up?" Teddy asked as he continued to cook.

"Sold your boat, that's what's up."

Unexpectedly, Teddy felt excitement. "You did?"

"Yep, got $30,000 for her. You'll have to kiss her goodbye today because tomorrow she's gone."

"That's great, Norm. Thanks a lot. When do you think I can get a check?"

"Got her right here in my pocket. See?"

Teddy took the check from Norm, unfolded it and looked at the amount. "Hey, $27,000? That's more than we agreed on."

"Ah, don't worry. I took my ten percent. Figured you could use it anyway. Fair is fair."

"Wow. Thanks, Norm."

When Norm left, Teddy stuck the check in his pants pocket and continued working.

CR&OR

The next morning was Sunday. They'd slept late and Teddy was first in the shower. He grabbed a towel to wipe his eyes as he stepped out and bumped into Zoey, standing in front of him in a white terry cloth robe.

"Hey, what's with you?" he asked, wrapping his towel around his waist.

Slowly Zoey untied her robe, slid it back off her shoulders and let it drop to the floor.

Looking at her naked body Teddy asked, "Wow! What's this about?"

Smiling mischievously Zoey said, "I want you to take a good look."

"Already have. Why, am I missing something?"

"Yes, it's going to be a year before you see me like this again."

"A year? Where are you going?"

"Nowhere, silly. I'm pregnant. "

Teddy opened his arms for Zoey, who stepped up and kissed him.

"Now, we're both wet," she said. "Dry off and come to bed with me. Hurry up. I'll get you some clothes for later."

Teddy dried off and was hanging up his towel when Zoey appeared at the door wrapped up in her robe again, holding a small piece of paper.

"Is there something you want to tell me?" she asked.

Teddy looked out of the corner of his eye and saw the check. "Oh, yeah. I forgot."

"Teddy Crodin. How do you forget a $27,000 check?"

"Well, I was busy, I guess."

Zoe turned him around so he faced her. "We need $20,000 to buy this café, and you forgot? You sold the boat yesterday, didn't you? And you didn't tell me? You aren't responsible enough to own this café. Do you know that?"

Teddy just shook his head.

Women. What's the rush. I would have told her today.

After a few drawers got slammed Zoey was dressed and announced she was leaving.

"Now, where are you going?" Teddy asked.

"Wilma's."

| CHAPTER 43

It was awkward getting around in the kitchen with Kent's wheelchair parked sideways so his left leg could rest straight out on the brace. They'd just finished eating supper when Tony spoke.

"Wendy and I have something we'd like to discuss with you, if this would be a good time."

While Kent studied Tony, Sarah spoke up. "What would that be?"

"Well, you need to know that Wendy wants to keep the veterinary clinic in the family."

Looking at Wendy her father asked, "Is that right?"

Wendy answered, "Yes, I'd really like to, Daddy."

"We've talked with the bank loan officer about buying the clinic and this house."

That surprised Sarah. "You want to buy this house? Where would we live?"

Tony motioned toward the stairs. "When Dad is up and around, he won't be able to climb those stairs any more. We thought if we bought this house, then you'd have the money to build a one story ranch, where he wouldn't have any stairs to negotiate."

Sarah looked over at Kent. "I never thought of that, have you?"

"Yes, I just felt it was too early to discuss it. But he's right. The doctor told me I couldn't climb stairs."

"Well, what were you going to do?" Sarah asked.

"I've been thinking about adding a master bedroom here on the main floor."

"And, I was going to learn about this, when?" Sarah's irritation had sidetracked the discussion.

"This is not the time," Kent said. He waved toward Tony. "I'm sorry for that. Please go ahead, Tony."

"Well, we've got all the loan papers in our bedroom if you'd like to see them. But the bottom line is that they show the value of the clinic, property and contents at around $400,000. If Wendy took it over, we're told the income is enough to live on and make the payments."

Wendy finally joined in. "But it's not possible. We need ten percent down to get the loan."

"I see," Kent replied. "And you want our help with the down payment?"

Wendy put her hand on Tony's arm to detain him. "Daddy, I can't ask you to do that. If we do this, I want us to do it on our own. Begging you for money is not the way I want to start."

Looking at Tony he asked, "Are you finished, Tony?"

"Actually, no. We'll need another $14,000 down for the home mortgage. $54,000 down is what we need to take over your business."

Kent nodded, and then asked Wendy, "You've never wanted to live in Clayton. Why now?"

Wendy took a deep breath. "It's true. I've said that. But I was much younger and didn't have a family. Quite honestly, Tony and I want Katie to grow up like we did, in a small town. My future in Kentucky would be only a servant to the rich horse owners. Tony thinks I'd get bored after a while."

"Do you, Honey?" Sarah asked.

"Yes. After a few years. Plus, the variety of animals, situations and of course the people make work here both challenging and rewarding almost every day." Wendy finally smiled, "And, Dad, you'd still have your lab to work in, besides consulting with little ole me, the rookie veterinarian."

Kent nodded. "I see. Well, let me share my views on this situation. Over twenty years ago, someone I've never met gave this house to me. Your mother and I have never made a payment. So, I can't sell it to you."

"You can't?" Wendy asked as Tony sank back into his chair. Her head bowed as she softly asked, "Are you serious, Daddy?"

"Yes, Honey, I am. Now, your ranch house idea is a good one. After some thought, we'd probably agree. We're fortunate enough that we can afford to do that ourselves. So, here's what seems fair to me. Since I was given this house, I'll give it to you."

Wendy looked quickly at her mother. "Really?"

Sarah nodded as Kent continued.

"Now, instead of a mortgage, you can get a home equity loan for your down payment on the clinic."

Tony reached across the table to shake Kent's hand and say thank you, while Wendy ran around the table to hug and kiss him. She turned to her mother, hugged her and started crying on her shoulder. In the middle of this joyous moment Katie woke up crying at the top of her lungs.

"I've gotta go, Mom," Wendy said as she headed upstairs.

Sarah placed a hand on Kent's shoulder. "I'll go help her."

"All right," Kent said as he continued his discussion with Tony.

Wendy was nursing Katie when Sarah entered and sat down.

"You were awful quiet. Is this what you really want to do?" she asked.

"Yes it is, Mom. I just didn't think it was possible. Tony just forged ahead through all the obstacles until we had a plan. I couldn't have done it."

"He seems rather level headed, Honey. I was impressed that he had thought everything through."

"Yes, he did. You guys giving us the house makes everything possible. I'm so grateful."

"Well, your Dad's right. We can't sell you something that was given to us. Plus, I'm going to just love having Katie so close."

"Wendy scrunched up her face, "Well, Mom, if Tony finds a job maybe you'll see more of her than you want."

"Not possible, Honey. So, what's Tony going to do?"

"We don't know. First things first, I guess. He'll take care of Katie. Once I'm up and running I'm sure he'll be bored enough to look for something."

"Have you kids thought about buying out the towing business?"

"Mom, of course not. We were just lucky to buy the clinic and this house."

"I see. Well, there are things called contract purchases where you can operate the business and make payments as you go along."

"Oh, Mom, you know all about that finance stuff. It boggles my mind."

Sarah rose and headed for the door. "Tell you what, Honey. When you're settled and Tony has that itch to work again, I'll talk with him about it. Ok?"

"Does the business come with a pair of overalls for Katie?"

Sarah hesitated. "I don't get it."

"You don't think Katie is going to want to ride with her Dad in his tow truck?"

Sarah broke out in laughter. "Well, what goes around comes around I guess."

As Sarah stepped out the door she paused to look back, "Just remember, you're the mom this time."

When Wendy came down with Katie, the kitchen was cleared and empty.

"We're out here." Tony shouted.

Champagne was open, glasses filled, and ready to toast something, either the deal to buy the clinic or the fact that Wendy was returning to Clayton.

CR&BO

It was eight-thirty at night when Teddy and Zoey closed the café, and drove to her parent's house.

Niki was surprised to see them, and opened the door with a smile. "Well, hello. How nice of you to stop by. We don't see you enough these days."

"I know, Mom," Zoey said. "We miss you too."

Oly came into the living room, "Hey, what's the occasion?"

"We've got some news to share. Why don't we all sit down," Teddy suggested.

When they were all seated in the living room he said, "You know, there are some things a woman's parents should be the first to know."

Niki jumped to conclusions and rushed to hug Zoey. "You're pregnant."

"Yes, Mom. I am."

"When? When's the baby due?"

"Next February. I just found out."

Oly rose to shake Teddy's hand. "Congratulation, Son. I wish the best for you two. This calls for a celebration."

Teddy cut Oly off. "Sir, there's one other little thing."

Oly seemed confused as he sat down again. "What other thing?" he asked.

Zoey made this announcement. "Well, Teddy and I want you to be the first to know that we bought Wilma's Café —we're now the proud owners."

Niki started jumping up and down, grabbing Zoey and dancing around with her. Oly motioned to Teddy and they headed for the kitchen. When they returned he had opened two bottles of wine and Teddy brought the glasses. They toasted the new baby and the new restaurant owners.

After a while, settled into the living room, Niki asked Teddy, "Have you told your parents yet?"

"No ma'am. It's the mother's family that should know about the baby first, you know."

"How sweet. You're so thoughtful. Wendy's over at the house now, you know. Wouldn't it be wonderful if both you kids settled here in Clayton?"

"Yes ma'am," Teddy answered, "But don't count on it. Wendy's never wanted to live in Clayton."

THE END

| ABOUT THE AUTHOR

 Don Wooldridge's newest novel, *Homecoming,* is the third and final volume in the Secrets of Clayton County trilogy. The preceding two books have rated at 4+ stars by reviewers on the Amazon Books site. Don's writing takes us back to our roots in the small towns of middle-America. Born and raised in Iowa, where this series takes place, Wooldridge is personally familiar with life along the Mississippi river. Add the author's creativity – developed from years of classroom instruction and the design of interactive learning systems – and his characters take on a life of their own. Don and his wife have lived in Mesa, Arizona for the past 21 years.

Thank you for taking time to enjoy *Homecoming.* Great has been my enjoyment as an author to bring my readers back to their roots with myriad memories of rural America and the culture created by bartering as a way for small communities to survive; to thrive on the support provided one another.

I would appreciate your sharing the story with friends and family members, and would be honored to have you leave a review for me on Amazon. All you need is an Amazon account and have purchased at least one product from them. Your review need not be long; the requirement allows a minimum of 24 words; I only ask that it is truthful and fair. Amazon requires that if you happened to have received this book as a gift, you make note that you were not compensated for the review, nor do you have any vested interest in the book's success.

Thank you for being a loyal reader… without you, writing would not have as much genuine pleasure and fulfillment for me as an author. I would be most appreciative if you were to rate this book on Amazon.
Customers who bought this book also bought:

The Secrets of Clayton County Book 1 of the Trilogy of Clayton County, Book 2 of the Trilogy of Clayton County, New Beginnings, and Bible Moments

Don Wooldridge

www.ingramcontent.com/pod-product-compliance
Lightning Source LLC
Chambersburg PA
CBHW061541170626
46811CB00001B/37